I0630765

AWAKENED

TREE OF LIFE

SHARLA WYLDE

Three Pups Publishing

GET A FREE NOVELLA

Building a relationship with my readers is one of the best things about writing. I occasionally send out newsletters with details on new releases, special offers, and other bits of news.

If you sign up for my newsletter, you will get a free novella – *Dragon Wings* - the prequel to *Awakened* which introduces you to one of the shifter clans.

See details at the end of the story on how to get your free copy.

PROLOGUE

A single event can awaken within us a stranger totally unknown to us.
— Antoine de Saint-Exupéry

1

128 BC

I can't sense them. My thoughts are void of their presence. Nothing has ever prevented me from sensing my men. They are in my head day or night—while they sleep or when they are miles away from me at the edges of our kingdom; a little niggling sensation in my head to let me know they are near. I have only to think of one of them and know what he is doing; what he's sensing; where he is. Now, for the first time in hundreds of years, I can feel nothing. Total numbness. I know in the depth of my soul that they are dead.

After all these years, I still crave the power and the way it courses through my veins. It's a heady experience. The first day I gained my power, I cursed it. My life would never be the same. A vicious cycle, the magic controlled the sex which would manifest more magic.

Enchantment initially linked these shape-shifters to me, mentally, physically, and sexually. Once the initial ritual was completed, my Guardians regained control their own actions. I realized generations ago, when I first came into my power, that I wanted lovers devoted to me—who would love me, guide me, and protect me—not ones just wanting sex for the sake of magic and power so I chose wisely.

The castle is silent. No women chattering while they work. No dogs barking in the courtyard. No men yelling insults to each other in jest.

Panic wraps a crushing hold around my heart. I struggle to breathe. I'm on my throne, collapsed, incapable of moving. Whoever has taken my men, my Guardians, has drugged me. I can barely see my afternoon tea cup, fallen onto the floor, the liquid pooling on the ancient stones.

All I can do is slump in my chair and wait. I can't lift a finger even if I wanted to. *Please make it quick.* I am not willing to live without my Guardians whispering in my head. They have been there forever. The silence is deafening and terrifying.

It's difficult not to panic. My heart races. A scream builds in my throat. I start to hyperventilate. How could this happen? *I am Queen. The Queen.* The thought screams through my head. I have powers others crave and covet. People call me a goddess. Now I'm powerless, as helpless as a babe.

I need to remain calm. Someone will come. Someone will save me. I compose myself as best as I can. I am determined to face whatever the gods have deemed for me; face it as the goddess and queen I am. I sit on my throne with its gold and jewels, the throne I have sat on for so many years

—years of passing judgment, meting out punishment as needed or praise when earned, bringing justice and prosperity to my people.

This hall is—was—my life. The tapestries on the walls depict my Guardians; my warriors, my counsels, my loves. The scenes show the power of my magic and how it touched our people, making us the most prosperous kingdom in the land. I have spent hours upon hours in this room, only to die here.

Then I see him. Carlton, the so-called ruler from a neighboring kingdom, has always craved my throne. Had he killed my Guardians? With a triumphant look, he strides toward me down the long hall. He's tall, broad-shouldered, handsome, confident. Women adore him. I hadn't and he hated me for it.

He smiles in triumph. He's won.

Something cold is pressed into my hands. I can't look down but small fingers wrap around mine, a child's grip, pressing a cold, solid object into my palms. A soft sob escapes me.

One of my Guardians created the small golden statue for my birthday, several years ago. The statue is in the shape of a tree with its branches spread out with intricate detail. There are animals and men depicting my Guardians within the branches and around the base of the tree. The details are so exquisite, a person could make out the fur on the animals, the muscled arms on the men, the individual branches, the eyes gazing out from between the leaves. The men call it the Tree of Life. I adore and treasure it.

A tiny voice whispers, "Your statue, my Queen. Camden told me to deliver it only to you." The voice is my godson, Trae, who has lived in the castle since his parents' death. He's six years old, the nephew of one of my Guardians.

Everyone dotes on him as he is one of the few remaining dragons. Now he offers me a chance at life.

Never tried before, I know what Camden's plan entails: store my power within the statue for protection until I can be summoned. Trae will stash it and keep it safe from my murderers. If Carlton gets his hands on my power, he will destroy my kingdom with his evil and spread his vile power across the world.

I can't voice my thoughts or grip the statue, but excitement rushes through me. Hope. Trae could save the kingdom. I have to rely on him to encircle my hands around the golden tree. When I feel the cool metal, I concentrate on my task. I have never had to drain myself of my powers before, but it is now or never.

My power is unimaginable. It has grown for years. Many people desire it. Others want to acquire the secret to how I not only maintain its strength, I increase it. The secret will die with me until another woman releases it. Just as I once did.

As Carlton steps closer to the throne, he notices the boy by my side and screams at his men to capture him. I feel Trae's sweet lips on my cheek and hear him whisper, "I will love you forever, my Queen," and then he's gone—taking the gold statue.

Weak, empty, and cold, my body refuses to respond. My hands fall lifeless into my lap. It has been too many years since I'd had no power, no energy flowing through me—such a long time since I was only human and vulnerable. Tears flow down my cheeks from the utter desolation.

Shouts can be heard in the distance. The guards and warriors are coming to rescue me but it is too late. Carlton is directly in front of me, demanding someone catch the boy. I send a quick prayer toward the heavens that Trae will escape and the guards and warriors will save me.

Carlton turns with an evil smile and plunges a knife into my heart. As it sinks into my flesh, my last thought is of my loves... my Guardians.

Chapter 1

Friday

How he ended up here, Ian Stone had no clue. The dark enveloped him, only emergency exit signs and safety lights running near the floor illuminated his way. The private museum off the beaten path of Chicago's Magnificent Mile had an older security system, easily bypassed for someone with his skills.

Ian might be the youngest in the wolf pack, but he had learned his thieving talents from a master—his father. Too bad he never used them. Since their father's death during a job gone wrong, Ian and his two brothers had given up thievery. They concentrated on their dwindling clan of wolves and the resort they ran in the Alaskan wilderness.

Killing time before he had to catch a flight back home, a sixth sense had pulled him toward the side street. Being a supernatural entity, he always followed his instincts, which had brought him to the museum, led him inside and up to the third floor where he stopped directly in front of the tree.

He stared at the small statue and knew immediately why its call had drawn him. Roughly six inches tall, the gold tree rested on a large pedestal with several other artifacts. A plaque directly underneath it read *"Tree of Life, circa 1,000 BC."* He'd heard of the infamous Tree and the destruction caused by humans trying to possess it. Leaning close, he discovered both human and animal bodies hidden within the branches. Obvious to him, the creatures lurking among the leaves were shifters. Not so obvious was what the tree was doing in this tiny, ill-equipped museum. He was surprised no other shifter had noticed it.

He remembered vague stories about an evil king who had killed half of their people then enslaved the other half. All in an effort to use the power of the Tree to control their people. All over three thousand years ago. To him and other pack members it had been a folktale—a story told to frighten children to behave, a myth to stab terror into the hearts of disbelievers, a legend to cause the elderly to weep.

Now that he had discovered the relic, nothing would stop him from stealing it. His brothers would probably beat him senseless for this little stunt but the urge to take the statue grew with every passing moment. Even if the Elder Council punished or even banned him from his clan, he had to acquire the statue. It was a link to their history, a forgotten past.

A little bit of sleuthing and he discovered there were no pressure plates or alarms directly on or under the pedestal. The only alarms he'd encountered had been on the doors and windows which he'd easily circumvented. In less than twenty minutes he made it in and out, tucking the statue in a backpack that contained resort brochures, swag, and unsigned contracts.

Once outside, he kept to the shadows, slinking away in the early morning stillness. Sounds of nightlife and people enjoying their Friday night, now early Saturday morning, could be heard from several streets to the east. April nights in Chicago were chilly, but not enough to deter weekend activities.

Slipping into a dimly lit alley, he pulled up short. Several teenage punks lounged near the back door of a restaurant. *Stupid. Stupid. Stupid.* If he'd been paying attention, he would have heard their chatter and smelled the cigarettes a block away. He needed to get his head out of his ass if he wanted to escape with his reward.

Their heads turned. Despite the limited lighting, his keen eyesight noted three boys with peach fuzz on their cheeks. *Damn.* He gritted his teeth. If he backed up now, he might bypass them and avoid any trouble. Then one of the young men took a step forward and flicked his cigarette in Ian's direction. Too late.

Protect the Tree. Protect the Tree. The words whispered through Ian's mind, insinuating themselves into the core of his being. Soft but insistent. A worm burying itself into his skull. His instincts warning him.

He shook himself and returned his concentration to the immediate threat. He had gone to too much trouble to risk losing the ancient artifact to a bunch of weak human teenagers.

His body reacted instinctively. The hair on the back of his neck rose. The familiar sensation of shifting rocked him —jaw tightening, bones thickening, muscles strengthening. His fangs descended. His eyesight mutated, enhanced with night vision. Scents permeated his nostrils, his nose expanding and lengthening, the bones and cartilage cracking.

Working desperately to control the shift, he shuddered and shoved his wolf's instincts to the back of his mind and soul. If he glanced in a mirror, his eyes would be a deeper, richer chocolate brown with flecks of gold that glowed in the dim light. His face would have taken on a wolfish shape, elongating into a snout.

Heightened senses brought about enhanced awareness. Trash cans overflowed. Flies swarmed and buzzed. The scent of rotting garbage, piss, and vomit overwhelmed the small area. The humans were immune to the stench but his wolf basked in it.

A snarl and a deep growl released from his throat. He snapped his jaws together, lips pulled back, fangs glistening in the moonlight. The boys, catching sight of his face, screamed. Terror mixed with a strong odor of fresh urine. Two of them scattered like frightened rats. Unlucky for Ian, the third kid jerked a handgun from the back of his jeans. The teenager, attempting to flee, pointed it at Ian. Stumbling backward, arms flailing, the kid fell.

Ian's keen eyesight watched the boy's finger tighten on the trigger a split second before the gun exploded. He twisted his body. A stab of pain ripped through his shoulder. The punk scrambled away, leaving the weapon discarded on the ground.

Fate sucked.

Protect the Tree.

The relentless refrain slithered through Ian's mind. Anxiety pulsed in his brain when he attempted to concentrate on the words. *Why is this happening to me?* Voices in his head. Gunshot wound. Never in all the years he'd been thieving had bad luck cursed him. The heist from the museum had been uneventful until he stepped into the alley.

Pain throbbed and burned along his right shoulder and arm, hindering rational thinking. His inner wolf whined. As fast as his transformation had begun, it now reversed. Even as his nose regained its natural form, a metallic odor assaulted his nostrils. Blood soaked into his shirt, making the wet fabric cling to his skin. He slipped his left hand inside his coat and applied pressure to the wound.

Protect the Tree.

He shook his head, the words irritating. He was not prone to hearing voices but this one persisted. The words rolled through his mind, a wave of insistence, and took over all thoughts. The mantra beat at his heart and soul. His chest pounded. A wave of nausea flowed through him. Doubling over, Ian sucked in air to calm his wolf and embrace the pain. Seconds passed before he straightened and wiped the sweat from his forehead. *Think.* Injured, bleeding, and freely shifting into a wolf was not a good combination in downtown Chicago.

A flight out of O'Hare was out of the question with his shoulder seeping blood. Carrying the statue to safety in his wolf form was not an option. Normally, he would shift and let his enhanced healing abilities take over. Shifting took seconds, but recovering from an injury could take hours. He couldn't afford to hole up in an alley and chance being discovered.

He would contact Waru, more commonly known as War, to request a favor. The alpha of the local leopard pack and a descendent of the great Maasai tribe, War would lend Ian his private jet to carry him home to Alaska. Shifters avoided the world but went out of their way to help their kind in crisis. The king of the leopards would not ignore a plea for aid.

With his free hand, Ian yanked his cell phone from his pocket, grimacing at the smeared blood on the device. He pressed speed dial, then held the phone to his ear. Instead of hearing War's live voice, a recording activated.

"Whoever you are, tonight's poker night. Call me tomorrow. Or call Emerson, if you dare." War's deep chuckle sent an ominous shiver through Ian. Damn, he hated when War taunted him, but in a recorded message the mockery dug even deeper.

Contacting War now would be impossible. No one interrupted him during his poker game. No one.

Beep. "War. It's Ian. I'm in Chicago and need a ride. Urgently. Call me when you get this." After leaving his message, he debated whether to call Emerson. Nope. Nada. Wasn't going to happen. Bleeding to death would be more enjoyable.

Putting the phone away, he pressed harder on the wound. He needed a place to stay overnight. His top priorities: stop the blood loss and escape with the statue. With the faint, relentless words still echoing through his system, he debated which was more important.

There was a safe place within driving distance, a motel that shifters could hole up in when in a crisis, but getting there presented a problem. He'd leave a trail of blood if he took a taxi. The cops would locate him within an hour. No, he needed another means of transportation. Stealing a car would be a breeze. Driving it without passing out, not so much.

He picked up the dropped gun and tucked it in the back of his jeans, then stepped out of the alley and cautiously glanced around. Staying off the main thoroughfare, he hurried down the almost vacant sidewalk. After several blocks he stepped off a curb and stumbled, catching himself before he face-planted on the dark pavement. The blood loss was more than he had expected. Desperate, he staggered across the street to a parking garage, determined to protect the little tree overwhelming all other sensibilities.

Chapter 2

The last five days were a blur for Ryder. She was running on a fraction of sleep, and exhaustion weighed her down physically and mentally. The conference should have been a breeze compared to her normal ER schedule but it was kicking her butt with dinners and late evenings shmoozing with other doctors. Back home in Dallas, her normal day was work then home. Once home, she spent most of her spare time researching.

Her adoptive father was dying of cancer. He'd been through treatments, shoved the disease into remission only to have it slink back into their lives, snarling and growling as it ate its way through his body. Once a strong man, he was now a thin version of himself.

Her father was the reason for her research. Scientific or holistic or witchcraft, she read them all. This conference had been part of her search. Several world-renowned specialists were present as speakers. She had cornered them, picked their brains, and listened to their lectures. Except there was nothing of substance for her dad.

Despite the lack of sleep, the national medical conference had ended. On a professional level, she had accumulated a paper notebook filled with suggestions and ideas to take back to work, not to mention the recordings and ad hoc comments on her phone. That didn't even cover the two swag bags of freebies she planned on sharing with her coworkers. On a personal level it was a bust. She was glad she had visited her parents before the conference and not now, after the disappointment.

Glancing at the dashboard clock, she realized it was almost two in the morning. Ry's last night in Chicago had turned into her last morning in Chicago. Her body begged for sleep. A weary moan escaped her as she imagined slipping into the over-sized, over-soft bed in her hotel room. She'd be in her own bed in her own house tonight. She looked forward to getting back to her normal, sometimes boring, routine.

Her flight home left at noon, which gave her a few hours to grab some shut-eye and finish packing. Calculating how much sleep she might get before checkout time, she drove into the self-park garage near the hotel and mindlessly wound the car up the multiple levels until she spotted a space.

She stuffed her cell phone and a smaller purse into an oversized tote, then grabbed the larger bag before opening the car door. The smell of the day's leftover exhaust fumes, old oil, gas, and heated metal assaulted her. She wrinkled her nose and coughed. Soon she'd be back in Dallas and back to her normal routine. With a quick flick of her wrist, she shut the door and juggled her bags.

Two steps away from the car, a tingling sensation began at the back of her neck and creeped down her spine. Not sure if it was a foreboding or women's intuition, she heeded the sensation and took a moment to observe her dim surroundings. Unprepared for the dark figure easing out from the shadows, she scrambled backward and bumped into the closed car door. Just her luck, the first open space had been on a poorly lit level with a stalker.

The man spoke in a soft, calm voice. "Excuse me." He hesitated a moment. "I'm sorry to bother you, but I need your help."

A polite rapist? Who would have thought?

Despite his tone, her senses screamed in warning. The hair tingled on her arms and the back of her neck. *Run. Don't listen!* The words shrieked in her head. Where was security when you needed them?

She was overreacting. Tired and alone in the dark would work on anyone's imagination. He looked ordinary. He didn't act crazy. Despite the shadows, he appeared neat and clean in jeans, t-shirt, leather jacket. Not what she expected from a thief or rapist. He didn't wave a weapon, just stood, nonconfrontational, and waited.

She scolded herself. *Stupid. The normal ones turn out to be the serial killers.*

As a doctor in the ER, she was familiar with what happened to women caught alone on dark nights. Stumbling on a stranger at two in the morning in a dimly-lit garage with no one else around scared the crap out of her.

She needed to buy time. "Let me call someone."

Not looking, she reached behind her for the car door. If she slipped inside, she would be safe. She refused to take her eyes off him as she gripped the handle and pulled.

Locked. *Damn it.*

He took another step forward. A metallic click sounded, followed by his hard, cold voice. "Don't. Move." Sharp. Harsh. Intense.

Startled, she narrowed her gaze on his hand and discovered a gun pointed at her. Adrenaline rushed through her. Terror constricted her chest like a tourniquet wrapped on the bloody stump of an accident victim.

So much for the calm, quiet type.

In the same harsh tone, he repeated the command. "Don't move. Do you have any weapons? Give me your cell phone and your bag. I need you to drive your car."

She froze as his words slammed into her. "What? My car?" She shook her head, confused. "No. It's a rental. You can't have it."

Scowling, she realized how idiotic that sounded. Not stupid under normal circumstances, she needed to snap out of this mind-freeze and fast.

Moving closer, he reached for her tote. Since she couldn't open the car door, she did the next best thing and tossed the bag as far away as possible. Pivoting to flee, she prayed he'd go for her money and keys, then cursed when she remembered her cell phone deep at the bottom.

Except he didn't take the bait. He moved fast—too fast for a normal human. Despite being several feet away, he grabbed her by the arm before she took a step. She must be more exhausted than she'd thought.

"Don't run. I won't hurt you if you do exactly what I say. I need you to drive." He didn't sound irate. She recognized furious and frightened people from the ER. He was neither. He sounded determined. He jerked her around.

She tried to keep her voice steady. "Take my car and let me go. I won't tell anyone." Her emergency training flooded back, helping her keep her composure. Remain calm under pressure. That was the first thing she learned on the job.

He shook his head, gripping her arm tighter, and thrust her toward her bag. With swift movements, he tucked his gun into his waistband, bent over, and collected her stuff with his free hand.

He maneuvered her back to the car and dropped the bag on the hood. Digging through it one handed, he yanked out her keys. Ry scowled. It normally took her ten minutes to locate those damn things. He'd found them in less than two seconds.

"I need you to drive." Clicking the unlock button on the remote, he reached for the driver's door.

Panicking, Ry darted her gaze around her surroundings. This was the fourth floor of the garage, and she questioned if the cameras worked or if security guards even monitored the levels.

Why had she refused to use the hotel valet? Next time, she would pay the extra money herself. If she got a next time.

Her uncle was a cop and always envisioned the worst-case scenarios. His lectures pounded through her brain. *"Always be aware of your surroundings, Ry. If someone tries to kidnap you, don't go with him. If you do, you forfeit your life."* She should have listened better.

"In ... *now*." The stranger shoved her toward the open door.

Ry recalled her self-defense training. Aiming for the top of her would-be kidnapper's foot, she brought her booted foot down but stomped on concrete instead when he pivoted. She twisted and brought her knee toward his crotch, but he shifted his body and she connected with his hip instead.

She opened her mouth to scream. He clasped one muscular arm around her waist and yanked her back, tight against his rock-hard body. The air in her lungs whooshed out. His other hand clamped over her mouth, overpowering her. Struggling was futile. She shuddered and froze. If she fought, he would only grip tighter.

His voice hissed in her ear. "Don't fight me. You *will* get in the car and you *will* drive me out of the city."

The moment she stopped struggling, he lifted his hand. She sucked air deep into her lungs and screamed. He slapped his palm back over her mouth.

He growled. "I can snap your neck in a second. I'd rather not, but if you don't cooperate, I'll kill you and take your car."

As his words sank into her brain, Ryder sagged in defeat. She remembered her uncle's words: *when all else fails and you can't escape, cooperate and survive.*

Do whatever it took to survive.

Always survive.

Seeming to sense she had accepted her fate, her attacker removed his hand from her mouth. When she didn't scream again, he reached for the driver's door, yanked it open, and shoved her inside. He slammed the door shut, trapping her.

Seconds later, he slipped into the passenger seat and shoved the keys into the ignition. Startled, she turned her head to stare. *How was he able to move so fast?* She'd missed glimpsing him in the brief flash of interior light. He stuffed her bag on the floor between his feet.

Motioning to the dash, he commanded, "Start it."

Ry opened her mouth to protest but remembered another of her uncle's common-sense advice. *Pick your battleground.*

She closed her mouth and shoved aside the snarky comment on the tip of her tongue. For now.

Chapter 3

Ry waited until they were out of the Chicago city limits and heading north before she gathered her courage. Her uncle would be proud of her.

"Where are we going?" She was surprised her voice didn't tremble. He shifted in his seat to face her. Not daring to glance in his direction, she stared straight ahead and continued to drive.

After a full minute of silence, the man answered. "The less you know, the better. Head north. I'll tell you when to exit. Simple as that." His voice, now smooth, quiet, and soothing, sounded normal. He didn't act like the crazed gunman she'd struggled with minutes ago.

Simple? Ha. He had kidnapped her. She snorted her annoyance and tried another tactic. "I can help you if you're in trouble. You don't have to kidnap me."

"I'm not kidnapping you." Clearly amused with himself, he chuckled. "Imagine me renting your car. Although I will need you to be my guest until my friend picks me up in a few hours. I can't have you telling the cops where I am. I promise I won't hurt you."

Hours? She'd miss her flight. Her family wouldn't realize she was missing until she didn't call them when she arrived home safely. Not until late afternoon. Anger mixed with her fear.

He returned to watching the cars speed along beside them. *Keep him talking.* If he perceived her as a person, as someone who mattered, who had a life, maybe he wouldn't hurt her. They were both humans, after all, and could work this out. If she kept his attention, he might not notice if she sped up or switched on a turn signal. Would anyone else notice or care at this hour?

Her kidnapper remained observant and on guard, clearly aware of their surroundings and the other vehicles. He ordered her to slow down twice before they left the city, letting cars zip past. The man anticipated her every movement. So much for that idea.

"How much will you pay me?" She bit her lip, waiting to discover what he would do.

His head swiveled back toward her. "Excuse me?" Her question had surprised him.

"You said you were renting my car. How much?"

He snorted a brief laugh. "Five hundred dollars."

"You think my time is worth a mere five hundred dollars?"

"No? More?"

When she didn't reply right away, he urged her, "How much? Name your price."

Glancing at him in the semi-darkness of the passenger seat, she considered her response. Ry wished she could see his face better.

"Twenty thousand."

He paused then countered, "Ten."

"Fifteen."

"Agreed." His grin flashed in the dim light. "I'll give you fifteen thousand dollars for the use of your car."

She wasn't stupid enough to believe there would be any money. It was an outrageous amount but it didn't matter. What was important was getting him to respond to her.

"Unharmed."

"Yes. I swear on my brothers' lives, I won't harm you."

"Ha. Do you even have brothers?"

"Yes. Two, and both are very much alive."

"And your parents? What would they think of this situation?"

He grunted and turned to stare behind them. She'd hit a nerve. She attempted to keep the conversation flowing with more questions and comments, but he continued to ignore her. As their banter dwindled, she ran escape plans in her head. If given half a chance, she would bash him over the head and run.

Not quite thirty minutes later, they crossed the state line into Wisconsin. He directed her off the interstate and onto a less-traveled blacktop road. As she slowed down to accommodate the bumps and dips, her heart rate rapidly increased and her thoughts turned ugly.

She wasn't stupid. Places like this was where most kidnappers killed their victims. On a deserted stretch of highway, in the middle of nowhere, after raping and torturing them. Leaving them for dead. *Great, I'll be the unknown body on the morning news tomorrow.*

He surprised her again when fifteen minutes later he directed her to pull into the parking lot of an old, dilapidated motel. The Vacant sign was unlit. Not promising. Huge garbage bins overflowed. She imagined the flies, bugs, and rodents living among the trash. Her last moments would be in a rat-infested, flea-bitten, stinking room.

A single car parked near the front showed someone was inside the place. Would they help her or assist him in her demise? She shuddered and slowed near the office.

"Don't stop. Park by the last room." He motioned to the far end of the long, low structure. The moment she stopped where directed, he reached over, shifted the car into Park, turned the engine off, and removed the key. All in smooth, precise movements flowing together before she blinked.

"Out," he growled.

She reached for the door handle but he opened it instead from outside. Geez, how tired was she? He had moved at lightning speed again. He maneuvered her to the last motel room, opened it, and ushered her inside. At her surprised expression, he murmured, "Prior arrangements." The entire time, his eyes scanned the darkness beyond the building. All she noticed was the pitch-blackness of open country with no lights or buildings or houses or cars. No sign of humanity.

Once inside, he closed and bolted the door, then slipped her car keys into his backpack. Dumping her bag on a small table, he began a thorough search of the room, checking the locks on the windows.

While he did his security check, Ryder stood in the center of the room, taking in her surroundings. A nervous gesture had her twisting a small pendant on a chain around her neck. It was one of the few items left to her by her biological mother; that and her unusual name. She played with the necklace in difficult times, hoping to gain some bit of courage from a woman she barely remembered.

Wallpaper with large yellow and orange flowers, ancient-looking with edges peeling, decorated the walls. A king-sized bed stood across from the open bathroom door, taking up one entire wall. The bedspread was thin in a

faded green pattern. The curtains matched the bedspread—
a decorative, once-coordinating match to the fading walls.

A dresser, a table with two wooden straight-back chairs,
and two end tables with lamps completed the furnishings.
The dull brown carpet boasted several stains. She refused to
contemplate what they came from, or whom.

"Great." Her father claimed she wielded sarcasm as a
defense mechanism. Probably not a good time for mockery.
Ready to bolt, she stayed still, refusing to touch anything.

"Don't knock it. It's clean." His comment came from
across the room. Cleanliness was not the top priority—
escaping was—but Ry agreed. Despite the age and decor,
the room was neat.

He drifted back into the bedroom from the bathroom.
Taking hold of one of the straight-backed chairs, he moved
it beside her.

"Sit and be quiet."

"I'd rather stand." She had no plans to obey his orders.
Besides, if she wanted to escape, she would move faster if
already on her feet.

Shrugging, he stepped away, tugging off his coat and
backpack. A hiss of pain escaped his tight lips. His fingers
came away stained with blood. The red blended in with the
black of his t-shirt; only the shine from the wet area on the
upper part of his right shoulder showed the mess. He
frowned at the lining of his coat, twisting it back and forth,
inspecting the damage.

"Damn, that's not coming out. I liked this jacket, too."

His nonchalance over a hole in his body stunned her.
What kind of man ignored blood oozing from his body?

Her immediate suspicion was a bullet or knife wound.
Both something she would expect from a man who
kidnapped women in a dark parking garage. *Good. Maybe*

he'll die before he kills me. Shame flooded her. She was an ER doctor, trained to help people. *If he keels over from blood loss, I can sneak away.* No, she berated herself. A doctor healed people. Even people like him.

Before she realized she'd spoken, the words rolling through her mind escaped out her mouth. "I'm a doctor. I can help you if you let me."

Damn it, Ry. She mentally kicked herself. *Mind your own business. Hello? What's wrong with you?* She ignored the sarcastic rant dashing through her head while waiting for his reply.

His head came up in slow motion, giving her a first good look. His soft, chocolate brown eyes met her gaze. Guessing his age to be somewhere in his early-twenties, younger than her twenty-seven, she assessed him.

At approximately six feet, he was pleasant-looking. He reminded her of several of the men she had dated in college —the nice guy next door. The little lines near his eyes and the corners of his mouth indicated someone who laughed and smiled. He didn't seem like someone who kidnapped women.

His hair fell to his collarbones. A bit wild and shaggy, but the colors caught her attention. It was a medium shade of brown, and a variety of blond and red highlights ran through the strands. The shading couldn't be natural but it suited him.

Three small silver hoops adorned his left earlobe and a single diamond stud sparkled in his right. Men with earrings didn't appeal to her but again, the look fit him. The image of a pirate flashed through her mind.

Ry recognized the pain and tiredness in his eyes. His face reflected his exhaustion and discomfort. Her heart twisted from his agony.

She read the doubt and distrust on his face even as he spoke. "Why would you help me?"

"I'm a doctor. Doctors help people. Besides, maybe if I'm nice to you, you won't hurt me." She always spoke her mind. *No need to stop now.*

He straightened. A small, annoyed frown marred his face. "I already swore I wouldn't hurt you."

Had she wounded his sense of pride and chivalry? Confused, she tried to sooth his male ego. "Let's call it an ace-in-the-hole I'll hold over your head."

"Poker. My friend enjoys the game." A smile flitted across his face. "Okay. Remind me of your ace when you're frightened. I swear I won't hurt you."

A compromise was acceptable.

Thinking she'd made headway, she continued, motioning toward the table. "There's a small first aid kit in my bag. There are antibiotics, needle and surgical thread, some bandages. I can stitch you up and halt the bleeding."

He nodded, wincing as he staggered toward the table. He picked up the oversized tote before dumping the contents and rifling through them. She had the distinct sensation he didn't trust her.

Certain he was rummaging for a weapon, she stood in the middle of the room waiting for him to complete his search. Crossing her arms over her chest, she worked to keep the disdain from her voice. "You won't find any weapons in there. I despise violence."

Except after tonight, she would carry a firearm. A gun, a Taser, some mace, an Uzi, or whatever it took to protect herself. Uncle Rick would help her buy something. She would not be vulnerable again.

Without glancing up, he continued searching. "Is that why you're a doctor?"

"No. My mother is a nurse. I enjoy hearing her stories and watching her work."

Why am I telling him my life story?

Appearing satisfied, he stepped back and motioned to her bag.

"Grab what you need." Weariness edged his voice.

Time to take control. Doctor mode came easy, putting her in charge.

"Take off your shirt and get on the bed. Lie on your back. There's not adequate lighting for surgery but this will have to do."

Ry retrieved the small bag of first aid supplies and selected the items she required. Pulling on surgical gloves, she turned around and froze. *Oh, baby. Breathe. Just breathe.* His face might be nice-looking but his body was gorgeous. All tan and muscled.

She never gawked at the men she treated in the ER. At this moment, though, it was impossible to maintain any semblance of professionalism. He was difficult to ignore.

His well-defined muscles rippled as he shifted on the bed. Dangling his legs off the edge, he attempted to find a comfortable position. *Is that a six-pack? Or eight? Wow. Stop counting, Ry.*

Too busy inspecting his wound, he didn't notice her leering. Good thing too. Glancing away, she worked at getting her hormones under control while metaphorically wiping away drool. An image of her running her tongue along his abs flitted through her mind.

Where did that come from? *Pull it together. Be professional.*

She shook herself then stepped toward him, batting his hands away. She had to stay detached and complete the exam. "Quit it. I'm the doctor. Let me look."

He grinned. She wished he wasn't so adorable when he flashed his wicked smile. His soft brown eyes reminded her of warm, melted dark chocolate. His lips looked so kissable. *Concentrate.*

After wiping the blood away, she inspected the seeping wound. To keep her mind on the task and not his abs or lips, she narrated while she cleaned. "The bullet went in the front and straight out the back."

She probed and prodded. He remained quiet, never wincing. "I can't be sure without further tests but there appears to be no internal damage. You need a hospital to be sure." At the mention of a hospital, he grunted, "No."

She halted her examination and reached for a needle and thread. "I have nothing strong enough to numb the pain while I stitch you."

He shrugged. "Do it."

Ry made quick work of stitching him up, then applying an antibiotic salve and a bandage, front and back. He didn't flinch. The man had nerves of steel. She reached into her bag and retrieved a syringe and a small bottle of antibiotics.

"No shots." He bolted upright and stood, shaking his head. "I can't take the chance you'll slip me something to make me sleep, then call the cops. Nope. No shots."

"It's antibiotics to prevent infection."

He shook his head again and stepped away.

"Well, when you die of an infection, don't yell at me. For the record," she spoke over her shoulder as she stuffed everything back into her bag, "I wouldn't call the cops." She turned and glared. "I'd leave you to die of infection, which is a good possibility. The motel owners can call the cops when your body rots and stinks. If they even smell it over the garbage outside."

He threw back his head and laughed. She stared in awe

as his throat muscles worked and his bare chest vibrated. A grin lit up his face.

Trying hard not to smile back, she ignored him and finished repacking her bag. *Sheesh, Ry, get a grip. He's your kidnapper, not your best friend.* She avoided looking in his direction. Still shirtless, he relaxed back onto the bed, propped up on pillows with the gun near his side. With an excuse to wash her hands, she hurried to the bathroom. She needed distance.

Ry locked the door before turning on the faucet. Waiting for the water to warm up, she attempted to cool down her hormones. She placed her hands on the edge of the sink and took slow, deep breaths.

Thoughts of his chiseled abs and muscular biceps bombarded her. The moment she envisioned him naked, she snatched up the bar of soap and vigorously lathered her hands, trying to erase the tantalizing images from her mind.

No. No. No.

Ryder dedicated herself to her career. She'd held down two jobs to put herself through college. She did not jeopardize her career with dating or even one-night stands. She lived vicariously through her best friend's affairs. In one year, Ry would finish her residency. She would become a licensed doctor. Until then, men, particularly sinfully sexy ones like the one in the other room, were off-limits.

Stop. Concentrate on escaping, not on his body.

Chapter 4

Exhausted and in pain, Ian pondered how much longer he might stay awake. His day began with a flight out of New York, then a layover in Chicago to meet with a potential client for the family business. He'd spent the rest of the afternoon and evening wandering around the city, killing time before his flight home late in the day. Then his day had gone bat-shit crazy.

Ian shut off the overhead lights, then switched on the TV. What to do with the woman for the rest of the night frustrated him. He should tie her up next to him on the bed. The idea sounded appealing. He grinned and shifted uncomfortably. Not normally attracted to humans, this one seemed different. She didn't have to treat his wound and yet she had volunteered.

A tiny thing compared to him, she stood around five-foot six, slim and cute with dark auburn, shoulder-length hair drawn into a short ponytail. When he had her locked in his embrace in the parking garage, he'd discovered her hair was soft and thick and smelled of flowers. He imagined running his hands through her tresses, clutching a handful and tugging her head back as he ran his tongue along her vulnerable throat.

Despite the ugly, thick-rimmed glasses she wore, her eyes caught his attention. They were a brilliant green. He imagined how they would brighten with passion when he kissed his way down her quivering body.

Ian jerked himself out of his thoughts and frowned. *Where had that come from?* He must have lost more blood than he imagined. She was his ticket out of the city. End of story. Distractions, especially from a human, would not aid him now. Although he was sorry about the comment in the garage about breaking her neck. He would never have done it but she didn't know that. He would have to apologize before he let her go.

If he closed his eyes for a few minutes, he'd be fine when she came back into the room.

SLIPPING OUT OF THE BATHROOM, Ryder glanced at the sleeping man sprawled on the bed. *Perfect. Now all I need are my keys.* Finding his backpack draped over a chair, she eased it off, attempting to soften any sound of jangling keys so she wouldn't disturb him. She slipped her hand inside and dug around.

Instead of a set keys, her fingers wrapped around something cold and hard. Tugging out the object, she discovered a small statue in the shape of a tree. Gold and tarnished, the six-inch object needed a good cleaning but the details were exquisite.

Whoever crafted the piece had been a master artisan. The intricate design revealed individual branches and leaves. Reclining at the base and lurking in the metal foliage were men and animals. Some only revealed bits and pieces of their bodies, which made identifying specific species difficult. The most distinct were three wolves lying at the base.

At the window, she held the statue up to a shaft of moonlight slicing through a crack in the drapes. Fascinated by its beauty, she inspected it closer.

"Wow. Hello, gorgeous." An overwhelming urge to caress the cool surface flooded her. She stroked the metal over and over, brushing the tarnished surface. Her fingers began to tingle, the sensation creeping up her arms.

The tree sparkled and shined, then glowed under her ministrations. As she stared in amazement, the statue burst into a cloud of dazzling dust like glitter at a little girl's birthday party. With her arms raised, the shimmering powder rained down on her upturned face. Instinctively she closed her eyes, allowing the tiny particles to drift over her. A laugh of pure pleasure and sexual desire escaped.

Heady emotions poured into her—excitement, lust, power. Sensations that frightened her for a split second. A surge of electricity tingled through her body. The air vibrated with energy and magic. She had never experienced such exhilaration. Ry opened her mouth. A gasp of amazement slipped from her lips, but she heard no sound.

Sucking in air, she drew more dust into her mouth and throat. Instead of coughing, a warm and smooth feeling slid into her lungs, like breathing in honeyed sunshine. She reveled in the soothing comfort.

Addictive. Craving more, Ry inhaled again, deeper, pulling in more of the golden powder.

Incredible. Another deep breath. More dust.

Intoxicating. Her limbs tingled with energy. Alive and full of life.

She opened her eyes. Her entire body hummed with power. Awareness of each pore and individual hair follicle caused the blood to race through her veins. Her heart beat faster and stronger. Her lungs filled with oxygen. Everything was new, fresh, and exhilarating.

Her gaze shot to the half-naked man on the bed. An instantaneous sexual awareness ripped through her. Her eyes devoured him. Her stomach quivered with excitement and anticipation. Her nipples tightened. As her lips drew into a predatory smile, she turned toward her kidnapper.

MARA SENSED the rush of power and pleasure as she took over this new body. *It felt so good to be alive again.* How long this time? Vanity had her hesitating at a mirror on the wall. She recognized her brilliant blue eyes. Those never varied with each body she claimed. Her face was pleasant, almost lovely. Brushing back a strand of hair, she smiled. She allowed her hands to drift over the body, *her body*, and found a well-shaped figure with firm breasts, flat stomach, and rounded hips. This form would suit her.

Glancing down, she realized she wore trousers. She scowled. What woman would wear men's clothing? The pants had to go. Her long, luxurious gowns made of velvets, satins, and silk would slide erotically against her bare skin. She would have to locate new ones.

Raising a hand, she smoothed the frown on her face. Or the other woman's face? No, it was hers. Not liking the feel of her mouth turning down, she smiled, causing her cheeks to lift, her lips to turn up at the corners. The movement sent tendrils of joy racing through her; she laughed with exhilaration.

A quick double-check confirmed that the woman's

consciousness remained tucked into the recesses of her mind, sleeping deeply. It was only temporary. Once Mara harnessed enough power, she would take over and complete the merging of this mind, body, and soul with her own. Until then, she could only control the situation sporadically as her own waning energy allowed.

More pressing matters lay before her. The first Guardian in this new life would be a wolf. The present would imitate the past. She understood what she needed to survive. There was only one way to acquire a Guardian.

Sex, blood, and magic.

The one part of acquiring a Guardian she disliked was using a binding spell. They regained control once the magical ritual was over which was the only saving grace to the process.

A handsome young man, shirtless and unconscious, lounged on the bed, his pants hung low on his waist. The top button was undone and caused a slight gap. Just the way she liked her men—gorgeous and sexy. The bandage on his shoulder confirmed a recent injury.

Gliding toward the bed, she discarded her clothes piece by piece. She would deal with wearing pants later. Besides, healing magic worked better when naked.

She eased the bandages off and placed one hand on the wound in front, then slid her other beneath his body to cover the exit hole in his back. Concentrating, she thrust her energy into his open wounds. Power trickled from her hands into his body. A pale golden light pulsed.

She used the small amount of magic she had to heal the wolf lying before her. She needed him strong. The quickest and most efficient way to regain her strength and power was through sex. Her magic would regenerate but healing his wounds took longer because of her weakened condition.

Mara released the young man from her thrall. Normally, she would allow him time to sleep and heal, but she had urgent matters. She needed sex. She needed power.

Tugging off his jeans, she admired the view for a moment before straddling his body. She ran her hands over his chest, leaned down, and whispered in his ear, "Awake, Guardian. Be mine." The simple incantation became the ritual she had completed twelve times in the past.

His eyes fluttered open. Such a lovely, deep brown. *My wolf.* She sensed his alter identity deep within him. He would be her first Guardian and her first lover in this new body.

Spellbound by the magic, he didn't question his actions as his hands drifted up her legs, skimmed her hips, and came to rest on her waist. Leaning forward, he took possession of her mouth, kissing her deeply and passionately. He tasted fresh and wild, his scent spicy and masculine. Taking control, he rolled them over, never breaking the kiss.

His magnificent body settled between her thighs. Mara adored his solid weight. He reminded her of her men—her previous Guardians. She had loved each of them. Pain slammed into her. Her last memory was of their agonizing deaths. Needing to concentrate on the task at hand, she shoved the memories away and focused on the man above her.

He rubbed his erection against her soft wetness. Tantalizing her. Teasing her. His mouth skimmed sensuously down her neck with little nibbles, licks, and growls. She shifted her head to the side and gave him access to her vulnerable throat. A low growl emanated from deep in his chest. The sensation rumbled through her body and triggered every erogenous zone.

"Bind me to you. Be mine," she commanded breathlessly. She nudged the compulsion into his mind with the last ounce of her remaining magic.

His mouth glided lower to her breasts to tease one nipple. Placing her hands at the back of his head, she pulled him closer, silently demanding more. The pressure increased on her breast as he sucked hard. She moaned with pleasure. She couldn't remember her last release. Had it been mere years or centuries? Her orgasm exploded. Her back arched. Her legs tightened around his body.

As he released her nipple, she watched with grim satisfaction as his wolf's fangs descended and he sank them into her breast. Pain shattered through her. She cried out at the agony. Absolute delight immediately replaced her distress. She thrilled at his fangs sliding into her tender flesh and moaned her satisfaction.

She craved the mix of pain morphing into pleasure. Her body arched up, quivering and shaking, carrying her to another full orgasm.

As her ecstasy receded, his fangs retracted, releasing her breast. His tongue laved the puncture wounds, his saliva sealing the holes and cleaning off her blood.

Changing position, he pressed his shaft to her entrance and slid home. With slow, sensuous movements, he glided out to the tip before easing back in inch by glorious inch. Balls-deep, he paused and ground his pelvis seductively into hers.

"Tell me what you want. Tell me what you like." His voice caressed her as smoothly as his movements. She missed this intimacy; the pleasure, the pain, and the rush of magic.

Pressing her lips to his shoulder, she kissed his skin before sinking her teeth into his muscled arm. His cock hardened. She reveled in her pussy tightening around his increased size.

Moving her mouth to his ear, she murmured, "Everything. I want it all. Make love to me for as long and as often as you like. I won't break."

He rumbled with pleasure before sliding his cock in and out of her body. He brought her to multiple orgasms before finally allowing his own release. As she floated on a cloud of euphoria, he held her and caressed her hair, running his hands tenderly over her.

When she regained her senses, he slid his body down hers until his head rested level with her thigh, his mouth near her mound. Her new Guardian instinctively sensed she needed multiple orgasms to increase her power, which he was eager to provide. Once the initial ritual was completed, her Guardians were in control of their actions but none had ever strayed. The power she gained had enhanced their senses and strength.

She glided into deeper pleasure as his tongue, lips, and fingers skillfully worked her body. She forgot about the woman whose form she now occupied, what place in the world she now lived, and what time period in which she now existed.

Only one thing mattered at this moment. Power.

Chapter 5

Saturday

Ry woke with a start, her limbs jerking. The glow from the television put the room in shadows and played over her bare skin. Groggy, it took several moments before she noticed her kidnapper lying beside her. Gloriously naked.

Frantic, she tried to remember what happened. Fragments came to her, but the memories were like gazing through a frosted window. Emotions, though, overwhelmed her. Mortification. Terror. Excitement. More mortification. One fact stood out. She'd had sex.

Lots and lots and lots of mind-blowing sex. With her kidnapper. Something she hadn't done in years while she devoted herself to becoming a doctor. And yet in the space of a few hours, she'd had hot sex in bed. Wonderful sex against the wall. Intense sex on the floor. Powerful sex with him on top. Passionate sex with her on top. Astonishing sex with him behind. Incredible sex in ways she hadn't known were possible. What had he done to her? What had she done with him?

Moving with extreme caution so as not to wake him, she slipped out of bed and tried to stand. Her legs refused to support her for a moment. Her muscles screamed with exhaustion. An unfamiliar lethargy caressed her limbs. A sticky wetness smeared between her thighs, confirming they hadn't used condoms.

Her mind struggled to accept the night's activities. Ry refused to consider her behavior. He must have drugged her. She had to concentrate on escaping and fleeing as quickly as possible without disturbing him. If he woke, she'd never get away.

The clock next to the bed read 8:17 a.m. If she drove fast, she might make her flight. In hours, she would be far away from this man and the events from last night. She had to leave and now.

Ry grabbed her clothes and hurried into the bathroom. She cleaned up and dressed in record time without making a sound. As she struggled with her bra, she noticed her chest in the mirror and stared in horror at the markings on her left breast.

A tattoo.

Not a simple one either. This was an exquisitely detailed wolf. His body wrapped around the plumpness of her breast with his head resting on his paws near her nipple. She visualized his tongue stretching out and licking her. The image made her tingle.

Stunned, she wondered how long she had slept. Wouldn't a design this complex take time? Days? Weeks? Months? How could anyone create a tattoo this detailed? She was not about to stick around and find out.

She threw on the rest of her clothes and slipped back into the bedroom. In seconds, she located her shoes, bag, and keys. The sun shone brightly outside, peeking through a slit in the curtains. She remembered holding a statue up to the moonlight. She envisioned the details, the wolves, and the thing disintegrating before her eyes.

Oh fuck. The statue! The relic must have been worth a small fortune. Her kidnapper would follow her and make her pay for its destruction. What kind of payment he would demand, she couldn't guess. Thrown in jail? Tied to his bed?

Giving him a last glance, she admired the naked body sprawled over the sheets. She took one long extra moment to appreciate him; his solid chest with an elaborate tattoo on one side, his broad shoulders, his chiseled abs with the happy trail leading down to.... Her face burned with embarrassment when she recalled the things they had done together.

Pivoting in a flood of mortification and confusion, she fled.

IAN WOKE AND STRETCHED, luxuriating in the strength and power racing through his body. Damn, he felt better than he had in a long time. Tossing back the sheet, he leaped out of bed then paused. Something wasn't right. Puzzled, he glanced back at the bed with tangled sheets and the scent of sex. He went instantly on alert, cocking his head to listen. Soft sounds from the TV were all he heard.

In mere seconds he realized the woman had escaped. He rushed to the window before pulling aside the curtain a crack. Her car was missing. His cursing filled the room. She'd probably called the cops. They might pull up to the door any second now.

As he stepped back from the window, Ian's mind whirled. Clothes. His gaze darted around the room and he spotted them near the far wall. His long strides swiftly took him to them.

When he bent down, a new realization dawned on him. No pain. Frantically probing his shoulder, Ian discovered that the bullet wound had vanished. No bandage, scarring, redness, soreness, or anything. It was impossible. Rushing into the bathroom for further inspection, he halted in front of the mirror. What he discovered stunned him.

A tattoo covered the left side of Ian's chest. An intricate design of Celtic scrollwork made its way over his breast, weaving around his side, under his arm, and up over his shoulder. In the center stood a tree that was approximately six inches tall. The tendrils of scrollwork meandered around the tree, merging with the branches and trunk to create one design. When had this shit happened? It reminded him of—

The statue.

Rushing back into the bedroom, Ian snatched up his backpack from the chair. Noticing the lack of weight, he dug through it frantically. No statue. He tossed the bag on the bed and cursed. Ian stormed around the room, shoving furniture aside in a futile quest for the treasure. After several minutes, he gave up. The only item left of the woman was her glasses.

Stunned, he concentrated on his predicament. *Unbelievable. The bitch stole it.* The golden statue was a priceless ancient artifact. Now some human woman had taken it out from under his nose. It was the ultimate embarrassment for a master thief. He would be the laughingstock of the packs when word of this got out. His actions would reflect on his brothers and their Alaskan pack and would devastate their reputation.

He needed to leave. Fast. He debated whether he should

walk out of the hotel on two feet or four. If he shifted, he would lose his boots but he would get away faster. Impossible to know when she had escaped, he had to hurry, especially if she called the cops. Now after ten in the morning, it might already be too late.

After stuffing his boots, jeans, and backpack under the bed, he used his t-shirt to make a bundle of his cell phone, wallet, and her glasses. Packing took mere seconds. He'd ask Waru to retrieve the other items later.

Ian realized he should call his brothers except he knew what their reaction would be and he did not want to deal with the drama when they found out what had transpired. Falling asleep last night had been reckless and irresponsible. He might as well have handed her the statue. He needed to find the woman and get the relic back before anyone else found out. No, his brothers would have to wait. War would be his best support in this crisis.

Cracking the door open, Ian used his wolf's senses to hear or smell if something was out of the ordinary. He grabbed the small bundle and hurried naked from the room and into the sunshine. In ten feet he turned the corner and stepped into a large group of trees behind the building. He always selected this room because of its proximity to the woods. Once hidden, he shifted.

The transformation came naturally, fluidly, in a shimmer of energy. In mere seconds, an enormous wolf with a mixture of brown, red, and white fur in perfectly blended shades stood among the trees. He knew from experience that his earrings remained, lost in the fur. Shaking himself, he grasped the bundle with his teeth and ran. Cutting across fields and a wooded area, he stayed away from main roads and houses.

He made good time, covering over ten miles before

shifting back into human form. Naked, he squatted behind a thick covering of bushes and yanked his cell phone out of the small pack. He dialed, and his body sagged with relief when he heard War's reassuring voice before the second ring.

"Hey, little brother. Beautiful day, isn't it?"

Despite his situation, Ian grinned. War called all his friends "little." Once a person stood beside him, they realized why. A large black man, he topped out at six-foot six, shoulders as broad as an ox's. With tattoos running over his bald head, neck, and shoulders, he presented an imposing image.

"You sound pleased. Poker night must have been profitable."

"It was. It was. I took the local police chief for over two hundred dollars. I'll let him win it back next week. You mentioned you needed a ride. What's up?"

"I fucked up." He was man enough to admit when he needed help. At least to War.

Instant alpha mode shifted his friend's pleasant conversation. "Tell me what's happening. Have you contacted your brother?"

Ian knew that War meant Jamie, his oldest brother. Jamie was his pack alpha and elder. Ian normally reported everything to him. Except this time, he had gone against orders by not heading directly home after meeting with their new client. Jamie would never believe that the statue had pulled him to the museum.

"No. I'm not calling Jamie. I need someone to bring me clothes and come get me. I'm over the border in Wisconsin."

War laughed. "Clothes? Seriously? Tell me it was a woman or I'll never let you live it down."

Humoring him, Ian half-heartedly joined in. "Actually, it

was. She took something from me and I need your help in getting it back."

"This is rich! Took? Or Stole?" War's chuckle mocked him.

Ian remained silent. *The less he knows, the better for me.*

War broke the stalemate. "Okay. I'll send someone, but you'll have to tell me more when you get here."

"Thanks, War. In the meantime, can you get the surveillance video from a parking garage? I can track her down from there."

"Depends on the garage. What's the name?"

Within twenty minutes, a sporty black BMW pulled up the dirt road and stopped. Stepping from the car, a familiar face greeted him and tossed him a wad of clothes. As the captain of War's men, Emerson ruled with an iron hand. The men feared but respected her.

She despised Ian. Roughly forty years earlier, Ian stole a woman from Emerson. He grinned to himself. He hadn't considered it stealing. To be fair, he'd tried getting both women in his bed. The other woman had come to him by herself. She had decided she preferred a man. Emerson turned into a royal bitch soon after.

"Nice tat. When'd ya get it?"

Fastening the jeans, Ian glanced at Emerson in confusion. Fists resting on her hips, she nodded toward his chest.

How did I forget? He snarled and yanked the shirt over his head, muttering through the material. "Not important."

Emerson shrugged and climbed back into the driver's seat. She revved the engine, taking her foot off the accelerator for a second and causing the car to jerk when he reached for the handle. Growling in annoyance, Ian slid inside. Before the door closed, she shifted gears and sped away. Neither spoke as they headed to Chicago.

Chapter 6

Home. *Finally.*

It seemed like forever since Ry had fled the dilapidated motel. After a mad drive back to the downtown hotel, she ran inside, using the valet service this time. Not caring about neatness, she tossed her clothes and personal items into her suitcase and carry-on. Without bothering to stop at the front desk to check out, she manhandled her luggage out to her rental car. She needed to get out of Chicago and as far away from *him* as possible.

She debated calling her uncle and spilling her guts. Being a cop, he would demand she remain in Chicago and charge the man with kidnapping and rape. The problem was, she knew he hadn't raped her. From what she remembered, it was not one-sided or forced.

Driving to the airport, she kept an eye open for him, aka Mr. Gorgeous Kidnapper. She swore she spotted him several times—while returning the car, checking in at the airport ticket counter, going through security, and on the tarmac as she waited for takeoff. He was never there.

Can you say paranoid?

She wanted to forget the previous night. Just put it all behind her. She had no reason to think her kidnapper would follow her. He didn't know her name. He didn't have a way to track her. Did he?

With a sigh of relief, she dropped her bags inside her front door. At least she had the rest of the weekend to recover before she had to show up to work on Monday night. Enabling her security system took mere seconds. Even knowing her home was secure, she checked and rechecked, then double-checked the locks on all the doors and windows, even wondering how she might reinforce them further.

Roughly thirty minutes from the hospital, her small three-bedroom rental house sat in the Dallas suburbs. Most of her furniture was secondhand. Student loans sucked up most of her money. The only brand-new items she'd purchased were her laptop, king-size bed, and the sixty-five-inch flat-screen television and media center in her living room. The big screen was her way to relax after an exhausting day in the ER. And jogging, when she found the time.

Her home was her sanctuary. After a twelve- or fourteen-hour day at the hospital treating everything from rashes to the flu to broken bones to gunshot wounds and knife stabs, all she wanted was to curl up on her sofa and kill time by vegging. Sometimes she would go out with her best friend for drinks, maybe a manicure—although ER work did not bode well for pretty nails—or a movie. She never dated, which her friend Lauren declared shameful.

Normally after a trip, the first thing she'd do was unpack, but she'd left Chicago without cleaning off the evidence of the previous night. Getting clean was at the top on her list. Once in the shower, she tried scrubbing off the tattoo but only managed to chafe her skin red and raw. Despite her attempts, the tattoo was real and permanent.

Giving up, she concentrated on scouring the rest of her body to purge any memories from the previous night. Eventually, she stepped out of the shower to dry off.

Determined to get a better look at the tattoo, she crouched naked on the bathroom countertop, leaning in close to the mirror. The details of the wolf amazed her. The fur was unique with brilliant shades of blond, brown, and red. The eyes were a deep, rich shade of brown with flecks of gold shimmering in the light. As she stared, the tail twitched. The eyes blinked. The mouth opened enough to show piercing canines.

What the hell?

She scrambled off the counter as if fleeing would make the thing on her chest disappear. Halting in the middle of her bedroom, her heart thudding, she gasped for air. *It is not alive. It is not alive.* Hallucinations were not something she normally experienced. But it had been a wild twenty-four hours and a tiring week. She wondered again if her kidnapper had drugged her.

Slowly controlling her breath, she cautiously slipped back into the bathroom and leaned toward the mirror. Examining the tattoo once more, she noted the similarity between it and one of the wolves on the statue. She had admired the three wolves lying at the base of the little tree. One had been curled up in the exact position as this wolf.

Wait a minute. She leaned in farther. The wolf's fur sported the variations in color as her kidnapper's hair. She frowned at the image in the mirror. *Don't freak out.* There had to be a logical reason why the tattoo reminded her of her kidnapper and the wolf on the statue.

Determined to cover up the marking, she tugged on

boxer shorts and a t-shirt that read, "Save the Earth. It's the only planet with chocolate." Once in the kitchen, she nuked a frozen meal before devouring it. She hadn't realized how hungry she'd become.

Now mid-afternoon, exhaustion weighed her down. She made another round to check the doors and windows before she collapsed into bed, falling asleep within minutes.

Then the dreams began.

The long flowing velvet blue gown sensuously caressed her bare skin. A matching cape lined with fur bundled her in warmth. She was dreaming but it was surreal, like she was someone else. Perched sidesaddle on a large white horse, she watched the countryside drift past. As she rode along, a man on another horse came into her sight on her left. He smiled. Handsome in a dark, rough, old-world sort of manner, he sported a couple of days' growth of beard. He wore leather pants with a heavy cape made from a solid gray material and edged with fur.

She smiled back, pleased with his attention. Then she frowned. Why was she delighted to see this stranger?

"Are you comfortable, my love?" He spoke with a Scottish accent. His actions and speech were similar to a player at a Renaissance fair.

My love. Was he talking to her? Puzzled, she stared at him and blinked.

His forehead creased as he frowned. "You appear to be miles away. What is wrong? Are you cold? We can return home if you wish."

She shook her head. She wasn't sure why, but she was comfortable and relaxed.

He took her hand, raised it to his lips, and placed a soft kiss on her palm.

"I would suggest I carry you in my arms and warm you up, but we have arrived at our destination. Perhaps we can indulge later."

He winked, grinning broadly. It was a suggestive action, making her stomach tighten and her body tingle.

As the horses came to a halt, she glanced around and found several men on horseback surrounding her. Some of them dismounted, including the one who had kissed her hand. Another one, as handsome as the first, stepped up to her horse. He placed his hands on her waist and lifted her off the animal, holding her close so her body slid suggestively down his.

The sensation of his strong, hard body against hers was amazing. His lips brushed her own before he released her. More tingling arose in various body parts. What was it with these men? Why did she react to them? Why didn't she shove them away?

Within moments of her feet touching the ground, a young couple with two small children and a baby greeted her. The woman struck up a hesitant conversation about her children before switching topics to farming, then to cooking. She followed the dialog although she didn't understand a thing about any of those topics. She enjoyed herself. It was a pleasant time. A pleasant dream.

During the chat, she darted glances at the men who had dismounted. Three of them had taken the husband aside and were discussing animals and crops. The others stood nearby.

Every time she glanced at any of them, they gave her loving gazes, winks, and smiles. These were not ordinary guards and soldiers. When she strolled past the ones on foot, they reached out with gentle caresses or brief kisses. None of them missed a chance to touch her.

When it was time to leave, they said their goodbyes to the young couple. The first man who had spoken to her lifted her up onto his horse and swung up behind her in the saddle. He held *her close. As they rode past open fields and a dense forest, he shifted her and slipped his hand inside her cape, inside her gown, and between her legs. He stroked her, his fingers sliding through her wetness. She trembled as his calloused fingertips glided gently on her sensitive bud. Every brush sent shivers dancing through her nerve endings. She leaned back in his arms and relished the attention. Her murmurs of delight transformed into cries of passion.*

RY WOKE on a whimper of pleasure with her sheets tangled around her legs. Her body tightened and trembled from her climax. She had *experienced* it. What had happened in her dream had affected her in reality. She quivered from the receding orgasm.

As she lay on her bed, confusion muddled her thoughts. With slow deep breaths, she realized that the woman in her dream had been her. And yet she hadn't been. She had gazed through another woman's eyes while Ry's every movement, thought, and word was being directed.

After crawling out of bed, Ryder stumbled to the kitchen for a drink of water. She'd been asleep less than an hour. Back in her bedroom, she sat on the edge of the bed and willed herself to calm down. Exhaustion overpowering her, she lay back and tumbled into sleep.

MEANDERING through a field of tall grass, she let her hands skim across the tops of the blades. Snowcapped mountains loomed in the distance. She was naked but she wasn't self-conscious. In fact, she felt wonderful, enjoying the freedom of her bare skin with the sun beating down and a cool breeze brushing and caressing her.

As she glanced down at her body, the wolf tattoo on her chest glowed. She traced the pattern. Her breast and body tingled with life and sexual energy.

She wandered through the field until the tall grass ended into a meadow with blue and yellow wildflowers. Standing in the open, she raised her face to the slight breeze, inhaled the scent of the flowers, and reveled in the silence. A sixth sense had her swinging her head to watch a wolf step into the field. He had the same coloring as the wolf inked on her breast.

Kneeling in the clearing, she experienced no trepidation and reached for the animal. It ambled closer. When it was directly in front of her, she wrapped her arms around its neck. It nuzzled and brushed against her naked body. She loved the soft and luxurious feeling of his fur.

He danced around, darting close before hopping away. His tongue lolled out of his mouth. Ry laughed at his playfulness.

When he quit bouncing around, he plopped beside her. She wrapped her arms around him again, burying her face in his fur. The wolf stretched out, his weight taking her to the ground.

As they fell, his furry body shifted until a naked man lay beside her. Gazing into his eyes, she realized he was her kidnapper. Unafraid, she snuggled close.

In a gentle move, he pressed her onto her back, his nakedness warm and hard against her. Ry tightened her arms around him, her lips caressing his neck and jawline.

"Did you miss me, my sweet?" He gently sucked on her sensitive earlobe.

A breathless sigh escaped her lips. "My sweet. Mmm. I like the way that sounds."

She was dreaming. She could do whatever she wanted with no repercussions. He had satisfied her the night before. He was a sexy, virile man. They had a connection.

Pressing her lips to his, she deepened the kiss. Time to show him what she wanted. He allowed her to switch positions and *straddle him. His erection lay snuggly against her heated mound. She grasped him and guided him to her entrance, sliding him inside. Arching her back, she cupped her breasts. With him holding her waist, she rode him fast and demanding.*

RY WOKE on a gasp of pleasure. Rolling onto her side, she hugged her knees to her chest, breathing heavily and trembling. The dream had been real. Too real. His hands, his lips, and his tongue on her skin had seemed genuine. Her body continued to tremble and tighten from her orgasm, the feel of him inside her still echoing through her.

It took several minutes to recover. A quick glance at the clock showed it was barely seven in the evening. Now too exhausted to relax, she hauled herself to the kitchen and downed two shots of whiskey. Back in the living room, she switched on the television. Then she curled up in her over-stuffed recliner with her favorite leopard-print blanket wrapped around her. She was asleep in minutes.

THE NIGHT SHONE bright with a brilliant full moon. She lay naked on a grassy hilltop, stretched out with the pleasant texture of soft grass against her back. Three wolves trotted up the hill. Excitement coursed through her body. As they reached her, the wolves shifted into human form.

Three gorgeous men knelt beside her. One of them was her captor. She had never seen the other two but they had similar features. His brothers? All three had rippling muscles, toned abs, broad shoulders, and strong chests. She imagined them gracing a hunk-of-the-month calendar. Now, however, they leaned close and showered her with kisses, licks, nibbles, teasing bites, and caresses from her lips to her breasts to her clit.

One by one, they made love to her. First, her captor, who moved slow and easy, drawing out her pleasure. Then the middle brother dove into her deep and fast, bringing her to an immediate climax. He slowed and drew another one from her body. The oldest brother with a bit of gray at his temples was intense. Positioning her on her hands and knees, he brought her to the brink of climax. He stopped, held still, and waited for her to calm before he moved, building her pleasure all over again. Every so often, he would smack her ass, adding a bit of pleasurable pain. Sweet torture she'd never experienced.

One brother wasn't any better than another. They each had their own specialties and talents and knew how to utilize them to the best advantage. What amazed her was that while one brother was deep inside her, the other two used their hands or lips and wrung cries of pleasure from her. She lost track of where she began and they ended.

RY WOKE; her body covered with sweat, tears ran down her cheeks. Her heightened senses caused the lightest graze of her pajamas against her skin to set off tiny sparks within her body. She whimpered and stumbled into her bathroom, ripping off her clothes as she hurried into the shower, crawling in before she could adjust the water temperature.

As the pinpricks of water hit her body, she wasn't sure if it was a good idea. Not until her body went numb from the cold did the sexual overload and sensitivity abate. Finally, in control of her senses, Ry staggered out of the shower and wrapped herself in a towel. Not bothering to dry off, she seized her cell phone.

She wasn't a virgin but she definitely was not the sexual creature in her dreams, she wondered if the experience at the motel had invaded her subconscious. The dreams must be manifestations of her fear or her guilt. Still unable to believe what she had done with her kidnapper, she was afraid she was losing her mind. Convinced she needed mental and emotional support, she called her best friend, Lauren, who was completing her psychologist residency. The two women were closer than sisters.

"Lauren. I need you. Please."

"What's going on?"

Ry sobbed, unable to control herself. "Please. I need you."

"I'm already out the door. Be there in ten minutes."

Ry clicked off her phone and slid down the wall. Huddled on the tiled floor in her bathroom, she calmed and relived the events of the past twenty-four hours. Kidnap. Sex. Tattoo. Escape. Dreams.

All revolved around a man with a gold statue.

Chapter 7

Saturday dragged for Ian. Hours after leaving the motel, he was no closer to finding the identity of the woman who had screwed him—both physically and mentally. He'd had plenty of time to think about what had transpired at the motel. The threat to snap her neck weighed heavy on his mind. He would never have followed through. He'd been desperate to get out of the city and she'd fought him.

Most of his thoughts though were on what had happened after he fell asleep. She had instigated the sex. He must have been too exhausted to protest. He remembered most of the night vividly.

By the time he reached War's home, the alpha was occupied with pack business. He kept Ian waiting for hours. Once available, the leopard shifter hacked into the security system at the parking garage. Using city-street surveillance videos, they tracked the woman back to a nearby hotel frequented by business travelers. That was when their hunt came to a screeching halt.

"What do you mean you can't access their security

system? You hack into everything." Ian realized he was pushing his luck by challenging the head of the leopard clan, but he couldn't bring himself to care.

"Watch your tone, little brother. I have people inside the hotel. We have to wait until they start their work shift. I won't jeopardize their positions by a little hacking."

Protect her. Protect her. The same voice ran through his head bringing back memories. Her tantalizing kisses. Her wicked mouth. Her perfectly rounded ass and lovely breasts. *God, I need some control.* He had no idea where these thoughts and infatuations were coming from. He had to find her.

War broke into his thoughts. "What's wrong with you? Does this woman have control over you or something?"

"I'm fine. I'm fine." He dragged his hands through his hair. He was *not* fine. His senses ran wild. He smelled her on his skin. The intoxicating scent of sex. The intriguing scent of her. The metallic scent of the unknown. The third puzzled him, but the combination of the three drove him beyond caring. "How soon can we get access?"

War studied him for several moments. Ian was familiar with a typical alpha stare and held still despite the urge to bolt. He put on his best I-don't-care face. He was good at not caring.

"Once I get the okay from my guys, we can head over, but it won't be until tomorrow."

Tomorrow? "I can't wait that long." Desperation tinged his voice.

"Sit. You're driving me crazy."

Ian ignored him and stalked from one end of the room to the other.

"Jamie should be kept informed on what's happening."

When Ian refused to reply, War stepped into his path,

forcing him to an abrupt halt. Ian glared up at his friend and mentor as annoyance and frustration surged through him. This desperate need to protect the woman was driving him out of his mind.

War set his hands on the younger man's shoulders. "Whatever is happening, it doesn't sound like you can fix it alone. Call your brother."

Ian jerked away from War. A low rumbling annoyance started deep in his chest—a warning to the leopard. "I can do this without him. I don't need my big brother to fix everything. Jamie sees me as his fun-loving younger brother who doesn't care about anything or anyone."

"Don't you?"

Ian snarled. Leave it to War to speak the gut-wrenching truth.

War switched tactics. "He's more than your older brother, Ian. He's your alpha. It's imperative he knows what's what."

"*Why?*" He struggled to regain a sense of calm. After several moments of battling his emotions, he shuddered and tried for a more normal tone. "Why? He'll end up acting more like a domineering brother than a reasonable alpha and try to repair everything. You know him. I need to take responsibility. I have to take responsibility." He was not about to let his brothers anywhere near the woman. *She's mine.* The truth echoed through his body.

He stalked to the far end of the room. Jamie thought of him as an irresponsible young pup, an Omega, just as other shifters turned a blind eye to his antics. He was the last shifter born to the packs. Since he'd been born one hundred and eighty-seven years ago, the shifter clans had begun to question the survival of their race. He heard what the packs said about him. *"Ian might be almost two hundred years old, but he looks twenty-five and acts eighteen."*

I'll prove them wrong.

He turned to War. "I need to make this right. You don't understand, but it's time I quit relying on Jamie or Colin to sort out my problems."

"All right, why this woman? What's your interest in her?"

The urge to protect her had become insistent. He didn't understand why. Partial lies were better at this point. "She stole something from me."

"You said that. It must be important for you to act this way."

Ian shot War a stony look and refused to explain his motives. War sighed and shook a finger at Ian. "Okay. Once we get her name and address, I'll leave it up to you. I can offer you twenty-four hours before I contact your brothers."

Ian grinned. War grumbled as he turned away. "I'm heading to my office. Don't leave the house if you want my help. You remember where the guest rooms are. Get some sleep. You look like crap."

Instead, Ian paced the living room floor. When he finally fell asleep on the sofa, images of her strolling naked toward him flooded his dreams. They romped and played in an open field of blue and yellow wildflowers before making love on a cushion of green grass.

Chapter 8

Lauren arrived in less than fifteen minutes. Ryder fell into her arms. Drained and embarrassed, she finally sighed and stepped back. "I'm sorry I panicked. I didn't know who else to call."

"You look exhausted. Where are your glasses?"

Ry plastered on a fake smile. "I must have lost them. I'm fine." She must have left the eyeglasses in the motel room. What was odd was she had no problems seeing without them. Now she had to tell Lauren about her dreams and her last night in Chicago. Lauren and Ry had become instant best friends when they met three years ago. They shopped, played, and took vacations together. If she couldn't tell her, whom could she?

"I've been having trouble sleeping since I left Chicago." On impulse, Ry pulled Lauren into a big hug, holding tight. "Seriously. Everything will be fine."

Lauren drew back, her eyes anxious as she scanned Ry's face. "*Will* be fine? Sounds like something is wrong."

Ry shook her head and released her friend. "Nothing I

can't handle." She followed her statement with a grin and a wink.

"Okay. I'll let it slide. For now. I'm ordering food and making drinks. You'll sleep tonight even if I have to sing you a lullaby."

AN HOUR LATER, they unpacked a bag of Italian food from Ry's favorite restaurant, Mama's on Main. They made the most incredible ravioli. The two women had already started on a pitcher of margaritas.

After piling two plates with pasta and garlic bread, Lauren raised her glass. "Here's to my cure for a sleepless night. A boring movie, several strong margaritas, and lots of carbs. You'll be in a sleep coma before you know it."

Ry raised her drink. "Here's to sleep comas."

They clinked glasses and set about enjoying their meal, relaxing into easy conversation. *This is what I need.*

Once finished with dinner, Lauren sat in the recliner browsing for a movie while Ry curled up on the sofa. She was asleep within minutes.

RY STOOD ALONE in the middle of her living room. She wore a little black dress and three-inch heels, one of her favorite outfits. As she waited, she trembled, her palms damp with anticipation. He would be here soon.

He entered through the doorway, wearing black slacks, a white dress shirt, and a loosely knotted black tie. She had to admire the way his clothes molded to his body. His movements were casual with an air of sophistication. He would be comfortable at a presidential reception or down the street at the local bar.

She watched the play of muscles through the fine silk of his shirt. This was her Mr. Gorgeous, the one who had kidnapped her.

Without a word, he took her hand in his, lifting it to his lips. He pressed kisses on her knuckles, turned her hand over, and brushed his lips against her palm. She shivered at the deliciousness of it all.

Placing her hand on his shoulder, she glided close when he swung her into his arms. Music played—soft, easy notes. He drew her into the small open area of her living room, keeping his gaze focused on her.

She closed her eyes and enjoyed the music, the movements, and the man. She loved to dance with a partner who knew how to move with the rhythm and take control.

When he paused, disappointment flooded her for the briefest of moments. He continued to hold her and sway with the music. He nuzzled her neck. She was helpless to protest or pull away.

With slow and sensuous kisses, he slid his lips along her throat. His teeth nibbled her ear. His hands roamed up and down her back. He cupped her butt, pulling her close to him. She could feel how much he wanted her. The hard length of his cock pressed against her stomach. He loosened his grip, twisting her around in his arms. Their gentle swaying slowed and gradually ceased as his lips continued to make love to her ear, her neck, her shoulder. His hands glided up her arms.

He slid her dress strap off one shoulder, giving him greater access to her bare skin. His lips lightly caressed along her neck and shoulder. A quick tug and his hands made short work of the zipper. With a whisper, the silky material slid to the floor. She stood in a black lacy push-up bra, matching panties, and black pumps.

He growled. It was definitely a growl. A shiver trickled down her spine. The atmosphere charged with erotic energy. Her nipples pebbled. Her stomach tightened. She leaned her head back onto his shoulder.

Placing his hands on her hips, he swayed their bodies to the music. Raising her arms up and back, she reached for his head. She was strong and sexy standing half-naked in his embrace with him clothed. When he skimmed his hands over her belly, she shivered. One hand slid up to cup her breast. The other slid down between her legs to tease her mound.

All the while, his lips nibbled on her neck and ear. The power zinging through her caused her limbs to tingle. Her body quivered in anticipation. Her legs wavered.

A breathy gasp was all she managed. "Please. I need you."

Her bra was off in a second. His fingers slipped inside the edge of her panties, ripping them. He left her shoes alone. Bending her forward, he positioned her hands on the arm of the sofa, tugging her legs back to widen her stance and lowering her back. His cock slid into her wet, demanding channel.

Her body recognized his touch. She instinctively pressed back, driving him deeper. He began slow, letting her relish every inch of his hard cock. Their movements took on a frenzied pace. Her moans and whimpers grew louder until she exploded in a climax.

He held still, allowing her breathing to slow. He gently stroked her chest and belly. From experience, she knew he would bring her to multiple orgasms before he came.

She smiled when two more pairs of hands slide across her body. Opening her eyes, she discovered the other two men from her earlier dream standing naked beside her. The older one dropped to his knees in front of her, placed his hands on her thighs before leaning in and pressed a kiss on her stomach before moving lower. The middle one turned her face toward him, then brushed his lips on hers while he caressed her breasts.

Chapter 9

Ry woke with a start, gasping from the sensations bombarding her. Lauren scrambled to her side.

"Shhh. It's okay. I'm here. You're fine." Lauren brushed the damp hair from Ry's face. Her entire body shook with fear. Her dreams hadn't quit. Her friend wrapped her arms around her and rocked. Ry burst into tears and held on as Lauren continued to murmur and soothe.

Minutes passed before Ry jerked away, wiping at her eyes.

"I'm sorry. I need to...." Not understanding what she needed, she shoved past Lauren and headed to her bathroom to be alone.

Splashing water on her face, Ry did her best to calm down. Lauren had witnessed her waking from her nightmares. Did her friend realize she'd been in the throes of a dream orgasm?

She trusted Lauren. She needed someone with a clear head to think this through.

When Ry emerged from her room, she found Lauren in

the kitchen. Every light in the kitchen and living room were on, driving out any remaining demons. A glass of water sat at Ry's usual place at the table. Lauren perched on the opposite chair, her hands wrapped around a similar glass. She watched Ry with a cool, professional gaze.

Seconds ticked by before Ry sank into the chair. She picked up the glass of water, gulped down half, letting it soothe her parched throat. The refreshing liquid revived her.

The uneasy silence grew between them until Lauren spoke.

"Tell me about your nightmares."

Ry sighed. She hoped Lauren wouldn't believe she was crazy. She raised her head and looked her friend in the eye.

"It's uncomfortable to talk about."

"If you can't tell me, who can you tell?"

Ry shifted in her seat. *She has a point.* "My dreams are about sex and men."

Lauren raised an eyebrow. She knew Ry limited her involvement with men because her career was her primary focus. That and saving her dad. She never dated, let alone spent the night with a man.

"Tell me about the dreams. When was the first one? What happened?" Lauren refilled both water glasses.

Ry contemplated where to begin. She spoke without looking up. "The first one had several men. I could tell by their clothing and their speech they were from a different era. It was like *Braveheart* or something." She waved her hand absently.

Lauren stared at her in amazement. "I don't know which comment to tackle first—several men or *Braveheart*. How many men?"

Ry's lips twitched. "Maybe six or eight?"

"Are you saying you and 'six or eight' men did the nasty?" Lauren fanned herself. Ry giggled.

"No." She rolled her eyes. "That would be a bit one-sided, don't you think?"

Lauren shrugged. "I don't know. I'd be up to trying."

Ry loved the twinkle in Lauren's eye and the smile on her face, but multiple men? She could never do that.

"No. It was only one of them, but all of them paid attention to me. They talked and kissed me and hugged me like they knew me intimately. I don't know who they thought I was. I mean, it was weird. It wasn't me, but I experienced everything."

They were silent for several minutes, sipping their water.

"The second dream was with one man. It began in an open field of wildflowers. A wolf walked up to me."

"Wait a second. A wolf? Aren't you the kinky one?"

"Shush. I'm telling you how it happened."

"Okay. Okay. But I might need to refer to my dream manual to interpret what wolves mean."

"Yeah, whatever. Anyway. The wolf changes into a man and things start to happen from there."

Lauren nodded wisely. "More sex. I get the picture. What's the next dream?"

Ry took a quick swallow of water. Holding the glass in front of her with both hands, she stared into the liquid for a minute. "There were three men. The one from the previous dream and two others who looked like him."

"Clones?"

"No, brothers." Ry had wanted to deny it, but she knew it was true. It was weird how her dreams resembled something her kidnapper had talked about. *Shit.*

"And you did it with all three?"

"In my dream, yes."

"Okay. That's three dreams. Any more?"

"Yes, tonight. The three brothers again. Here in my living room."

"Nice." Lauren grinned. Ry glared. The grin disappeared from Lauren's face as she cleared her throat. "What's wrong with three? Or is it the living room you disapprove of? It sounds like a delicious sexual dream."

Ry shoved back her chair, stood, and paced away from the table. She had to make Lauren understand. Whirling around, she addressed her friend. "It's intense. Powerful. I can't control the dreams. When I wake up, I can still feel the orgasm ripping through me. My entire body still feels *everything*."

Lauren set down her glass. "Ry. They're called wet dreams and everyone has them sometimes during their lives. It usually happens when we're younger but—"

Ry threw up her hands and cursed. Lauren meant well, but she wasn't helping. "I know one of the men."

Lauren frowned. "What do you mean you know one of them?"

Ry tugged on the medallion around her neck. Normally cool under pressure, she handled the bloodiest, most horrific cases in the emergency room. Now, she was shaking because of a few silly dreams. On the verge of tears, she took a long, slow breath to remain calm. "He kidnapped me last night."

Lauren opened her mouth but snapped it closed when Ry cut her off. "Technically, it was early this morning."

"Wait a minute. Kidnapped? Were you hurt? Did you report it?" She leaned closer. "Are you saying the guy in your dreams is the guy who kidnapped you?"

"I was in the parking garage near the hotel in Chicago. It was early in the morning. He had a gun and forced me to drive him out of the city. We ended up at this sleazy little motel. He had a bullet hole in his shoulder. I stitched up the wound." She clamped her rambling mouth closed.

Lauren's stare was a mixture of disbelief, anger, and exasperation. "You stitched him up? You should have jabbed something in him and twisted it."

Ry shrugged. She should be experiencing the same rage as Lauren, but she was mentally and physically exhausted.

"Okay, so you patched him. What then? You obviously got away. Did you report him? Call the cops?"

Ry shook her head. She wouldn't meet Lauren's eyes.

"Oh shit. Ry. Please tell me he didn't rape you." Lauren's voice had gone quiet.

"No." She glared at the other woman. Ry's fists were white as she clenched them tight. "He didn't rape me. I seduced him." She didn't understand why defending him seemed so right.

"I don't believe it." Lauren stood, her arms crossed, her foot tapping. "You do not seduce men. Your only experience with a man was in college, and he turned out to be an egotistical ass. You haven't dated in ages."

"Well, believe it. I don't understand how it happened. He fell asleep. All I remember is trying to locate my keys in his backpack so I could escape. Instead, I found this little gold statue. I was holding it and looking at it, and the next thing I remember was waking up next to him in bed. Naked."

She paused, confused and frustrated as she tried to decide how much more to tell Lauren. She raised her gaze. Her lower lip trembled. Tears threatened. "We were both naked. We'd had sex. We didn't use condoms. I distinctly remember initiating all of it."

Lauren reached for her again, but Ry held her hand up to stop her. Coming to a decision, she inhaled and let out a long slow breath.

"You need to know everything." Ry tugged her t-shirt over her head. Standing half-naked in front of Lauren, she displayed the tattoo.

Lauren stared openmouthed at the elaborate markings. She raised her hand toward the tattoo, but jerked back. She glanced at Ry's face, then back to the wolf image.

"When did you get that? And *why*?"

Ry tugged her shirt back on, pushing down a shimmer of annoyance. *What's wrong with the tattoo? What's wrong with me for defending it now, after I wanted it gone yesterday?*

Scowling, Ry got her emotions under control before she spoke. "I didn't *get* it. When I woke this morning, it was there. I didn't wait to ask questions. I ran. When I got home, I tried scrubbing it off, but it's permanent."

She straightened her clothes and determination filled her voice. "I'm done feeling sorry for myself. I need to figure out what happened in Chicago, who the man was, and why he continues to haunt me. I refuse to let a few nightmares and an unexplained tattoo torment me."

"You go, girl. Let's figure this out. Tell me about the statue."

"The statue?"

"Think about it. Why would he have it? He might have been transporting it somewhere. Maybe for him or someone else. I doubt it, though. People don't transport a valuable item around without a guard or without protecting it in some fashion. Not unless it's junk. You said it was gold, so it's more likely he stole the statue. What else would explain his injuries and wanting to get out of the city?"

Ry sensed a slim, tiny sliver of hope. "I wonder if

someone reported the statue missing. It's possible the police may have a lead on this guy."

"Exactly. We can go to the police and—"

"No. No police. Not in Chicago. My uncle will get involved. Then my parents will find out. My dad can't take any excitement now, not with his weakened condition."

"We need someone to get details for us and manage the investigation. We have no idea how to track down a stolen statue or a kidnapper."

"Not my uncle. He'll interrogate me."

Lauren snorted. "*Interrogate* is a rough word."

"Not with Rick." She shook her head. "Trust me, it will be a full-blown interrogation minus any torture. I could never get away with anything growing up." She brightened. "I do know someone we can ask."

She hurried into her office and grabbed her tablet from her desk. Doing a quick search on the internet, she turned the device to show Lauren.

Her friend peered at the name on the screen. "Swift Private Investigations." Surprised, she looked up at Ry. "You know a detective?"

Ry hiked one shoulder. "I've never met him, but the owner plays poker with Rick every week. They've been doing it for years."

She turned the tablet back around and swiped through pages.

"Rick trusts Waru with his life. They've worked together on several cases. If I ask, he won't tell my uncle. I hope he'll help me because of his friendship with Rick."

Lauren glanced at her watch. "It's after midnight. We can call his office now and leave a message. They'll get it first thing in the morning. You can try sleeping in the meantime."

Doubting she could sleep, Ry agreed anyway. Picking up her cell phone from its charging station, she dialed the number listed on the agency's website and was surprised when someone answered.

Chapter 10

Sunday

After midnight on Sunday, Ian slouched in a recliner and nursed a tumbler of Glenlivet. War had agreed that the least he could do for making him wait was to share his liquor. Luckily for Ian, War had nothing but the best. Half-drunk and working on the other half, Ian glared at War who sat across the room typing away on his laptop. The man hadn't even tried to hack into the hotel's computer system. He was not taking this situation seriously.

The woman could be hurt. Or dying. Or married. *Oh crap. Please, not married.* At least War had been kind enough to print her image from the garage cameras. The grainy picture showed only a side of her face in shadow.

When War's office phone rang, Ian jumped, splashing whiskey onto his hand. War glanced at the caller ID and frowned. He snatched up the phone.

"Swift Private Investigators. Waru speaking."

Even from across the room, Ian's sensitive hearing heard a gasp from the other end. A woman's voice, faint but discernable sounded through the phone. "Mr. Swift. This is

Ryder Hoffman. You startled me. I didn't expect anyone to answer."

Ian heard the fear in her voice, but was more intrigued by her voice itself. It sounded familiar. He leaned forward to eavesdrop on the conversation. At least this was more interesting than drinking himself into a stupor and staring daggers at War.

War spoke gently. "Of course. Your uncle has spoken of you often. I'm sorry if I frightened you. My office phone rings here at my house. Is everything all right? Did something happen to Rick or your parents?"

"Yes. I mean, no. Rick is fine. Everyone's fine." She hesitated, stumbling over her words. "I have this, um, situation I can't discuss with them. I'm hoping you can advise me but keep it quiet. I'll pay you, but I need you to promise that you won't involve Rick."

War spoke without hesitation. "Of course, you have my word. I won't mention this to him. How can I help?"

The silence stretched, only broken by her unsteady breathing. Something or someone had frightened the woman.

"I was in Chicago this past week for a medical conference. I..." She stumbled. "Someone kidnapped me last night."

At the mention of kidnapping, Ian came to his feet. *It can't be this easy.* Taking a step toward War, he halted at the death glare the leopard sent him. He was not an idiot. No one crossed an alpha, especially when he was annoyed.

War continued his conversation, his voice calm and steady, his gaze glued to Ian. "That's a serious charge. You should discuss this with the police."

"I told you, I don't want my uncle involved," she bit out,

sounding annoyed. "I don't want my parents to find out either. Dad's sick. The stress could kill him."

"Okay. I understand. What do you need from me?" War kept his glare focused on Ian, daring him to move.

"I want you to locate the man who kidnapped me. I can describe him and the motel." She hesitated. "Also, he had a statue."

Excitement exploded through Ian. He did a fist pump into the air. This was the woman. *Ryder. What kind of name is that for a woman?*

"A statue?" War's eyebrow rose. "Couldn't be very big if he was carrying it. What did it look like?"

"It wasn't big. Maybe six or seven inches tall. It was a tree with animals and men hiding in the branches. He probably stole it because it looked expensive. If someone reported it missing, we could have a lead. He might have a record. Will you help me?"

"Of course. Give me the details. Don't worry about payment. You're family."

A sigh of relief drifted through the phone. Guilt and distress plagued Ian. He had made her afraid. He hadn't meant to. He had every intention of letting her go this morning. Was she hurt? So far, she hadn't mentioned being injured.

"Thank you." She told War everything Ian had refused to tell him. Her detailed descriptions of him and the motel were flawless.

War's glare at Ian turned into a death ray. He changed the topic. "Ryder, how are you? Did he hurt you?"

Ian knew where the questions were going. Humans didn't normally survive during sex with shifters. Their superior strength and sexual appetite killed or gravely wounded most humans. The thought had only added to Ian's concern over the past several hours.

He took two steps closer, trying to hear better.

She muttered, "No, he didn't hurt me. I'm exhausted. I can't sleep. I'm having nightmares. I need closure on this, Mr. Swift," she added, seeming to gain strength.

"War. Call me War. I'll do whatever I can. Is anyone with you? Someone you can stay with?"

"My friend, Lauren. She's staying the night."

"Good. Give her my phone number in case she needs to contact me. I'll call you when I have an update."

"Thank you."

A dial tone replaced her subdued voice. Ian couldn't believe this was the same woman. The woman from the previous night had been feisty and argumentative. This one was passive and compliant.

War calmly set the phone aside before standing, a quiet storm brewing in his eyes. This would not be good.

"Do you want to tell me what you were doing with a stolen statue? One, might I add, that caused the destruction of half our ancestors and enslaved the others?" he ground out with a distinct precision.

Ian set aside his drink and held up his hands. He sensed his friend's underlying fury. "I can explain."

War bellowed, "I hope so." He sucked in a breath and quieted his voice. "Even your brother won't be able to save your ass if the clan council hears about this."

A tiny bit of nervousness pushed thoughts of the woman aside. He would deal with the council when the time came. For now, he had War's confirmation that the statue truly was the Tree of Life.

"I was killing time before I flew home. I snuck into this little museum and there it was. The Tree of Life."

"It's the Tree of *Death*!"

Ian winced. "I never expected to discover it, let alone hold it. I thought the stories were lies. I didn't believe the statue existed. But when I saw the Tree, I couldn't leave it. I had to have it. *We* had to have it." He smacked a fist to his chest, grinding out his words. "It's our history, War. Why should that shabby little museum stuff it onto a shelf for people to gawk at? They have no idea what it is, what it was. The power it holds for us. The history, good or bad, it holds for our people. I had to steal it. I had to protect it. I had to have it."

War sadly shook his head. "All I'm hearing is 'I, I, I.' What were you thinking? Your brother can deal with you. If Ryder has it, she'll give it to me."

"Ryder? Is that really her name? How do you know her?"

"She's Rick's niece." War turned to his laptop. He showed Ian the screen plastered with a professional head-shot of a woman. His woman. The woman who had tormented him for the past fourteen hours. Fascinated, he hurried closer to gaze in awe at the picture.

"This is her, isn't it?" War questioned. "This is the woman you kidnapped and fucked?" Too engrossed in the picture, he ignored War's questions and his own screeching internal alarms.

Breathless and excited, he straightened. "Where is she? Tell me."

Before he could react, War seized him and threw him against the wall. Ian was too shocked to fight back. The leopard stood half a foot taller and weighed at least fifty pounds more. An expert in hand-to-hand combat, War had a definite edge. The outcome of a brawl between the two men would not end well for Ian.

War snarled in Ian's face; one hand wrapped around the

younger man's neck. The other gripped the front of his shirt. War held him against the wall while his canines dropped, a low menacing growl rumbled from his chest. His eyes shifted to yellow, showing his leopard.

"What did you do to her? If you hurt her, I'll kill you." War trembled with fury.

"I've told you everything. She didn't sound hurt. She even said she was all right."

War roared. He dropped Ian, who stumbled to regain his footing. War stepped back and drew in several deep breaths. Halting several feet away, he glared as he gathered his composure. His canines gradually receded.

Ian watched him warily while the alpha straightened his shirt and collar then waited to discover what War would do.

"She lives in Dallas. Her name is Ryder Hoffman." War's voice sounded strained. Ian knew War had a choice to make —choose his people or a human. Any association with a human was a tiny blip in a shifter's lifetime and he would be alpha for an extremely long time. "My best human friend is her uncle. I *will* protect her." He ran his hands over his bare head.

Seeming to make up his mind, he faced Ian. "Do you remember me talking about Rick Meier? My poker buddy?"

Ian nodded. "Yeah, the local chief of police, right?" Realizing what he had just said, he cursed, scowling. "Shit. Chief of Police. Great."

"Don't worry. She won't tell him any of this. She doesn't want him involved. Ironic, isn't it? She remembers him talking about me and thinks she can trust me. I played poker with him Friday night. Now I'm advising her kidnapper."

The poker game Ian hadn't interrupted. If he had, they wouldn't be in this mess.

Fate sucked.

"You know where I store the keys. Take my Tahoe. Go to the airstrip. I'll arrange a flight for you to Dallas. Like I told you yesterday, I'll give you twenty-four hours to fix this, then I call your brother."

Yes! Ian grinned. Pivoting on his heel, he hurried to the office and snagged the keys from a filing cabinet. He'd almost made it to the front door when War bellowed, "*Emerson.* Go with Ian. Keep him out of trouble."

Chapter 11

Ry and Lauren survived the night by staying awake and talking about everything except men and sex. Lauren left for the hospital promptly at a quarter after six in the morning, promising to be back for lunch.

Once her friend left, Ry decided she would try to sleep and to hell with her dreams. She had thirty-six hours before she was scheduled for work. Any amount of rest would make her feel better. Exhausted and nauseated, she tumbled onto her mattress. Within seconds, she was fast asleep and dreaming.

DRESSED IN A LONG, *flowing gown of deep blood red, she sauntered through an extended corridor. Large rocks made up the walls, held together with mortar. The floor was a pattern of stepping-stones worn smooth by years of feet strolling across them. This was a castle. An ancient, drafty castle.*

Large tapestries adorned the walls. One in particular caught her eye. On it was the image of a beautiful blonde woman with striking blue eyes. Her hair hung loose around her shoulders. She wore a long red gown and sat on a throne. The crown on her head epitomized royalty. Reclining, kneeling, and standing around her were several men. They were large and would have dominated the scene, except they scattered themselves behind the woman, making her the focal point.

Ry recognized the man standing directly behind the queen. He was the same one who had pleasured her on his horse in her first dream. Several of the other men seemed familiar. She took a step closer to get a better look, then hesitated.

Dreaming of the same men was impossible. But then, she'd dreamed of the three brothers twice already. Stepping away, she decided now was not the time to delve into the unknown. Hugging herself, she turned away from the tapestry and continued striding down the corridor.

At the end of the passageway, she stepped into a large open room lit with candles and oil lamps. Although they threw shadows into the corners, the middle of the room was lit up brilliantly. Chairs, chaise loungers, tables, and a bed were scattered throughout the room. The bed was enormous and piled with furs, blankets, and pillows.

In the center of the room three men sat on chairs. As she moved closer, they stood and bowed. One was the man on the horse from her previous dream. The other two had been stitched into the tapestry.

She blushed when the hottie from her ride strode toward her. He had made her body sing with his hands under her cape and dress. His smile was brilliant when he halted in front of her. Putting a finger under her chin, he raised her face so her gaze met his.

"You have the look of a young blushing girl. What thought is making you shy tonight?" His voice was deep and soft with a beautiful accent. His speech had an old-world charm. It caressed her body, inside and out.

"I'm remembering a certain horse ride with you."

All three men chuckled. "I'm sure we can all remember similar outings with you. It's a convenient way to get you to ourselves."

All?

What was he insinuating? Had she done the same thing with these men? She glanced between the other two men in alarm. She hadn't, but they obviously thought she had.

He took her arm and led her to the other men, who greeted her warmly but respectfully. Each one took a moment to address her with an endearment, a caress, a brush of his lips, all of which fueled her senses. Flames licked along her belly and breasts, between her legs. It amazed her at how they stirred her passion with such slight movements.

The three men bore a strong resemblance to each other. Brothers. Hottie Number One appeared to be the youngest. All three were strong, fit, and handsome. She wouldn't mind giving them physicals.

He tilted his head and gave her a half smile. "Some days you make me wonder if you are yourself, lass. If you do not want to play games tonight, we can make it a quiet evening."

Games? She breathed easier. After his comment about her and the other men on their outings, she had wondered if they would expect more from her, something similar to what they'd done on the horseback ride. Games would be an innocent distraction.

"No. No, I'm fine. I wouldn't mind some games. It'll take my mind off things. Do you play poker?"

He grinned. "You know we do." Sounds of agreement came from the other two. He reached for her and ripped her gown from neck to navel in one swipe. She gasped and realized she wore nothing underneath as a rush of cool air slapped her skin. Before *she could respond and pull the ripped material back together, he grabbed the two shredded sides and finished tearing it.*

A fire flared deep inside her, licking down her limbs and through her body. All thoughts of protesting fled. Despite the cool air, her body burned hot. Unable to move. Unwilling to move. Something deep inside her wanted whatever was about to happen.

She stood naked, except for golden slippers. He grasped her wrists, pulling her hands behind her back and turned her around for his brothers' view. The position thrust her breasts up and out. Held in place, she watched as the two other brothers sauntered up to her. Each one caressed a breast using their hands, their mouths, their lips to tease her. They didn't touch her anywhere else.

Their caresses heightened her senses. Her body trembled with desire. She moaned with each lick, each suck, each graze of teeth and tongue. As she exploded in a quick climax, her body shook with the intensity. Her screams of pleasure echoed through the room.

They gave her a moment to relax before they rotated and continued. This time, the youngest one with a riot of tri-colored hair knelt in front of her. His fingers spread her drenched folds, sliding one thick digit inside her. His tongue lapped at her sensitive bud. Repeatedly, they teased her to a climax, let her calm down, changed positions, and went right back at it again. She lost track of how many orgasms rippled through her. When she sagged in the arms of the oldest brother, the youngest scooped her into his arms and carried her to the bed.

Laying her down, he stretched out next to her, one hand propping up his head with the other one resting on her middle. Her eyes were barely open as she watched the middle brother lie down at her other side. He smiled at her before leaning over and brushing a kiss against her lips. She could taste herself as he delved his tongue inside her mouth. Breathing heavy, he pulled back and grinned wickedly down at her.

"Ready for more games?"

Her eyes widened. More? If this was their idea of games, she definitely wanted to find out what was next. A fever burned in her. She wasn't satisfied yet. Despite climaxing time after time, she was desperate to have something, someone, inside her. She wanted much, much more.

Opening her mouth to beg, she froze as the oldest brother climbed on the bed and settled between her legs. He was bare-ass naked and magnificent to watch. His muscled chest held a smattering of hair that trailed down his stomach. The edges of a Celtic scroll tattoo reached over his shoulders and around his neck. His trim waist sported strong, well-defined abs. His muscled thighs flexed as he knelt between her legs and widened his stance.

He seized her ankles. With a grin, he drew her down the bed until she stopped spread-eagle against his thighs. She lay wide open in front of him with his cock teasing her entrance. One hand on her thigh, he used the other to hold himself at her opening. If he didn't put it in her, she would scream in frustration.

But he held himself still. Glancing away from the magnificent sight between her legs, she found him watching her. Waiting. Puzzled, it took her a moment to realize he was holding off until she gave him the command to continue. They would do nothing she didn't want. They would never hurt her. He held himself still, gazing into her eyes for permission.

With a moan and a breathy please, she pressed herself toward him, trying to get him to slip inside. She needed him. Now.

The man lying next to her stroked her belly. "Shhh. Go slow. Let Camden take the lead."

Camden. The hottie had a sexy name. She lay still, staring up at him. Her body quivered with anticipation. Inch by slow inch, he pressed himself in. She shifted her hips to accommodate his marvelous size as he slid deep. By the time he was all the way inside, her breathing was heavy and her body trembled. She tried to make him move, but he held her still by gripping her legs while his two brothers held her shoulders.

"You have the touch. She's right on the edge." She didn't care who had the touch, she wanted movement. She needed him to move and let her come. She looked down at the joining of their bodies and him buried deep inside her. This is a dream. What an amazing dream.

"Please," she pleaded. Her voice was a whimper of agony and desperation. She tossed her head from side to side, wanting him to move. He pulled out an inch and paused.

He continued to tease her by withdrawing an inch or two, then thrusting back in. Agonizingly slow. Every little movement he made was such an extreme pleasure. His hard cock rippled through her sensitive folds. She spiraled to a climax, only for him to deny her and send her plunging back down to earth. His teasing was for her pleasure, taking an extraordinary amount of concentration on his part to control his own reaction.

She wasn't sure how much more she could take.

Her channel tightened around him. It wouldn't be long before she exploded and he wouldn't be able to stop her. He moved in long, sure thrusts as he gripped her hips, moving her in time to his rhythm. This time he didn't pause. She gasped for air and cried out for more. When she climaxed, she arched her back, reached out, and gripped the nearest pair of arms. Her screams of pleasure filled the room as she sank her nails into flesh.

Recovery came slowly. When she opened her eyes, she found three pairs of brown ones staring back. Who was next?

Chapter 12

Ian ignored Emerson on the flight to Dallas. Neither spoke more than a few words to each other. He fidgeted, hating the fact they'd been waiting over three hours for the jet to be readied. He suspected War had stalled the takeoff on purpose. Though he was glad War had offered his private jet, he disliked having Emerson with him.

The woman sat across from him onboard the plane. She continued to fiddle with a gold-hilt knife she carried everywhere. Ignoring him the entire time and being her glorious asshat self.

He was even less than thrilled when War did not supply him with Ryder's address. Ian tried calling, but War refused to answer.

Cradling his head in his hands, he wondered once more what had drawn him to the statue. He'd been strolling past the museum, heading to a restaurant when he found himself inside, staring at the Tree of Life. He wasn't sure when the idea of stealing the statue took root or why.

With a sigh, he shifted his thoughts to the woman and getting the statue back. Within a couple of hours, he would be with her. He wanted to embrace her again and run his hands through her hair and over her body.

Unable to control his thoughts, he tried calling War again. No answer.

Exiting the jet after it landed, Ian halted on the private tarmac. Shielding his eyes from the early morning sun, he spotted his best friend in the world. Leaning against a large red pickup truck stood Zachery Brinkman, an attorney in Dallas. His private practice represented shifters in the Southwest. Zach would eventually inherit half of the family cattle ranch in West Texas. Imagining tiger shifters managing a cattle ranch caused a smirk to flicker across Ian's lips.

"Don't tell me. War told you to keep me out of trouble." How many more people would he dispatch despite giving Ian twenty-four hours? Now racing toward twelve.

Zach chuckled. He was the epitome of a Texas cowboy from the brim of his battered Stetson down to his faded jeans and the tips of his worn boots. His smile had the ability to charm women out of their clothes. Ian had learned all his seduction techniques from this man.

"War called to inform me of your visit and mentioned you might need a ride. Do you?"

"Depends." Ian contemplated his friend. "Did War give you the address?"

"Yep. He did."

"Then I guess you're driving."

RY WOKE, unsure of what had disturbed her latest dream. Squinting at the clock, she realized she'd been asleep less than two hours. No wonder she felt horrible, worse than before she'd fallen asleep. Sighing, she lay back down. The dream had been as intense as the other ones.

Her doorbell rang, the noise stirring her. She groaned. It rang again. Someone was desperate. It definitely wasn't Lauren. She would have used her key. Pushing against the mattress, she rolled over and fell off the bed with a thud, tangling herself in the sheets. She winced thinking of the bruises she'd have later.

The doorbell rang again. In deliberate movements, she forced herself to her feet then stumbled down the hallway. Whoever was on the other side of her front door was about to get a piece of her mind.

Without looking through the peephole, she flung open the door, prepared to lay into the intruder but gasped, frozen in place. Terror slammed into her. Her kidnapper. He had found her.

Reaching for the door, she tried to slam it shut but he shoved his arm in the way and shouldered it open. Stumbling backward, she grabbed a vase on a side table and clutched it as a weapon. Only then did she notice the dismay on his face.

I don't look that bad, do I? Glancing down, she noted the rumpled t-shirt and baggy shorts. She turned her head to the side and stared at herself in her hall mirror. Lauren had commented on her crappy, exhausted appearance the day before. Now Ry agreed. She had dark circles under her eyes, a pale complexion, and wild, tangled hair.

His booted footsteps sounded loud in the small space. She whirled back toward him, brandishing her vase. "Leave now and I won't call the cops." Her voice was steady while she silently prayed he would leave.

"We have business to discuss." He turned his head slightly to speak over his shoulder. "You two wait outside."

Only then did Ry realize that a man and a woman stood behind him. They glanced at each other then left, closing the door behind them. No help from those two.

Turning back to her, the man who sexually tormented her in her dreams spoke. "You look like shit."

"People keep telling me. I told you to leave."

"Here. You left these." He held out her missing glasses. The prescription ones she hadn't needed since fleeing the motel. When she didn't move to take them, he set them on the side table where her vase turned weapon had stood.

"We need to talk."

She blinked; her face scrunched up in confusion.

"I have nothing to say to you. Leave." She pointed at the front door directly behind his back.

"Not until we talk."

"Go to hell." She whirled and took a single step before he gripped her shoulder in one hand and spun her to face him. Off-balance, she stumbled, the vase slipping from her grip. He grabbed it in one hand and her waist with the other, steadying both.

Lust slammed into her. The intensity staggered her against his solid body. He stared, mesmerized by her face before dropping his head to capture her lips with his. Intense desire shone in his eyes.

Images of her and this man, naked in a field of wildflowers, sprang unhindered through her mind. Instead of frightening her, it excited her. Yearning ran rampant. It spun through her body, heating her from the inside out.

When his lips met hers, she leaped on him and wrapped her legs around his waist. He caught her, his hands cupped her butt, and hauled her close. The vase crashed to the floor. Ry was starving for him. She needed more. She clasped her hands on the sides of his head to hold him still as she devoured his lips.

Neither slowed. Their mouths licked, nipped, bit, and sucked on each other. He fumbled with his jeans as she stroked herself up and down against his deliciously hard cock. Their frantic movements unbalanced him. They stumbled, hitting the wall with a loud crack.

He straightened and steadied himself before making short work of his zipper. His cock slid against her butt. Her loose shorts were wet, clinging to her thighs. He slipped one hand between their bodies to tug them aside, giving him access to her dripping pussy.

Ry pressed down against his hand. His long fingers slid into her. First one. Then two. He pumped them in and out. Stretching her. Sliding through her slickness. Pulling his hand back, he gripped his cock to slip it past her shorts and position himself at her entrance. One quick thrust and he buried himself deep inside her. They both paused, groans of pleasure filling the air.

When they finally moved, their actions were fast and frantic. Their lips fused, tongues sliding against each other. Within minutes, their climaxes slammed together. Ry threw back her head and screamed while he bellowed his release. They clung to each other. His cock throbbed inside her. Her body wanted more, but the enormity of what they had done panicked her. She didn't even know his name.

Unwrapping her legs from around his waist, she dropped to her feet. He reached out to steady her, but she brushed off his hands. Ry shoved her hair back from her face and put distance between them. In an attempt for some semblance of decency, she tugged at her shorts. She took a good look as he straightened his clothes, tucked his cock away, and fastened his jeans.

He was gorgeous. How could she have ever believed he was merely "nice-looking" when she'd met him? She examined his face for something, anything to give her an idea of what he was thinking. Nothing. His face was void of all emotion. Even after one of the most amazing orgasms of her life, he gave nothing away. *How can he be cold and emotionless now when minutes ago we were smashing walls?*

Moving into the living room, she hurried to the far corner, pausing for a moment before turning. When she faced him, Ry found keeping her distance difficult. The attraction and pull between them demanded she race into his arms. Determined not to leap on him again, she tugged on her medallion and focused on his forehead. Nothing sexy or alluring about a man's forehead.

He paused in the doorway before striding around the perimeter of the living room, casually looking at her possessions. Neither spoke for several minutes. He kept his back to her as he inspected her sound system.

Finally, he turned toward her and cleared his throat. "I'm Ian Stone. I want to apologize for what happened just now. I usually have more control."

Ry stared into his soft brown eyes before she tried and failed to redirect her gaze back to his forehead. His eyes drew her gaze back and reminded her of the wolf tattoo. She crossed her arms over her chest before speaking. "I would have thought you'd apologize for kidnapping me, too."

His eyes lit up, his gaze traveling over her body. "I will never apologize for that." His voice was low and sexy.

She lowered her eyes and tried to conceal her pleased smile. Why did his comment make her heart quicken and leap into her throat? Shoving aside her unusual thoughts, she looked up at him. "You can't stay. I don't want you here."

"Don't you remember? I owe you fifteen thousand dollars. You left before I could pay you."

Confusion set in, then she remembered their conversation in the car while she drove him to Wisconsin.

She quickly shook her head. "I don't want it."

"Nonsense. I made a promise. I can offer you the cash, but I need you to answer a question first." He waited for her to nod before continuing. "Do you remember seeing a small statue of a tree in the motel? About this big?" He held his hands out to show her.

The pleasure and thrill she'd experienced only moments before vanished as a chill splashed over her body. Her stomach dropped. This is what he really wanted—the little tree and not her. Was the money payment for her silence? *Why hadn't he come for me?* The words niggled through her mind like someone whispering hateful doubts.

Irrationality and annoyance flooded her. Her hands tightened into fists. The statue was in a billion dust particles on the floor of a ratty old motel room. How would he react to that bit of news? Not well, but in that moment, she didn't care.

Distrust and suspicions weaved into her heart and soul. He'd made wild love to her in her front hallway, shoved up against the wall, and all he wanted was that stupid statue. Her blood simmered. Her rage rose rapidly. Building faster than she could control it.

"Damn you. You think I stole it." Her shriek sounded harsh, but she couldn't control herself. "Is that the only reason you're here? The only reason for all of this?" She motioned between the two of them.

He blinked in disbelief. "Ryder. You're freaking out. Calm down."

How the hell does he know my name?

"Tell me the truth. Did you come here to seduce me so I'd tell you where the statue is?"

He opened his mouth to speak, but she cut him off. "Don't bother. I can see it on your face. You need to leave. Now." She gritted her teeth. She couldn't remember ever being this irate. Something was wrong. She sucked in a breath, trying to understand what was happening. Her lack of sleep was making her unreasonable. There was no other reason.

"Ry. Sweetheart. Please listen. I can explain everything." He took a step toward her with his arms spread wide.

"*No.*" Fury controlling her, she whirled and slammed her fist into the wall. Sheetrock cracked and split. Pain exploded through her fist and fingers as she connected with a wall stud. Agony shot up her arm. She immediately realized she had broken her hand. Cradling it against her chest, she cursed and doubled over in pain. The anger had overwhelmed her fast. Faster than she could wonder where it had come from. She was not a violent person.

Ian was by her side in a second. Scooping her into his arms, he carried her to the sofa and set her down. She rocked back and forth, tears of pain streaming down her face.

He ran to the kitchen and rushed back with a cold pack from her freezer. "Why did you do that? Why did you get so upset? Let me see your hand. I promise to be gentle."

He knelt at her feet not touching her, not speaking, and waited for her consent. Just like the men in her dreams. Waiting for her permission.

As Ry looked into Ian's eyes, the tattoo on her breast grew warm. Heat flowed through her chest and spread across her middle. It seeped into her limbs. Her body flushed hot as the sensation tingled through her. Hesitantly, she reached out to Ian with her swollen hand and laid it carefully on the side of his face.

"Kiss me," she commanded in a quiet yet authoritative voice.

He rose onto his knees, leaning in so as not to hurt her, and pressed his lips against hers.

A shock of pleasure blasted through her. The heat raced from Ian's mouth into hers as if a living, breathing entity flowed between them. Ry sucked in his breath, pulling in his heat and energy. The warmth traveled through her body and into her hand, making it tingle. The bones in her hand mended and healed, the swelling receding. She touched his warm skin with her fingertips and stroked his cheek. No more pain. No more agony.

When their lips separated, she smiled, letting the fingers of her once-broken hand slide through his hair. There was no discomfort, only the soft thickness against her skin. She felt drugged but had taken nothing, only his intoxicating kiss.

Ry dropped her gaze to her right hand and flexed it. Impossible. Her hand had healed itself. Her mind struggled with the enormity of what had happened.

"Ryder. What did you do?" Ian sat on his haunches. His whisper was a mixture of awe and confusion.

"I have no idea." Why were bizarre and unnatural occurrences happening after she met this man? Which brought up another question. "How did you find me?"

He hesitated. "I went back to the parking garage and asked around. People talk when inspired by enough money." He cleared his throat. "A lot of odd things are happening. This attraction between us. You healed your hand and my bullet wound. My tattoo."

"Your tattoo? Let me see."

Ian hesitated for a split second before pulling his shirt over his head. She immediately wished he hadn't. Her hand seemed to have a mind of its own and wanted to stroke his skin. Ry swallowed hard and forced her hand back to her side. Her gaze dropped, and landed on his tattoo.

She scrutinized his chest. "It looks like a tree. I saw it when I left."

He must have sensed her growing attraction because he stood, stepped several feet away, and pulled on his shirt. "I didn't have it when we met. It happened after I fell asleep and before I woke yesterday morning."

She wanted to shout for joy. Finally, something she could relate to. "Mine too." Without hesitation, she yanked her t-shirt off and bared herself.

Instantly, she realized her mistake. A low growl sounded from across the room. Like a wolf's. She blinked. Ian focused his stare on her breast and the tattoo emblazoned there.

She yanked her shirt up to hide her chest.

"Don't." His voice, low and thick, ordered her to pause. "I want to see. The details are amazing. It's very lifelike."

The air sparked with tension. Sexual hunger shone in his eyes. Ryder was sure he would leap across the room and toss her onto the floor. Her respect for him rose when he mumbled something incoherent and turned around. She took the moment to tug her shirt back into place.

"There's something else."

He waited, allowing her to gather her courage. "I keep having erotic dreams. About you." She refused to mention on the other men. It was difficult enough admitting just this much.

He turned, his face pale. "In a field of blue and yellow wildflowers." It wasn't a question.

"How did you know?"

Instead of answering, he strode toward the hallway and the front door. "I'll be back." He was clearly agitated.

Ryder hurried after him. "How did you know?"

His hand on the front doorknob, he paused and looked back. She kept her distance, remembering their previous encounter in this exact spot.

"I had the same dream."

Chapter 13

Zach and Emerson sat in the truck parked across the street. Heading toward them, Ian didn't make it twenty feet from the front door when he heard it smack open.

"Don't you walk away from me."

He halted and turned. The woman was nuts. Slamming her hand into the wall and now chasing after him in her pajamas. She looked like a banshee. With blue eyes blazing, she stormed toward him barefooted.

Uncertainty tugged at his memories. *I thought she had green eyes.*

Coming to a halt in front of him, she jabbed a finger against his chest. *Ow.* She meant business.

"Don't drop a bombshell and stalk away. You do not understand what you're dealing with, do you?"

Who is this woman? "What are you talking about?"

Behind him, the truck door clicked open. She whipped her gaze to a spot behind him. "Stay out of this." Her voice was cold and deadly. Alarm wrapped an icy grip around his heart.

When she turned her gaze back to him, he sensed her wrath for a brief second. Then her eyes softened. Her lips lifted into a genuine smile. He managed not to flinch when she caressed his cheek.

"I'm sorry. You don't deserve my anger. I'm not myself. Please stay. I'll have use of you later." Her expression sagged with sudden weariness. "I need sleep first. Healing exhausts me."

One moment she was talking, the next she was tumbling to the ground. He snatched her up and swung her into his arms. Once inside, he let his senses direct him to her bedroom, where he laid her on her bed. Her eyes opened and she gazed wide-eyed up at him. Green. Her eyes are now green. *What the hell?*

More confused than ever, he pulled away. *Protect her.* The same voice that had chided him into protecting the little gold tree now persisted. *Protect her.*

I'm going crazy.

"What happened?" Her whisper sliced through him. He needed to talk to War or Jamie. Between the two alphas, one of them had to understand what was happening.

"You fainted. You need to sleep. I'll stay for a bit. Don't worry."

She blinked sleepily. "I'm so exhausted. Lauren's coming for lunch. You don't need to stay." She yawned, curled onto her side, and was immediately asleep.

Ian snagged the pile of discarded blankets and sheets from the floor, shook them out, and covered her. On impulse, he leaned over and brushed a kiss to her forehead.

"Is she a whack-job or what?"

Ian growled at Zach's question and whirled on his best friend, who was standing in the open bedroom doorway.

"I don't know what's happening, but she's not a whack-job." He noticed Emerson hovering behind Zach. "We need to find the tree."

"What tree?" War must not have kept Zach in the loop.

Emerson pulled out her cell. "The Tree of Life. Or Death, depending on if you ask War or not."

Zach cursed and turned toward her. "I thought it was a legend. You mean it exists?"

"She stole it from him." Emerson seemed to relish that idea.

Zach barked out a laugh. "That little human stole it from Ian? That's priceless."

Ian shoved past them. "Doesn't matter. If she has it, we need it. I swear it's here."

Emerson turned her cell toward Zach. "This is what it looks like. About six inches tall. All gold. It contains all the animals from our clans and then some." She pointed at one spot. "Personally, I think this is a dragon, but they don't exist so maybe a giant lizard."

Zach frowned. "She could have given it to a friend or sold it by now."

Ian paused on his way to the living room. It was as good a place as any to start his search. *No. It's here.* He looked at them. "I can't explain it. I sense it. It's in this house. Too many weird things are happening. There has to be a curse or something associated with that thing. We'll find it, then we'll hand it over to War. He'll put it in a safe place and all of this will go away."

The other two looked at each other, exchanging an unspoken understanding. Ian knew they thought he was crazy, just like they clearly thought Ryder was. Then Zach walked up to him, slapped him on the shoulder. "Whatever you need. You can count on us."

Chapter 14

Hours later, Ian wanted to slam his own fist into a wall. There was no sign of the statue and yet he sensed it was in Ryder's house, just as he could when he was at the museum. So close and yet invisible. When he remembered her friend would be there within half an hour, they left.

Ian slouched in the backseat of Zach's truck as the day's events shuffled through his head. Nothing made sense. As soon as he could, he'd call War to get his take on what had transpired.

Sensing the truck slowing down, he glanced up and cursed. No need to call War. Three large black SUVs were parked outside Zach's home, signaling that War, Jamie, and Colin were here. How many other shifters would respond to their summons? The wolf pack and the leopard pride operated in a military fashion. When the generals, aka alphas, called for backup, their men responded.

Zach stated the obvious. "Looks like we have company."

"Don't stop." Despite Ian's protest, Zach pulled into the driveway and parked. *Maybe if I stay here, they'll ignore me.*

But as much as he wanted to avoid his brothers, he needed answers about the statue in order to help Ry.

As he walked into the house, his suspicions were confirmed. Several large, overbearing men and one tall, slim woman filled the living room.

Ian glanced at War. "Twenty-four hours, huh?" He had known all along that the leopard alpha could change his mind, but did he seriously have to gather every wolf and leopard shifter in a five-state radius?

"Don't be insolent to an alpha." The dressing-down came from his brother, Jamie.

Ian shoved down his annoyance and met Jamie's gaze. He would not back down on this. Ry was his top priority. *Protect her.*

Minutes ticked by. The silence in the room thickened until Ian wanted to yell. He had gone against the pack and his alpha by stealing an item considered off-limits, not reporting in, and keeping vital information to himself. He even had sex with a human and risked the anonymity of their kind. He may be Jamie's little brother, but he was in deep shit. Jamie wouldn't treat his brother any differently than he would anyone else in his pack.

Jamie finally looked to Zach. "Any luck on locating the statue?"

Damn him.

Zach answered, drawing Ian's attention and wrath toward him. "No. We found nothing although we spent several hours searching her house."

"You think she sold it?"

"That was my first consideration, but she's had less than a day to do it. Unless she knew about the statue ahead of time and already had arrangements, I doubt she could have sold it this fast." He darted a glance in Ian's direction. "She also seems sick. She passed out and has been sleeping ever since."

Jamie considered Zach's reply before addressing Ian. "Did you hurt her? She is human."

"What? No. She already told War she wasn't injured."

"They had hot monkey sex as soon as we arrived," Emerson interjected, probably hoping to discredit him. She crossed her arms over her chest and grinned in annoying satisfaction. She'd throw suspicion his way any chance she found.

Ian growled in her direction and flashed his fangs until he heard a low rumbling coming from War. Emerson took a step forward, exposing her own fangs.

Jamie stepped in. "Everyone out. I want to talk to Ian alone." In seconds, the room was empty except for the two brothers. He swallowed hard at the stern look on Jamie's face, knowing he was in trouble.

Jamie was the epitome of authority. All three brothers were similar in their looks, but Ian used his to get laid. He wasn't sure his brother had been with a woman in the past year, possibly longer. Jamie had been searching for a bride but was painstakingly slow with the process.

"You should have called me instead of War. Do you realize how this looks to the rest of our pack?"

Ian shifted, uncomfortable at the question. "What do you want, Jamie? An apology? My submission? Just tell me. Get it over with."

The silence stretched between them.

"She means that much to you that you would defy me?"

He let his thoughts drift back to Ry for several seconds. "Yes. She intrigues me."

Jamie let out a deep sigh. "I swear, Ian. Someone dropped you on your head one too many times when you were a baby. She's a human. Any way you look at it, nothing good can come of a relationship between you two."

Ian rolled his eyes and huffed out a breath. Jamie never trusted him.

The silence spoke more than Jamie ever could. Ian quickly continued. "What bothers you more? The statue or the woman?"

Jamie slammed his fist on the tabletop beside him. "Both."

Ian winced at his tone.

"You're an excellent thief, almost as good as Da, but you know the rules. We don't steal. Not after what happened to him. I refuse to let you throw away your life on stealing. I need you. We need you. Our clan is too small and too important for us to take chances with being thieves. I thought you understood that."

Ian understood his brother's concern. Their main business was an extreme-sporting resort in Alaska. They catered to people who wanted to challenge the elements with climbing, skiing, snow mobiles, and a number of other sports. They didn't offer hunting except with a camera. Their clan of shifters were the only hunters allowed. And to them it wasn't a sport. No one would jeopardize The Wolves Run with their thieving profession—a trade passed down from father to son. Ian had broken the family's cardinal rule.

"Be reasonable. I have it under control." Except there wasn't anything reasonable about this situation.

"Really? Are you fucking kidding me?" Jamie's fury filled the room as he paced. "Because that's not what I'm seeing. The statue is in the hands of a human woman you've been screwing and you can't find it. If you'd quit thinking with your dick, maybe you could understand the situation you've put us in."

"You won't believe me even if I explained."

"Try me."

Ian still hesitated.

Jamie stepped close and placed his hands on top of Ian's shoulders. Back in control, his voice was quiet and sincere. "Ian. Even if I doubt you, I'll stand by you. Right now, you're my brother and I'm concerned. You're acting irrationally. I want to understand what's going on."

Ian noted the worry in Jamie's eyes. This wasn't his alpha. This was his big brother.

"It spoke to me."

Jamie frowned.

"I heard a voice in my head. A woman's voice, telling me to protect the tree. That was when I stole it. Now it's telling me to protect her. The woman. Ryder."

Jamie's expression was unreadable. In a split second, he was the alpha again. He stepped back. "Protect her from what?"

"I don't know. From everything, I suppose. I'm torn, like I should be there, watching over her."

When Jamie didn't respond, Ian dove into explaining everything else—the tattoos, his wound healing, her hand mending, and their shared dreams. He even told his brother about her eyes changing colors and her extreme mood swings. As he finished, relief eased through his system. Keeping everything to himself had been stressful.

But Jamie's expression was not encouraging. It was filled with doubt and something he hadn't seen in years—fear and confusion.

"You believe me, don't you?"

His brother shook himself out of his thoughts, his control in place again. "I want Abby to examine you." Abby was Zach's sister and the doctor at their resort.

Ian protested, but Jamie held up a hand. "Humor me. If there was some drug on the statue, I want to know about it. It could have affected you and most likely the woman too."

He hadn't considered that angle. With their accelerated metabolisms, drugs and alcohol didn't stay in shifters' systems long. If this drug was something they'd never encountered before, though, it could have affected him. The statue was over three thousand years old and had survived the most devastating events in their history. Who knew what was lingering on it?

"All right."

"Good. I don't want you going near her. Understood?"

His head throbbed. "I should go to her. She needs protecting."

"No, Ian. You fucked up. Now do as I say. Once Abby finishes with you, get some sleep. You look like shit."

Funny, Ian had told Ryder the exact same thing.

Chapter 15

The doorbell woke Ry. Again. She desperately wished someone else would answer it. Gritty eyes, dry mouth, stomach roiling, and dizziness all forced her deeper into the blankets. Barely able to open her eyes, she wondered if it was Ian again. Had he even left? She couldn't keep track of what day it was or what had even happened over the past few hours. She barely remembered Lauren popping in before leaving for the hospital. Although she definitely remembered the crazy sex with Ian in the front hallway.

Groaning, she rolled out of bed and tugged at her clothes before making her way to the front door. Unsteady, she zigzagged, but stayed on her feet. What was this compulsion to answer the door every time someone knocked? She'd have to puzzle it out later. Ignoring the summons hadn't crossed her mind until she was standing in the hallway.

Peeking through the peephole, she gasped. The man standing on the other side was one of Ian's dream brothers. Seriously? She peeked again. *Holy shit. He is real.* He was staring straight at the security device as though he realized she was watching him.

His muffled voice reached her. "Ms. Hoffman. My name is James Stone. I'm Ian's brother. I'd like to speak to you."

She hesitated. He knew her name. Even worse, he'd admitted he was one of Ian's brothers. *Shit. Shit. Shit.* Talk about dreams coming true.

"Without the door between us, if possible."

Taking in a slow deep breath, Ry was amazed at how calm she felt when she unlocked the door. She opened it and took several steps back. He remained on the doorstep, critically assessing her.

"May I come in?"

The man was polite, nothing like the dream version who had made her scream in ecstasy.

"Yes. Of course. Please."

She would recognize his body anywhere, with or without clothes. He looked like an older version of Ian, possibly late thirties to early forties. But whereas Ian's hair was multicolored, James's was a thick, deep brown but with a hint of gray at his temples. He didn't have the laugh wrinkles around his eyes that Ian did. Instead, there was a slight furrow between his eyes as he studied her. She wondered if he had the same four jagged scars like claw marks on his back. In her dreams, she had traced them with her tongue.

He stepped in, casually closing the door behind him. "I apologize for intruding, but I'd like to talk to you about what happened."

She stared at his chest.

"Ms. Hoffman?"

Ry dragged her eyes back up to his face. She nodded. She couldn't open her mouth to respond. *Damn. So much for being a normal, intelligent person.*

"My friends call me Jamie. Ian is my youngest brother. Would you mind if we talked?" At her hesitation, he added, "I promise I'll make it quick."

Pull on those big-girl panties, Ry. She needed to tell this voice to get out of her head and these brothers out of her life.

Ry grumbled accusingly, "I resent the fact that you and your brother seem to think you can knock on my door whenever you want. I should call the police after what Ian did."

"Please accept my apologies. He sometimes does foolish things. I wanted to make sure you ... recovered from Ian's little scheme. I've reprimanded him for what he did in Chicago."

"Reprimanded? He's not...." Concern raced through her. She took a step forward before pausing. Why did she even care about Ian? After what he'd put her through, she should be pleased he'd been "reprimanded."

"I hope he wasn't disciplined too harshly." She tried for casual. "I wasn't hurt." Her voice was low. Something about this man brought out an insecurity in her and she didn't understand why. Unlike the ER where she knew what she was doing and what to expect, where she didn't question her actions. She hated the current uncertainty and struggled to suppress it. *Look him in the eye.*

Jamie continued to watch her every movement. "It was more of a verbal dressing down than anything. He's too old for me to take him over my knee." The corners of his mouth turned up, as though to reassure her.

A rush of excitement raced through her. Why did the image of her naked and sprawled over Jamie's knees dance through her mind? *Don't go there. You do not want a spanking.* Her face flushed with embarrassment. Turning away, she walked into the living room. When she reached the sofa, she turned back to Jamie, who had closely followed. She hoped her cheeks weren't as flushed as they felt.

"Why did you come? Just to tell me you punished him?"

"As I mentioned, I wanted to express my concern. I was worried about how you were recovering from your experience. You must have been frightened. Most women would have."

She narrowed her eyes at his words. "I'm not most women."

One of his eyebrows raised slightly. "My apologies. I didn't mean to insinuate anything. I wanted to make sure you weren't afraid."

Afraid was the word she would have used yesterday. Today's words were irate and annoyed. Ian had kidnapped her. As she thought about that night, her emotions worked their way up through her stomach and chest, like a wave of fury rolling over her as it had earlier in the day with Ian. The doubt and uncertainty were shoved aside.

"I'm not afraid. I'm angry. I'm lucky your brother fell asleep and I escaped. If I hadn't fled the next morning, there's no telling what else he would have done." The rage overtook her—a living, breathing beast hovering inside her, wanting to burst free. Her body shook as her hands clenched into fists.

"I'm sorry. I didn't mean to upset you."

His words soothed her. The heat backed off. Her hands unclenched. *What the hell is happening to me?*

"I wish you would leave now. I don't feel well." This time her voice trembled. One minute his words barely annoyed her. The next, irritation poured from her. She was acting like a hormonal teenager. Could she stop it the next time or would she end up hurting him or someone else? She had lost her temper and fractured her hand earlier. She did not need a replay of that scene.

"Okay." Jamie drew out the two syllables.

The bottom of Ryder's world fell-out. Her body turned cold, nauseous, and faint. She swayed and Jamie grabbed her upper arms before she toppled over. She closed her eyes and breathed.

At his touch, Ry's emotions flipped to being hot, excited, and craving his caress. A wave of passion began at her toes, making them tingle, drifted up her limbs, and across her torso. Her nipples peaked. Heat flooded between her legs, warming all her most private places in delicious ways. A flashfire of sensual delight.

Jamie turned her in his arms and held her from behind. His hands reached around her body as she leaned back against him. One of his hands cupped a breast. The other dipped into her shorts. His fingers slid through her wetness. He stroked and teased her sensitive bud. His other hand pinched and twisted her nipple. The heat burned, rapid and fierce. She shuddered as an orgasm rocked her body.

Gasping, she opened her eyes and looked into his.

Jamie stood in front of her, not behind her. His hands were on her upper arms, not stroking her intimately.

Jerking away, she stumbled several steps back. Horrified and frightened by what she had imagined, she wrapped her arms around herself. He seemed unaware to the fact she had experienced every aspect of a climax. In fact, her body still hummed from her orgasm. *Great. Now I'm having mind-blowing sex dreams while awake.*

"Go away. *Now.* Please." She gasped the words out as she backed away.

Without a sound, he left.

· · ·

Ry HAD TO GET AWAY. No more sleeping. No more thinking. Just exercising. She changed from her pajamas to jogging shorts and t-shirt, then headed out for a run. With her earbuds in and her classic-rock playlist queued up, she set out on her usual route.

The conference the week before hadn't been conducive to working out, and she'd been preoccupied with the kidnapping and her dreams since returning home. If she could immerse herself in exercise, maybe she wouldn't fly off the handle. Not a great possibility, but hey, a girl had to have hopes, right? Not wanting to think about dreams or strange men, she headed down the street.

After five minutes, she wasn't having any luck with blocking out the thoughts darting through her head.

Lovely thoughts of gorgeous dream men.

There was Ian. He was tender and loving. Kissing her body all over and heightening her senses. She enjoyed when he slid his cock deep inside her while he moved slowly and sensuously, allowing her to experience every single inch of him.

The older brother, Jamie, was a take-charge kind of man. She'd seen it in her dreams. He'd made sure she enjoyed every moment, but he always wrung a little bit more from her. She was convinced she would pass out from lack of oxygen from screaming. He also had a thing for spanking. The idea made her shiver.

The middle brother was the playful one. He would heighten and sharpen her senses by tickling and teasing her sensitive spots until she begged for more, then a single breath on the back of her neck would spin her out of control.

Ry shuddered. What she needed was a cold shower. She couldn't continue to think about the three brothers. She shook her head to clear her thoughts, attempting to get her mind back on track so she could complete some work this afternoon. Her emails at work would be piling up.

Not concentrating on her jogging, Ry stepped off the sidewalk and into traffic. Her arm jerked as someone yanked her back from the jaws of death in the form of a red SUV.

She found herself held in the arms of a tall, broad-shouldered black man. He towered over her, well over six feet tall with muscles on top of muscles stretching his shirt. Tattoos crisscrossed his bald head and snaked down his neck to vanish underneath his clothes. They were intricate markings that must have taken years to complete, but then again, who knew? Hers had shown up overnight.

As she gazed up, the same intense sexual reaction she'd had with Ian and Jamie rushed over her, sinking into her pores, making her tingle in anticipation.

His mouth moved. He was talking. She watched his lips, curiosity moving her to gently press the fingertips of her right hand to them. They were soft despite the rugged, hard appearance of the rest of him. Surprise filled his eyes.

Rising onto her toes, she slid her hands up around his neck, pulling his head closer to hers. She murmured, "Nice kitty." Their lips pressed together. His parted with a sigh. Their heads tilted and the kiss deepened, slowed, and turned sensuous. His eyes closed. Hers remained open. She watched the masculine beauty of his face the entire time.

Ry broke the kiss, lowering her heels to the ground. Her forehead and hands rested on his chest for a moment. Stark realization of what she had done with a complete stranger smacked her. Taking a step backward, she turned and ran. A sob broke from her throat.

Now she was kissing strangers on a public street.

Chapter 16

"Where the hell is Jamie?"

Ian cringed at the sound of War bellowing through Zach's house. The leopard alpha strode through the living room and into the kitchen, stopping in front of him. "Where's your damn brother?"

"Over here. What are you yelling about?" Jamie's cool, collected voice came from the entryway to the garage. "Did you get patrols set up?"

Ian studied them. Something had happened. Jamie might not appear upset, but the index finger on his left hand was tapping against his leg. Never a good sign.

War growled. "I saw her."

"When?"

"Just now. Well, twenty minutes ago. She was jogging. At least until she kissed me."

Jamie's eyebrows raised. Ian's heart stuttered. She'd kissed War?

"Did you recognize you?"

The big man shook his head. "No. I don't put my picture

on my website. I don't do selfies with her uncle either. I doubt she has any idea what I look like. Where were you?"

"I went to talk to her. She became upset. She must have gone for a run and come across you."

Ian interjected, "Why did you upset her?"

"I didn't." Jamie let out a slow breath. "Her eyes changed color."

"Yes!" War shouted in excitement. "I couldn't believe it."

"Ian told me about it earlier, but I thought it was his imagination. Sorry, Ian." Jamie's apology was a relief, as he'd begun to doubt what he'd seen.

Zach stepped into the conversation. "Her eyes change color? How does that happen?"

Everyone turned to Abby, who threw up her hands. "Don't look at me. There is no medical condition that'll make someone's eyes mutate like that in an instant."

"She became upset. The more I talked to her, the angrier she got. Then she looked panicked and began to faint, so I grabbed her." Jamie paused, collecting his thoughts. He looked directly at Ian. "Her eyes changed. I swear, all I did was grip her arms."

Ian instinctively grasped that he would not like what came next.

Jamie shifted his weight from foot to foot, struggling with what to say. "I had an image flash through my mind. One of her and me. In an embrace. Nothing happened in reality, but when she stepped away, I would have sworn we'd made love. It was freaky weird."

War added to the turmoil. "She called me a nice kitty."

Silence took over the room. They would normally have laughed and teased War for someone calling him that. Instead, Ian could tell they were all wondering how she could have known he was a cat shifter. And how had she disturbed Jamie so much?

"And you're both saying her eyes switched colors?" Abby asked.

They nodded. "Her eyes turned blue when she yelled at us earlier," Ian added, motioning to Zach and Emerson.

"She's a whack-job, I'm telling you." Zach's answer to everything. Ian rolled his eyes.

Jamie took control. "No. It has to be the statue creating this chaos. We know bits and pieces of the old stories. She can tell what type of shifter we are. No human can. We need to keep an eye on her. A close eye. Ian, I hate to say it, but I think you should visit and stay overnight if she'll let you."

"I'm on it." He stepped forward, more than eager to be at her side.

Jamie's lips twitched. "I thought you wouldn't mind. I'll send Colin over tomorrow to relieve you."

"I'll be fine."

Emerson snickered. "You'll be shagging. Don't deny it." Everyone threw her annoyed glances. "What? You know he will."

Ian bumped into her shoulder hard as he pushed past. He headed to the front door, excited to see Ryder again, but hesitated, eavesdropping when Jamie spoke from the other room.

"We'll make a plan and decide what to do with her. We need to determine if she's a danger to herself or others."

War's booming voice followed. "You think the statue did something to her? Do you believe whatever happened to our ancestors will happen to us?"

"There's not enough of us to stop it if it does. Something's not normal about any of this," Jamie said. "I understand she's the niece of your friend, but I need your promise that you'll choose us over her. If necessary, I will kill her in a heartbeat if I have to, to save our people. We've been friends for a long time. I don't want you standing in the way."

Jamie and War were both the alpha and elder of their packs. Their people were their number-one concern.

Ian, hand on the doorknob, waited for War's reply.

The leopard alpha did not disappoint. "If it comes down to it, I'll kill her myself. But what are you going to do about Ian? The boy is protective of her."

"Don't worry about him. I'll deal with him if the situation arises."

Horror and anger gripped Ian. He wouldn't let them hurt her, let alone kill her. She wasn't a threat to them. The statue was hidden in her house. He'd locate it and offer it to the alphas for safekeeping. Everything would go back to normal.

Ian slipped out the front door and headed to one of the spare cars. Thoughts of Ryder had bombarded him since he left her house hours ago. He was over one hundred eighty years old and had been tupping women since he was fifteen. No one had generated such intense sexual feelings in him before.

LATER IN THE EVENING, Ry ordered Chinese food to be delivered. Lauren had stopped in twice, over lunch and again after work. Ry had convinced her that she was fine and sent her home. Now, taking the food, a glass, and a bottle of wine, she headed to her small but private patio. She loved the quiet of the spring evening. After finishing her meal, she leaned back in her lounge chair with her wine and watched the moonless sky.

She was confused. What was happening with her and Ian was not normal by anyone's definition. And her hand? What was that all about? Squeezing her eyes shut, she took a deep breath, determined to address each issue from the past few days.

The intense sex with Ian, the dream sex with multiple men—the same men who changed from wolves to men, the detailed tattoo, her attraction to men she'd only just met, her broken hand, the voice in her head. None of it made sense. She should talk to Ian, but she wasn't sure how to reach him. She shouldn't worry. Tonight was for her. The patio was peaceful and soothing. She dozed.

A sensation tickled over her little by little. It started as a tingling at the site of her tattoo, making her nipples peak. Sexual awareness drifted through her body. Opening her eyes, she turned her head. Ian stood at the edge of her patio, tall and commanding. How long had he been there?

Her libido kicked into overdrive.

Ry set her glass on the patio table. The second she stood, he was beside her. When his hand met hers, her desire intensified. She wanted to grab him, wrap herself around him, and pull him close. There was no need for words.

She raised her arms and draped them around his neck. Their lips met. Their tongues tangled together. He held her close and deepened the kiss.

Ian gathered her up and carried her into the house and to her bedroom. After setting her on the bed, he stepped back and stripped off his clothes. Hungry to taste all that hard-male flesh, she scrambled to do the same.

Naked, they stared at each other for several moments. The sight of his tattoo clicked something in her brain. It puzzled her for two seconds before she gave up and let her gaze roam over his entire body. His cock hardened and lengthened. A low growl rumbled in his chest before he knelt next to the edge of the bed and tugged her body toward him. He buried his face between her thighs.

IN THE EARLY MORNING HOURS, Ian and Ry sprawled across her bed. Ry relaxed against him, their legs intertwined, her hand resting on his chest. She ran her fingers across the light dusting of hair, following it down his sternum to his belly button and back up again. Their breathing was slow and synchronized. She couldn't remember the last time she'd been this relaxed and tranquil.

Ian broke the silence. "We need to talk."

She hid her face in his chest and groaned. "Not the statue again."

He chuckled softly. Placing a finger under her chin, he lifted her gaze to his.

She shivered. *How did he do that?* A minute ago, she lay exhausted in his arms, but the trace of his fingers on her skin ignited her passion. Tingling spread between her legs and up to her nipples. She pressed her thighs together to thwart the sensations. Flustered, she tried to think of something to discuss besides the damn tree. She'd never had a conversation naked before; it was disconcerting.

"You're not my usual type. I mean, I don't have a usual type. I don't date." She cringed as she realized the words sounded foolish.

Ian only chuckled from deep in his chest. "I'm not sure this counts as dating."

She blushed. He was right. There was no dating involved, just major hooking up.

She scrambled to correct her blunder as she motioned

to their bodies tightly wound together. "It's been years since I've done... *this*." How did she describe their lovemaking and what seemed to be their whirling into a relationship? She didn't want the distraction of a man with her hospital workload.

A horrifying observation struck her. "We didn't use condoms." Her voice rose with each word. She sat up, not caring about her nakedness. "We didn't use condoms. I'm a doctor and I didn't use condoms."

"It's okay. I'm sterile and I'm clean. I'm guessing from your reaction and your previous comment that you don't tumble into bed with every man, so I'd say you're clean too."

She blinked. "You're sterile?"

A faint sadness crossed his face before he smiled. "Makes it simpler. Tell me about you. I want to know everything about you. What color do you like? What's your favorite drink? Favorite movie? Tell me about your family."

After a moment, she settled against him and talked. He didn't disclose much about his family and she didn't mention Jamie's visit. She definitely didn't mention the stranger she had kissed. She learned about their family business in Alaska. Maybe one day she could visit. He learned about the couple who had adopted her when she was three, how she barely remembered her biological mother and had no idea who her father was.

They snuggled and whispered. Laughed and talked. She put the statue, their tattoos, and all the crazy happenings out of her mind. The world only revolved around them.

Chapter 17

Monday

Ry woke with the sun shining through the blinds. She stretched, feeling healthier and stronger than she had since leaving Chicago. So much had happened in two days. Interestingly, her erotic dreams had stopped overnight.

The slide of sheets against her naked skin reminded her of her late-night visitor. Everything they had done together had been incredible. Ian made love to her in more ways than she'd ever imagined possible. His well-placed kisses had driven her mindless and boneless. They had talked into the early morning hours, he made them a snack of sliced apples, then made love again, and fallen asleep in each other's arms. Curious if he was still here to continue their activities, she hurried out of bed and into the bathroom.

After a quick shower, she dressed in lounging pants and a t-shirt. The moment she stepped out of her bedroom, she smelled delicious scents coming from the kitchen. Cinnamon rolls. *Yummy.* Ian must have gone out for breakfast. *Double yummy.* Ry's stomach rumbled. Then something else assaulted her nostrils—bacon.

She winced. Being a vegetarian, she didn't relish the smell of meat.

Ian.

He was still here. A wave of excitement raced through her. She rushed down the hall, sliding to a halt at the kitchen doorway. He stood at her stove, his back to her.

Breathless, she eyed his ass. "Ian."

He turned around. "Sorry, sweetheart. Jamie is grilling him. You're stuck with me."

Ry stumbled backward into the wall. She reached for a nearby chair and shoved it between them. Impossible. It wasn't Ian. It was the middle brother from her dreams. *He's real.*

An older version of Ian and younger than Jamie, this brother appeared to be in his early thirties. Like Jamie's, his hair was thick and a deep, rich brown.

He raised an eyebrow, the gesture similar to both of his brothers, and frowned.

"Are you all right? You look like you've seen a ghost." Setting down his fork, he stepped away from the stove and headed toward her. He made it past the counter before she screeched and fled back to her bedroom. Slamming the door, she locked it, wishing it had a bolt.

Of course the third brother is real. Why had she ever doubted it? She had already met the oldest one in person but seriously, life did not imitate dreams. The thought shocked her. Leaning against the door, she tried counting to ten.

One.... This is not possible. Two.... People from dreams cannot be real. Three.... Close your eyes and breathe. Four.... He'll go away. Five....

The man from her dreams, or was it nightmares now, knocked on the door. The pounding vibrated through her entire body. Leaping back, she whirled around to stare at the only barrier between them.

"Ryder? I'm sorry I scared you. I'm Ian's brother, Colin. You can call him so he can verify who I am. He said he left his business card on your bedside table."

Silence. *If I'm quiet, he'll go away.*

"Ryder? I can hear you breathing, so I know you're there. Talk to me."

Damn. How could he hear her breathing? Wolves have extreme hearing. She shoved away the thought. "Why are you here? How did you get in my house? I need to go to work. You'll have to leave so I can get ready." The words rushed out of her mouth.

He burst out laughing. It spread through her body, warming her from the inside out. Some of her dread faded away. *What is it with these brothers?*

Colin chuckled. "When you let loose with questions, you definitely let them fly."

She imagined him smiling at her through the door.

"Okay. Let me think. I'm here because Ian didn't want you to be alone and he's busy. I came in when Ian left early this morning. As far as work, it's Monday and I have a friend who confirmed you're not scheduled until tonight."

Stunned, Ry opened her mouth, but nothing came out.

"Did I answer all your questions?"

She cleared her throat. "Yes, but I don't like this. I want you to leave. Tell Ian I don't need a babysitter and I resent a stranger coming into my home."

"If you'd come out of your room, we could discuss this face-to-face. Then we wouldn't be strangers."

Ry decided silence was her best move now. She was

afraid. Afraid that if she left her sanctuary, the same thing would happen with this brother that had happened with Jamie. Or worse, what was happening with Ian. She wanted to berate Ian for leaving her alone. The only way not to end up kissing this brother or imagining herself being pleasured by him was to hold her tongue and stay in her room.

"All right. I'm going back to my breakfast. If you'd like something to eat, come out. I made enough for us both."

She heard him step away, then soft footfalls retreating. She needed to contact Ian. Hurrying away from the door, she snatched up the plain white business card from beside her bed. Not finding her phone, she darted around her room looking for it. It wasn't here. *Think. Where did I leave it?*

She groaned. On the patio. It was the last place she remembered having it. Ian had shown up last night and all thoughts of a normal evening had vanished. Ry sagged against the bathroom doorway as her mind whirled. *Now what should I do?*

No. This is my house. My home. I will not hide. With newfound courage, she pushed away from the doorway and paced to the bedroom door. She hesitated before grabbing the doorknob and yanking it open. She kept up her bravery until she stepped into the kitchen.

Colin sat at her table, eating. He looked up and smiled. "There's more, if you're hungry."

"I don't eat meat."

His eyes widened and he choked on the bite he was chewing before swallowing quickly. "Excuse me?"

"I'm a vegetarian and I would appreciate it if you did not stink up my home with your nasty cooked-flesh odors."

His lips twitched. "I'm sorry."

"Thank you."

"No. I mean, I'm sorry you're a vegetarian. Do you have any idea what you're missing?" He raised a long, crispy slice of bacon and sank his teeth into it, then moaned in exaggerated pleasure.

She stared in fascination while he chewed. Realizing she was gawking, she jerked herself out of the mesmerizing trance, glared and stormed past him to the patio door. Heat spread across her face.

"Wait a second." He rushed to her side, blocking her path.

"I need my phone. It's out there." She tried to brush past him but he was a solid mass of male flesh. "Move."

He hesitated a moment before opening the door and stepping aside, then followed, keeping within a foot of her. His breath tickled her neck. Ry scanned the small patio until she spotted her phone on the chair she'd occupied the night before.

She quickly retrieved it and glanced at the calls and messages she had missed. One was from Ian. With two swipes of her finger, she held her phone to her ear and listened.

"Sorry I can't be there when you wake. I'll stop by later. I know you don't want to hear this, but please, baby, please. If you have the statue, you need to give it to Colin. We think it's making you sick with a drug we haven't identified yet. You're tired. You keep having those dreams. Consider it. We'll talk later."

A flare of irritation rose at the mention of the statue, but she shoved it down. She hadn't considered drugs or even poison. It made sense. When the little tree disintegrated, she had inhaled most of the particles. Maybe some of the freaky things she'd experienced lately were hallucinations.

Dread and panic replaced her anger. She whirled and found Colin a step away. His gaze focused on her face.

"I need to...."

He raised an eyebrow.

God, I hate arrogant men like him. She held back an exasperated sigh. "I need to talk to Ian. Now."

"If it's about the statue, you can tell me. I'll get rid of it."

If only she had it, she'd get rid of both him and it.

"You don't understand."

He crossed his arms over his muscular chest. "Try me. I've been told I'm fairly intelligent."

She snorted, but she realized it was time to explain what had happened to the statue.

Colin grinned. "I'm not an ogre. Trust me. Did you sell it?"

Ry rolled her eyes and headed toward the house.

He grabbed her arm and stopped her. "We need the statue."

She stared into his brown eyes only seeing genuine concern. It was time to tell. "It disintegrated at the motel."

His eyes narrowed. "You don't have it?"

"No. I never had it." She jerked her arm from his grip and hurried into the house, leaving Colin in the back yard reaching for his own phone. She made it to her living room when her phone chirped with a text. A quick glance showed Lauren's name. *Let's grab coffee. Meet me out front in two minutes.* Finally, a break from these men.

She glanced back to find Colin but he was nowhere in sight. He must still be outside and on the phone. Not wasting time, she ran into her bedroom and tugged on a pair of socks and shoved her feet into her running shoes.

When she hurried down the hallway toward the front

door, she heard Colin shout her name from the kitchen. She paused and glanced back toward him. She truly didn't know this man and his brothers. Ian had kidnapped her. His brothers were inserting themselves into her life, watching her.

He stepped toward her, frowning. "You're leaving?"

"Look. You know everything about the statue. There's no need to continue to harass me. I'm going for coffee with Lauren. Make sure you're gone when I get back."

Rushing outside, she ran to the curb but slowed as a Land Rover SUV pulled up and stopped. This was not Lauren's vehicle. The back door opened. A man stepped out, holding Lauren in his arms. He dumped her, unconscious, on the lawn and grabbed Ry's arm when she knelt beside her friend. Ry screamed in frustration. The man picked her up despite her kicking and punching him.

Colin shouted from inside her house, his yelling becoming louder and more frantic. Looking over her shoulder, she watched him sprint at an amazing speed toward her. She screamed at Colin to help her. The man holding her stuffed her into the SUV and they sped away.

Scrambling into a sitting position, she tried to move away from the man who had held her, only to realize there was another one on her other side.

"What's going on? Why are you doing this?"

Settled in the front passenger seat, a third man twisted around to run his gaze over her. His leer sent chills streaking down her spine. The evil she recognized on his face made her shudder with terror. She wrapped her arms around her frame as a creepy sensation skittered down her spine. She controlled her shudder.

"I'm Ethan Dunbar. I was hoping I wouldn't have to

resort to this, but I have no alternative." He gave the man next to her a slight nod. In the next second, a large male hand smothered a cloth over her nose and mouth. Struggling, she recognized the sweet smell of chloroform as darkness seeped over her.

Chapter 18

I an was irritated with the current discussion. His mind drifted back to the past few hours. In the early morning, the alphas had summoned him from Ryder's bed and back to Zach's house. Then they dispatched Colin to watch over her. The thought of another man in her house made Ian nervous and jealous. He should be there. No one else. She was his. His to protect.

Jamie and War informed him that they would relocate Ryder to a safe place. Her home was not secure enough or large enough for multiple guards to watch her. Moving her would offer them the chance to interrogate her about the statue while letting their men do a more thorough search of her house. They would begin the process after her neighbors left for work.

Now he sat, with Jamie and War, in one of the black SUVs two blocks away from Ry's house. They were listening to Markus, Jamie's security advisor, discuss the best way for extraction. Markus, a bear shifter, was as enormous and muscular as War. Whereas War was bald, Markus sported a short mohawk, the sides shaved. A tribute to his American Indian heritage.

Markus was meticulous and thorough with his reports, and today was no exception. Ian wished the man would summarize his observations. Annoyed that Jamie refused to let him visit Ry, he tuned out the other three men and stared at her front door.

Jamie's phone buzzed. "It's Colin." He answered it, putting it on speaker phone.

Colin spoke. "She doesn't have it. She said it disintegrated at the motel. I suggest we send someone there to confirm. Maybe no one has cleaned the room yet."

Focused on the conversation, Ian shook his head. "I can sense it in her house. I know it's there."

"I don't know about that but we can't find it here. It's the first time she's even mentioned what happened to it. I believe her." He paused. "Hold on."

They heard his muffled voice then he spoke into the phone. "She's going for coffee with her friend. Should we look again?"

The two alphas and Markus exchanged glances. Markus shrugged. "Wouldn't hurt. Ian can tail her and warn us when she'd heading back."

A shout from Colin broke their discussion. "Stop that car!"

Scrambling out of the SUV and onto the street, Ian spotted Ry racing across the front yard while his brother stormed out the front door. A dark gray SUV rolled up in front of her house and blocked their view. Ian sprinted toward her with the other three men matching his strides.

Colin had a head start, but even he didn't reach the car before it pulled away and had sped away for half a block. Leaping onto the hood of the moving car, he snarled a warning and smashed his fist into the windshield. Cracks splintered across the glass. There was no doubt in Ian's mind that Ry was inside the fleeing SUV.

Picking up speed, it headed directly toward them. The four men dodged the vehicle, Jamie and War rolling to one side, Ian and Markus to the other. The two biggest men, War and Markus, slid in behind the SUV and grabbed the bumper. With their massive strengths combined, they braced themselves, planted their feet, and forced the vehicle to a skidding halt. They hoisted the back end, and the tires spun as the driver revved the engine.

They had to resolve this in the next few seconds or risk drawing attention from any neighbors who were home, or War and Markus losing their grip. Whichever came first.

The man in the front passenger seat screamed obscenities at the driver. Ian smashed a partially shifted fist at the back-side window as Jamie pounded on the other side, and Colin continued to beat on the windshield. The sound of the SUV being dropped to the pavement echoed across the street and through Ian's soul. War and Markus had lost their hold. Tires squealing, the car shot forward. Colin flew off the hood, rolled across the blacktop, and leaped to his feet as he came to a stop.

Poised to shift, Ian froze when a large hand gripped his shoulder. He whirled, baring his teeth and ready to rip out the throat of whoever dared to interfere with saving Ryder.

Markus held up his hands. "Easy, boy. Let's act smart."

Ian stared in the direction the car had disappeared. Terror slashed a hole in his chest. His heart thudded with a now-familiar beat.

Protect her. Protect her.

Chapter 19

Ry fought against the dark. Voices whispered in the void—some encouraging, some berating—all urged her to wake. She stretched, but something held her immobile. Forcing the cobwebs from her mind, she opened her eyes, blinked several times, and assessed her predicament.

Her back was against a wall and her arms pulled tight over her head. She looked up to discover that her wrists were locked in handcuffs with a chain looped between them and bolted into the ceiling.

Puzzled, she took at her surroundings. She was in a large room with a picture window and a dingy, dilapidated couch. The view outside showed dirt, scrub grass, and dusty tumbleweeds as far as she could see. Nothing else. Based on the condition of the furniture, tattered carpet, and worn drapes, she doubted anyone had lived here in years. Why couldn't she be kidnapped to a luxury hotel or a secluded island?

Hearing footsteps, Ry swiveled her head. The doorway filled with several men. She recognized the three from the

SUV. The shorter one on the right had chloroformed her. She glared at them all.

Two of them halted halfway across the room. The third man, Ethan Dunbar, stopped and faced her. His expensive and immaculate suit angered her. His evil and sinister smile sickened her.

"Ryder Hoffman." He paused, tilting his head slightly as he watched her for a reaction. "I will ask you a question and I want an honest answer. First, you must understand how serious I am."

Before she asked what he was talking about, he backhanded her. Her head snapped to the side and pain flashed through her face and head. Tears pricked her eyes. No one had ever struck her before. *No one.* Surprise and anger warred within her as her face throbbed.

Tasting blood, she ran her tongue around the inside of her cheek before turning her head. Ry opened her mouth to curse him, but he backhanded her on the other cheek. Back and forth, he slapped her until her ears rang and she cried. Finally, Ry sagged in the handcuffs, tucking her face into her shoulder to avoid the next slug.

When he finished, the only sound in the room was her sobbing. He stepped closer. She flinched and pulled back, only to be stopped by the chains. His chuckle grated along her spine and sent shivers racking her body.

Dunbar motioned to the two men across the room. They stalked toward her, then halted beside her, pinning her between them. They tilted their heads and leaned in, one on either side of her neck. She jerked away again, but the chain and handcuffs kept her in place.

The two men inhaled her scent deep into their lungs. They rubbed their faces against the sides of her neck. Their animalistic movements horrified her. She screamed and struggled. As abruptly as they started, they pulled away.

First one spoke, then the other.

"She reeks of wolf. She's fucked the youngest one."

"Only the wolf. No one else."

Ry had no idea what they meant. She didn't particularly want to understand either. "Look. I have money. Let me go and I'll give it to you." She tried to remain calm, but the panic settled high in her chest, a huge weight suffocating her. Her stomach ached to heave.

"It's not money I want, sweetheart." Dunbar stared at her intently. His voice grated on her ears as he spoke quietly. "Where's the statue? Tell me where it is and I'll let you go."

The pain raging in her head made thinking difficult, but Ry didn't believe him. He'd lied about Lauren. Fear for friend's safety shoved bile up into her throat. What the hell was so important about the little relic that everyone wanted it? Would he even believe her if she told him? Ry blinked back tears and glared.

"It's gone."

Dunbar stood motionless for several seconds, his face inches from hers, before his fist slammed into her stomach. Ry doubled over, pulling the chain tight. Instead of an agonized scream, the air in her lungs whooshed out in a whimper. Breathing hurt. She gasped, attempting to take shallow breaths. Tears streamed down her face. Her brain ceased to function. Reflexively, her body bowed away from her attacker, but the taut restraints held tight.

He grabbed her hair, yanking her close to his face. The force on her head increased painfully for several seconds, then released. When no more jabs or punches hit her, the pain eased to a steady throb.

Her breathing ragged, she straightened. Her interrogator

stood near the large picture window, gazing out at the bleak landscape. She scrutinized him while he spoke into a cell phone. He was too far away for her to hear the conversation, but she watched him tilt back his head and laugh.

Horror washed over her. The word *psychopath* screamed through her brain.

Ending his call, Dunbar tucked his phone into an inner suit pocket before he turned toward her. The laughter on his lips faded into a cold expression and sent tremors through her body. Straightening his suit jacket, then tugging on his cuffs, he strolled in her direction and stopped a couple of feet in front of her. His silence grated along her skin before he spoke.

"What happened to the statue?"

Ry wanted to go home. She wanted Ian. She tried to answer but fell into a coughing fit instead.

Dunbar stepped farther away and waited impatiently. When she quieted, he spoke again. This time he almost convinced her of his sincerity. "Tell me about the statue and I'll let you go. It's simple."

Her voice was a mere mumble. "It disintegrated. It's gone."

Dunbar blinked. A frown crossed his face. He threw a glance at the men across the room, then threw back his head and laughed. This side of him frightened her more than his evil smile. He rubbed his hands together in excitement, reminding her of an evil mastermind.

"Miss Hoffman, I don't believe you. All I want is the statue. I've been searching for it for years. Take some time and think about your answer. I'll be back later."

She let her thoughts go out to Ian, a silent plea for help. Dunbar motioned to the two men. "Take care of her, Carter."

Seconds later, a fist crashed into the side of her head and everything went black.

Rʏ ᴡᴏᴋᴇ, lying on a bare mattress in an equally bare room. Sitting up, she glanced around and discovered a small table with a chair. Nothing else. No windows. An open door showed a bathroom. She assumed the closed door was the way out. Taking advantage of the solitude, she hurried into the bathroom.

She examined herself for injuries, but found none. There were no bruises, no scrapes or cuts. She scrubbed away the dried blood. She should have signs of the beating, even pain. The punch to her head alone should have given her a massive headache, concussion or a nasty bruise.

Exiting the bathroom, she stared across the room at the only way out, which was most likely guarded. The door loomed, a forbidden exit. Dragging in a slow deep breath, she stepped around the bed, clasped the doorknob, and turned it. Surprised, she took a quick step backward.

A man stood in the hallway, his military stance imposing. A scar ran down one cheek, detracting from his otherwise pleasant appearance. His eyes on her, he barked out, "She's awake." He must have had a radio intercom system on his body somewhere, because he clearly wasn't talking to her.

He gestured for her to move back. When she didn't, he took a menacing step forward. Ry turned and fled into the room, slamming the door behind her. She fumbled for a lock. Unable to detect one, she hurried across the room and sank into the farthest corner, sliding down the wall. Huddled into a ball, she stared at the door.

Minutes passed. No one entered the room. Eventually, she drifted in and out of sleep, dreaming of Ian. The familiar sexual hunger returned. Shoving it aside, she concentrated on her current situation.

Losing track of time, Ry jumped when the door opened and a young man peeked in. He looked barely old enough to shave. Ry watched him from behind lowered eyelids as he walked around the room. He placed a tray of food on the small table, then motioned to the bathroom.

"I'm Devon. You should clean up and eat something. Dunbar won't be back until morning. Take advantage of his absence." Without another word, he left.

Could she trust him? Not knowing who was trustworthy or not, she could only go on her instincts. Hurrying into the bathroom, she closed the door. At least she'd found a place to lock herself in. She slid to the floor next to the tub and sat numbly staring at a blank wall. The enormity of her situation weighed heavily on her mind. Dunbar would be back. Tears rolled down her cheeks unhindered.

Where was Ian? All she wanted at that moment was to be held tightly in his arms. She thought about him, pictured him in her mind.

A shower would be wonderful, but she was not about to trust anyone in this place. *To hell with that.* She needed to escape. Pulling herself together, she stood and stepped out of the bathroom.

Ry headed to the table and looked at the now-cold food —a grilled chicken breast, baked potato, and vegetables. A glass of wine and a glass of water sat on the tray. Being a vegetarian, the chicken didn't interest her. Her stomach growled, but she wasn't sure if someone had contaminated the meal. A sniff of the water provided no peculiar odor. She sipped, found no noticeable taste, and drank.

After she drank, she paced the small room and considered her options. If she got past the guard outside her door, she could slip out of the house. She had no idea where they were holding her, but at least she'd have a chance.

Her stomach churned and rumbled, clenching in agony. Rushing to the bathroom, she puked up what little she had in her stomach.

Something must have been in the water, because she was soon convinced she was dying. Sprawled on the bathroom floor, she lacked the strength to raise her head. When the young man found her, he stroked cool fingers across her cheek.

"I'm sorry. Hopefully you'll forgive me later." He pressed his lips to her forehead. Ry closed her eyes, wishing the room would stop spinning.

"What the hell are you doing? I thought I told you to take care of her," the man who had punched her earlier hissed at Devon. Ry would recognize his obnoxious voice anywhere.

"I'm sorry, sir. I don't know what happened. She ate the same food everyone else did. Maybe it's the flu?" the boy stammered, obviously frightened. Ry attempted to sit up, but fell back to the floor exhausted. She was amazed at how weak she had become in such a short time.

The man snorted when Devon mentioned the flu.

"Get Levi up here to give her something or take her downstairs. I don't care. I need her ready by daybreak when Dunbar returns. Do you understand me?"

Ry was barely aware of him leaving or when a pair of muscled arms plucked her up and transported her down the stairs. Someone commented on weak humans. She ignored everything when her world shifted and her stomach revolted again. She took slow breaths to keep her guts at bay.

As the strong arms laid her on another bed, relief flooded her. She'd made it without spewing only because she had nothing left in her stomach.

She slipped peacefully into sleep and her dreams, barely noticing a slight pinch in her arm or the boy tucking blankets around her.

THE MOST MAJESTIC tree she ever laid eyes on stood tall with its branches sweeping wide and full. Ry stepped up to it and placed her hands on the trunk. The bark texture was smooth and emanated a comforting impression. Something in the back of her mind recognized she was sick, but she couldn't remember why. Later. She would remember later. Then again, maybe she wouldn't want to remember.

She walked around the massive tree, gazing up into the branches, her hand trailing along the trunk. She marveled at the immense size. It was magnificent. She let her hand reach up to a low branch and gently grazed her fingers against a leaf.

"It's beautiful, isn't it?" The voice was soft and lyrical.

Spinning around, Ry spotted a woman in a long flowing red gown striding toward her. She was gorgeous with long, straight, blond hair parted in the middle and hanging to her waist. When she smiled, her brilliant blue eyes reflected her happiness.

The woman stopped under the tree and ran a hand over the trunk.

"It's called The Tree of Life. I've always found comfort standing here. A light brush on the trunk is all it takes to erase my troubles and problems. Do you sense the same thing?"

Ry nodded numbly at the woman. This dream was like her other dreams—surreal. Only this time, she instinctively realized she was staring at the woman from her dreams.

The woman laughed lightly. "Don't be afraid of me, Ryder.

I'm here to help you understand. You don't need to know every-thing now, but over time, you will. You'll learn how to return here whenever you want answers or whenever you're in pain."

Ry understood what she was talking about: all the bizarre things no one could explain. She asked, "Why is this happening? I want my life back."

The beautiful woman smiled warmly, similar to a mother reassuring her child.

"It's Fate, my dear. Your Fate. Your bloodline determined your path long before you were ever born. You cannot alter or halt its progress. You were never warned and prepared for this. For now, remember that the pain won't last."

"But those men...." Ry shuddered, thinking of Dunbar and the others.

"They can't hurt you unless you let them into your mind. Your body will heal. You're stronger than they are." She took a step toward Ry. "You need to trust your Guardians. You'll recognize who they are. They'll keep you safe. You need them in your life. You must trust me on this. Trust them."

Out of the corner of her eye, Ry caught a slight movement. When she looked in its direction, she saw three wolves sauntering up to the woman. One by one, they gently nuzzled her outstretched hand. Then they turned and trotted toward Ry, brushing up against her and rubbing their furry bodies against her bare legs.

She savored the luxuriousness of their fur on her naked skin. As they wound themselves around her, they shifted into the three brothers from her dreams. Ian, Colin, and Jamie.

The voice floated in her head, growing fainter. "Trust them."

Chapter 20

Tuesday

In moments, the sun would burst over the horizon. The man in black leather stood near a Harley. He absently fiddled with a pack strap on the back of the bike while overlooking the quiet farmhouse and buildings. Dew settled on the grass and a slight fog shrouded the buildings. The woman was inside. He had sensed a power explosion several days ago and tracked it. Someone had released a shitload of magic into the air. He had followed her slight tremble of magic to this place. Whoever she was, she had great potential for destruction.

A massive hulking creature materialized beside him, emitting no sound. The smell of death and sulfur wafted off the foul beast and wrapped around them. The immortal being was the size of a small hippo. It stood on two legs and was covered in a black shroud. There was no way to tell if it was male or female. Not that it mattered.

When called from the Darkness with black magic, death demons heeded their master.

"I want all the men dead. I sense two women. Leave them alone."

The creature began to leave.

"One more thing." He paused, his eyes fixated on the house below. He absently ran the backs of his knuckles against the scruff along his jaw. "Make the men scream before they die. I want them to experience the pain and agony of what they've done to her. Be quick about it. There are others moving in to rescue her."

Too far away to see anything in the dim light, he stood watching the buildings nonetheless. When the screams began, a satisfied smile crossed his face. His work complete, he drove away on his vintage motorcycle.

Chapter 21

In moments, the sun would burst over the horizon. It'd been almost eighteen hours since Ryder's kidnapping. The now-familiar voice had begun to whisper in Ian's head the moment she disappeared. When the voice switched to Ryder's, he was startled. She pleaded with him to save her; begged him to end her pain. Images of him holding her close shifted through his mind.

The original voice returned, directing him west, out of the city. Jamie and War put a stop to his initial frantic heroics to save her by himself. They gathered all of the shifters present before letting Ian lead them. Not knowing what they would run into, Markus equipped them all with handguns. Ian didn't question the voice. Of all the odd things happening between him and Ryder, it had been the one constant.

He was surprised that Jamie didn't question him when Ian told him what the voice wanted. His brother had simply nodded his understanding and ordered the others to follow Ian.

Zach drove while Ian pointed the way. War and Markus

followed with their men, struggling to keep him in their sight. Eventually Ian halted the caravan in the middle of a dirt road, miles from nowhere. Jamie sent him a questioning glance.

"She's in that direction about a mile. We can wait here for the others," Ian explained.

When the vehicles pulled up behind them, Markus and Emerson took over and ordered security sweeps. In moments, reports came in of the surrounding area. A small run-down farm lay nearby with a two-story house and three outbuildings. It sat far out in the country with no one around for miles.

The sun had broken in the east when shrieks burst through the silence. Glancing at each other, the group of shifters hesitated for a split second before exploding into a sprint heading toward the farm buildings. There was no mistaking the sound of men screaming in horrific pain and suffering before being silenced with death.

They found the first body near the barn, decapitated, warm, and twitching. The head lay several feet away, a horrified expression on the man's face. A scar crossed his cheek. Blood had splattered across the grass and the side of the building. The smell of death hung heavy in the air.

Death, sulfur, and burned flesh.

Ian was familiar with violence and horror. Shifters did not lead gentle lives. However, the thought of Ryder in the midst of such a horrifying situation sent terror racing through him.

On high alert, Markus took control. "Ian, you and Colin concentrate on finding Ryder and get her out of here. We'll meet up with you after we take care of the rest of this mess."

Hurrying toward the house, they passed more headless bodies. Jamie and Markus stopped to inspect several of them. It was a gruesome sight, especially since they couldn't determine who or what had done the deed. Ripping someone's head off their shoulders took tremendous strength and most shifters weren't that powerful.

Slipping into the house through a side door, Ian followed the beacon in his head. Colin remained behind him. Emerson and War provided backup with guns for the two men while they sought out Ryder.

Ian quickly located a small bedroom on the first floor. Halting outside the doorway, his wolf scented the air and discovered two women inside—one was Ryder. One step inside and he confronted a woman dressed like a man who stood beside a small cot. She welded a knife in an effort to protect Ryder. Lying on the makeshift bed, Ry looked tinier than normal.

The moment he set foot inside the room, she tossed the knife to the floor. Her voice remained steady, but her hand shook. "I'm Devon. I'm unarmed. I've been protecting her."

Ian jerked his head to the opposite side of the room. "Stand over there."

She hesitated, glancing at Ry. But after a moment, she hurried to where he had directed.

Keeping his eyes on Devon, Ian closed the distance to the cot. Colin inserted himself between them and Devon. A thick blanket covered Ryder. She appeared unharmed.

"She's drugged. It was the only way to keep them away from her. Dunbar is coming back within the hour in his helicopter. I want to go with you."

"Dunbar?" Ian shot the woman a curious look.

"A human who hired us. I don't like him. The money was good, but not enough for beating a woman senseless over a statue." Her fierceness and anger suggested she wanted revenge.

Hearing a growl from the doorway, Ian turned to see War. None of them condoned abusing innocents, especially human women and children. With a slight nod toward the other woman, War spoke, "I'll see she gets out of here. She might know a wealth of information about this Dunbar. Take Ryder and circle around to the trucks. Head west. We'll catch up with you once we deal with this place."

Zach and Abby's father owned a ranch farther west which was isolated and protected. They needed time for her to heal and time to uncover who Dunbar was and what he wanted. It would be safer for her there than in Dallas.

Ian scooped Ry into his arms and marched through the doorway. He slipped out the back door this time, hoping to get Ry as far away as fast as possible. Colin turned around and paced backward as they left the house, keeping his eyes peeled for anyone who would prove a danger.

They were moving away from the last outbuilding when they heard the crack of a rifle. Dropping to the ground, Ian covered Ry with his body. Colin crouched over them, scouring the area for the shooter. Another rifle shot sounded. Ian heard a thud, then Colin's grunt.

Taking a quick glance to his right side, Ian found Colin on his feet. Several more shots rang out but none directed toward them. Ian heard shouts and people running. When no more rounds sounded, he raised his head to see what was happening. Zach and Markus rushed toward one of the taller outbuildings, but Ian couldn't see who they were heading toward.

"Come on, let's get her out of here." Colin continued to provide protection.

Picking Ry up, Ian hurried away, with his brother several steps behind. The others would deal with destroying the house and buildings, along with the headless bodies.

THEY TRAVELED FAST, Ian carrying Ry's unconscious body with little effort. They ran for several miles before looping back toward the trucks. The terrain became rocky and more difficult to navigate. Discovering that Colin wasn't behind him anymore, Ian halted and turned. His brother leaned against a boulder, blood seeping through his shirt. Ian realized then why Colin had kept a slight distance behind him: to hide the smell of blood.

They wouldn't make it to the trucks without stopping for Colin to heal. Ian glanced around, spotting a sheltered overhang under a rock outcropping. The others would come looking for them, but in the meantime, they would hole up and rest.

Ian conveyed Ry toward the rock wall, gently setting her on the ground. The drug Dunbar's people had given her must have been powerful. She hadn't woken once. He cleared debris from a spot on the dirt, breaking off pine branches that had younger, softer needles.

Colin stumbled to the small clearing, moving past several large boulders and flopped down with a thud, his hand pressed against his shoulder. "I'd help but I'm afraid I'll get blood all over."

"You move and I'll beat you with a rock."

Colin laughed, moaned, then winced. "I can't believe I got shot."

"Getting old, dude. You're slowing down. Can you even track a moose anymore? I mean, they are huge. You should be able to at least spot one, or is the eyesight going too?"

"Shithead."

"Asshole."

Ian halted in front of Colin. "I'll make a pallet for Ry,

then head to the trucks. You can shift and heal, then stand watch while I'm gone."

Colin gave a short nod before closing his eyes and leaning against a boulder. As a shifter, he would only need a few hours in his animal form to heal enough to continue their journey.

Ian spread the branches on the dirt ground, then he stripped off his clothes, covering the pile. He eased her down onto the pallet, wishing it was more comfortable. She deserved something special after her ordeal, not a bed made of branches and sweaty clothes.

With that thought, he joined Colin. His brother had removed his clothes, preparing to shift. They stood naked, enjoying the warm Texas spring air. Colin shuddered when Ian probed his wound. He smacked his hand away.

Ian poked again, harder than necessary. "It went straight through. Why didn't you tell me you were shot?"

Colin yanked his shoulder back, glaring at his younger brother. "We had to get her out of there."

Ian grunted, then stepped away. "You should shift. You won't heal before I get back, but at least you'll slow the bleeding. Keep an eye on her. I'll secure the area before I head out."

With a quick nod, Colin shifted into his wolf form. He lay near the boulders, which gave him a good view of the area. Ian shifted and trotted away. He would do a quick loop to make sure they were alone before he ran to the trucks.

Chapter 22

Groggy, Ry drifted out of sleep slowly. She wasn't sure where she was, but she soon realized she was lying on something extremely uncomfortable. On top of that, she was shivering from the cold. Opening her eyes, she stared up at sky, clouds blotting out the sun. Puzzled, she turned her head and discovered huge boulders surrounding a cleared area. Beyond that, she could make out the shadows of juniper trees.

Why did she continue to wake up in unusual locations and situations? She was tired of it and all this kidnapping.

Standing, Ry noticed the clothes spread on the ground. Inspecting them, she realized from the quantity and style that they belonged to two men. Based on the amount of blood on one shirt, someone was seriously wounded. She instinctively knew the clothing belonged to Ian and Colin.

She heard a howling in the distance. Were there wolves in Texas? Was she still in Texas? She shivered, unsure if it was from the howls or from the cool spring breeze. If one of the brothers were hurt, she had to help. Not knowing how to defend herself against wolves, she carefully made her way to a gap between two boulders.

Instead of finding a man defending himself from a pack of ferocious beasts, she discovered a giant brown wolf. He stood several feet from the boulders, his head thrown back and his muzzle raised to the sky. She watched as he howled again, the sound riveting her to the spot. From a distance, she heard answering howls. He was calling his pack.

She was the one in trouble. She must have made a noise, because his head whipped around and his gaze focused on her.

The wolf's entire body shuddered. Preparing to hide, she watched, mesmerized, as the fur disappeared, leaving bare skin behind. The head, body, and limbs morphed into the shape of a man. In a matter of seconds, the wolf vanished and in his place was a broad-shouldered man who straightened and stood on his two bare human feet.

Colin? She stumbled back against the rock wall.

His eyes were still slightly wolfish but rapidly faded away to show his soft brown human eyes. How in the world was he able to do that? A man did not shape-shift into a wolf and vice versa. It was impossible. Except she had seen the brothers change from wolf to human in her dreams. Was she dreaming again? No. She felt the cool spring air. She smelled the scent of juniper trees.

The man was a werewolf as were his brothers. Werewolves that were so incredibly sexy she couldn't take her eyes off his naked form. Her gaze drifted down his body, taking in the smooth, streamed lines of his masculinity. She noticed the wound in his shoulder. The bloodstained clothes were his.

He stepped toward her. Her breathing quickened. Her

heart raced. He halted when only a hands' breadth separated them. She watched as he leaned in slightly and took a deep breath, inhaling her scent. She trembled with excitement.

Ry's eyes drifted to the hole in his shoulder. She raised her hands slowly. When he didn't stop her, she carefully placed one hand on the front of his shoulder and the other over the back, covering his wounds. Not knowing exactly what she was doing, she closed her eyes and concentrated on envisioning the injury closed and healed.

A soft moan escaped Colin as he shivered. Ry continued to clasp his injury with her hands for several minutes before dropping them. The wounds had disappeared.

When she gazed up at him in surprise, he placed his hands on her hips and pulled her close. Dipping his head, he pressed his face to her neck. His teeth nipped her skin, his lips pressing light kisses against it, his tongue trailing up her throat to her ear.

Her head fell backward, giving him complete access to her neck and throat. Heat flared through her. A spontaneous inferno.

This wasn't right. Although she had no commitment to Ian, she couldn't betray him with his brother. She moaned. "Tell me this is a dream. Tell me we shouldn't be doing this."

He paused, his breathing ragged against her neck. He hid his face for a few seconds before answering, "No, sweetheart. It's not a dream."

"What about Ian?"

"There's no stopping this. He would understand more than anyone."

Although she wanted to move away, a wave of desire flooded her core. He was a man and a wolf. Her brain shut down. Her senses took over. She was lost to the sexual craving.

"Colin." She breathed his name into the air near his ear. Ry turned her face toward him, seeking his lips. She kissed him hungrily, demanding more, wanting more, needing more.

Stepping back, he ripped her clothes off. Picking her up by her waist, he pulled her legs around him as he carried her across the clearing to a large boulder. Setting her on her feet, he kissed her fervently while bending her over backward. With her arms around his neck, she held on tight although his grip was solid.

His lips trailed down her throat, down her chest to her right breast. Her body tightened, certain parts tightening more than others.

He froze the tiniest bit before shuddering. Turning her gaze on him, she found his mouth partially shifted. His wolf fangs flashed, but she wasn't frightened. Quite the opposite, in fact: the change excited and intrigued her.

Ry ran her hands through his hair, pulling his head and mouth closer. He sank his fangs into her breast. A quick stab of pain followed by a rush of exquisite pleasure. Ry gasped as it pulsed through her, her body throbbing. Fascinated, she watched his fangs slide deeper into her flesh. He disengaged them, then his wolf's tongue lapped at the wound, licking up the trickle of blood.

It took Ry several seconds to realize she now sported another wolf tattoo. This time, it rested on her right breast. Colin raised his head, his gaze locking with hers. His face shifted back into human form. His human tongue licked the blood off his now human lips.

Swinging her around, Colin pressed her body forward, bending her over, and placing her hands on the boulder. Ry waited breathlessly for him to touch her. Several anxious moments passed before his hands claimed her hips. Slowly, deliberately, he glided his hands down them to her thighs, slipping between them. He gently pressed her legs farther apart. Ry breathed slowly, her head hanging, as she tried to control the excitement and anticipation.

Then he pressed his cock against her, sliding exquisitely slow up and into her. He slid in, inching his way deeper inside. Once he settled in her, he hesitated. Ry did her best to control her breathing. He filled her, stretched her. His hands ran up and over her hips, sides, and back. Soothing her. Her body clenched around him.

Colin's grip on her hips tightened. He pulled out in a swift movement before shoving back in fast and hard. He withdrew until only the tip remained, then slammed back inside.

Ry sobbed his name. She begged him to move faster and harder. Her cries and screams echoed through the clearing. When she climaxed the first time, he gave her a moment to recover. When he resumed his strokes, he slowed to let her feel the entire length of him each time he slid in and out.

She lost track of time. Eventually they made their way to the clearing and pallet of clothes where Colin continued to make love to her time after time.

HOURS LATER, Ry lay on the makeshift bed with her legs over Colin's shoulders. She clenched his upper arms, her fingernails digging into his flesh. Colin moved in short, slow strokes. A noise caught her attention, causing her to turn her head.

There, standing a few feet away, was another wolf. His

head hung low as he watched, his sides heaving from exertion. Fangs flashed. A snarl escaped. She recognized the wolf's fur. It matched the one on her left breast. When she whispered his name, the wolf shifted into Ian.

Gloriously naked, he stood, breathing heavily. Rage pulsed off him. His fists clenched and unclenched at his sides. His gaze poured over them as he took in the sight of their lovemaking.

Seeing Ian sent her into an immediate climax. She kept her eyes on him as she arched up into his brother. A moment later, Colin came with an explosive bellow. They stayed together for several moments, working to control their breathing. Their bodies throbbed from their exertion. Colin rolled off her, stood, and faced Ian's wrath.

Before he could explain, Ian rushed in swinging a fist at his brother. Colin scrambled backward as they both avoided stepping on Ry.

She rolled to her knees. "*Ian.* Stop. Colin didn't start this." She knelt on the ground, staring at the two brothers, wanting to avoid bloodshed.

"*Ian,*" she screamed, finally getting his attention.

He turned toward her, snarling, his face partially shifted into a wolf's angry glare. Frightened, she scrambled backward. Ian immediately stopped, his face shifting back to normal.

He begged, "I'm sorry. Please, please forgive me. I didn't mean to frighten you."

Stepping toward her, he reached his hand down to tug her to her feet. As soon as she touched him, she sensed her soul slip away. Similar to when she was still half-asleep but unable to wake or move, Ry wanted to scream. If she would only relax, she would fall back asleep and wake once she had rested, but this was different.

Ry wasn't asleep. She was on her feet, standing naked in front of two equally naked men. She struggled mentally for control but something held her back. A woman's soft voice soothed and calmed her. It was the one she had heard in her dream under the tree, asking Ry to trust her. Ry let herself go, giving the woman control over her mind and body.

Ian dropped to his knees. Taking her hands in his, he pressed his lips first to the backs of her hands, then into her palms. Only then did he look up, searching her face for some semblance of Ry. This was not the woman he'd fought his brother over.

This face had the bluest eyes he had ever seen. The power flowing from her caused him to hesitate. She held herself differently, tilting her head slightly while she smiled. Her movements, when she reached out and ran her hand through his hair, were distinctly not Ryder's.

This woman was regal, confident, sensual. When she spoke, she had a slight accent and a sophistication Ryder didn't have. Not sure how to react, he decided on respect due to the power emanating from her.

"My deepest apologies. Can you forgive me for frightening you and leaving you unprotected?" he asked.

"You're forgiven, Ian. You didn't understand the depths my enemies will go to." Her voice was strong and commanding but compassionate.

She let her hand drift down his cheek and under his chin, then tilted his face up. "Now you do. There'll be no tolerance from now on, do you understand? Someone must protect me at all times."

"I will never fail you again. I swear on my life."

Her indulgent smile focused on him. "Let's hope it

doesn't come to that. I'm counting on you to guide Ryder through the initial process. She'll be fearful about what's happening, especially the intense sexual feelings. She's not a sensual being."

Not understanding what the process was, he considered his own extreme encounters with Ry. That was something he understood. Time after time, he'd been drawn to her, driven to protect and love her. Now it seemed his brother had been sucked in too.

The woman speaking for Ryder continued. "Once she gains the first level, she won't crave the all-encompassing passion. She'll still require it but she'll be able to control it. You all will."

She turned her body slightly toward Colin, holding her hand out to him. "Make love to me. I need more power. I spent too much energy healing Ryder and you." He took it, placing a kiss on her palm before stepping behind her and brushing his body against her backside.

Leaving her hand in Colin's grip, she caressed Ian's cheek with the other. Standing between the two men, she leaned her head back and rested it on Colin's shoulder. She closed her eyes and sighed. The two brothers watched her breathing quicken. Her body trembled with excitement.

Ian sensed her power. The waves of authority rolled over him, as if he were floating in the ocean: gentle and peaceful, seductive and powerful. He glanced at Colin and saw the awe and respect on his brother's face. He suspected his own looked similar.

In a bold move, he placed soft kisses on her belly button, his hands on her hips. His caresses grew in intensity with her answering moans and sighs. He added licks and nibbles. Colin wrapped his arms around her, pressing their joined hands to her breast, controlling their strokes.

She laughed lightly, pressing forward into their joined hands while spreading her legs for Ian's licks, kisses, and caresses. With his hand and tongue busy between her thighs, she shuddered to an immediate climax. The sounds coming from her were pure pleasure. She pressed back into Colin.

"Shhh. Relax. Let us take care of you," Colin whispered in her ear and leaned over her back, inching her forward toward Ian.

Ian stood and focused on her breasts. With a slight movement of his hips, Colin slid his cock inside her. He ground slowly, causing her to moan and whimper with pleasure. She spiraled out of control into another orgasm.

Ry was lost. She couldn't move. She couldn't think. The entity inside her had faded away, allowing her to experience the intense sexual vibrations streaking through her. They were stronger than they had been during her previous encounters with Ian. Ry panicked. The soft voice echoing through her mind quickly calmed her fears.

With the energy flowing through her, she met the sensations head-on; adjusting to the intense pleasure, she relaxed. She laughed, tears streaming down her face, her body shuddering with desire. Her dreams continued to turn into reality.

The two men took turns making love to her. She relished the attention they lavished on her. While one of them slid inside her, creating a wondrous friction, the other watched intently. The brother observing would caress a sensitive spot or support her. Her orgasms came fast and strong. The number of times and intensity weren't humanly possible.

By nightfall, exhaustion set in. Colin transferred her to

their makeshift bed. Ry lay behind Ian, pressing her front against his back. She slipped an arm around him, pulling her body tight against his. Colin lay behind her with his hand resting on her hip. Sleep was a welcome haven.

Chapter 23

ednesday

Colin lay sprawled on a sofa in Robert's office. He couldn't remember the last time he'd been so fatigued that his brain refused to make sense out of the conversation around him. Ian dozed on a matching recliner across the expansive room. Exhaustion would not explain either brother's physical state. They'd been sleeping on and off from the time Markus and his men surrounded the rock outcropping the night before.

Colin now understood Ian's craziness and confusion over the past few days. He remembered the odd metallic scent when they had made love the first time. He couldn't place it but he knew Ian had experienced it too. He absently rubbed the right side of chest. The image of a tree spread across his skin replicated Ian's. Through it he was aware of her breathing, her movements, and any threats to her.

Back in the clearing, a voice inside his head had alerted him to Markus's presence even before the bear shifter had shown himself. Ian had also gone on alert. Once they realized who the intruder was, Colin had shielded Ry's nakedness from prying eyes while Ian pulled his shirt over her head to cover her. She'd remained asleep the entire time.

Ry now had a replica of his wolf tattooed on her right breast. He had seen it blossom under his fangs. Safely ensconced in an upstairs bedroom, she hadn't awakened since their last bout of lovemaking. The woman was insatiable. Or should he say the entity living inside her was? He and Ian had no doubt that they were dealing with someone or something possessing Ryder.

"Colin. *Colin*." War shouted his name a second time. Colin shifted his gaze toward War and the others.

"I was saying," War continued, concern evident in his frown, "we need to understand more about why this Dunbar kidnapped her. I've talked to Devon. I sense we can trust her, but she's still under house arrest. She claims he wants the statue."

Growls and snarls vibrated throughout the room.

"Everything keeps coming back to that damn thing Ian stole," War added.

"At least we know what happened to it now," Ian mumbled from the chair he'd draped himself over. Zach and Abby's father had opened his home to the group.

"I thought you were sleeping," Jamie said. "I wonder if Dunbar knows it disintegrated. Either way, he'll probably continue to look for it and her. But why the interest?"

"There's that third party too. Don't forget them," Markus said. At Ian and Colin's puzzled looks, he continued. "Someone killed Dunbar's men. Someone shot Colin from the barn loft. We don't know if it was the same person ripping off heads and shooting people. Either way, he, or they, escaped."

"Anyone who can rip men's heads off is not someone to mess with," War chimed in. "We need to proceed with caution. I believe eliminating Ry is not the right thing to do. Yet."

A niggling sensation began at the base on Colin's skull, and his new tattoo tingled. Ryder. Ian must have sensed the same thing, because he swung into an upright position. Colin sat up, eager to be at her side. He had never acted like a love-sick pup but he didn't care. The rush of endorphins alone was worth crawling into her bed.

"That's the million-dollar question, isn't it? Why all the interest in a normal human woman?" Ian answered. "Except she isn't normal anymore."

In an unspoken agreement, both brothers stood and headed to the door.

"Where are you going?" Jamie demanded. "Don't walk away from me while I'm talking to you."

Ian kept walking as he spoke over his shoulder. "She's awake."

"Stop," Jamie snarled. Colin halted with his hand on the door handle. He had never defied his brother, at least not since Jamie had become alpha. Ian hesitated too. They turned back toward him.

"We're not done here. Sit." When neither obeyed, Jamie took a menacing step toward them while pointing at the sofa. "*Sit.*"

Colin glanced at Ian, meeting his confused gaze. Neither wanted to anger Jamie, but the pull from the woman upstairs urged them to leave. Finally, they moved in unison and sat back in the seats they had just vacated, hovering on the edge ready to bolt.

Jamie questioned his brothers. "How do you know she's awake?"

Colin and Ian glanced at each other before Colin

answered. "It's hard to explain. It's a sensation. An awareness of her and where's she's at."

Ian added, "It's the same way I knew where to look for her after Dunbar kidnapped her."

"None of this is normal, Jamie," Markus interjected, waving a hand toward the two brothers. "If Dunbar was after the statue, we have to assume that's the key to whatever is happening. If we understood the statue, we might understand what's happening."

"I've been asking around about the statue." All eyes turned toward Robert. The patriarch of the tiger clan was dying. Everyone could see how his heart was failing him; his body had withered, his strength had diminished, and he tired easily. Despite his illness, the clans respected his knowledge and honor. He would remain in power until his last breath. "There aren't many people who have any knowledge about it or even want to discuss it. I've narrowed my search for an expert down to one man in Spain. I'm trying to reach him."

Jamie nodded. "Keep us updated. Do whatever it takes. Use whatever resources you need." He turned to his brothers. "Stay away from her unless she asks for you. We can't predict how she'll react. She is human. I want her calm. Keep her away from any stressful situations. We've seen hints of her uncontrolled anger."

"She's not human anymore," Markus stated. "You know it's true."

"We'll have to deal with her soon."

Ian took a menacing step toward War. "If you so much as raise a hand against her, you'll answer to me. I don't care if you're an alpha or not. I will kill you."

Jamie and War glanced at each other. When Ian hadn't been present the day before, they'd discussed the possibility of killing Ryder. The trouble was, they now realized that Colin wouldn't be as willing to kill her now as he had been the day before. In less than twenty-four hours, the woman had altered his opinion and ensnared him into her bed.

Jamie held up his hands and stepped in front of his brothers. "Look at it from our point of view. She's changing right before your eyes and you can't see. Not to mention Dunbar is out there looking for her."

Colin walked up to his younger brother's side. He glared at the alphas. "Right after I kill you myself. No one harms her."

Ry squeezed her eyes shut tight when the memories raced through her mind. She remembered falling asleep with Colin pressed behind her as she wrapped herself around Ian. She groaned. She was a sex addict. There was no other explanation for her behavior. What would happen to her career plans now? She'd have to see Lauren professionally for her new addiction. *Great.* At least Lauren would keep it quiet.

Her life was now officially a hot mess.

Burying her face in the pillow, Ry tried not to think about the previous night's events, but the images kept swirling through her head. As she relived the time she'd spent with the two brothers, she remembered them shifting from wolves into men.

Her thoughts, wild and chaotic, skipped from one crazy idea to another. She remembered the wolves striding toward her through a field of wildflowers in her dreams. She'd seen the wolves changing into Colin and Ian at the clearing. That had been reality. Images and sensations of fangs sinking into her flesh caused her to shiver.

She knew she hadn't been hallucinating. Werewolves didn't exist, did they? She was a reasonably open-minded woman of the twenty-first century. Surely, if a species like that existed, humans would have known by now. *Right?* There was no time or need to panic. The only way to find out was to ask.

First things first, she needed the bathroom, then she would figure out where she was.

Cautiously she opened her eyes to discover she lay naked in a canopy bed. She sat up and gazed around the quiet and peaceful room. It was enormous. Her living room, kitchen, and dining areas would fit inside it with space to spare. One entire wall was covered with luxurious brown velvet curtains. Reaching up, she ran her hands over the rich and lush material.

Where am I?

She turned her head and found her old blue terry-cloth robe draped across the foot of the bed. Someone had gone out of their way to make her feel comfortable except she wasn't feeling it. She picked up the covering and pulled it on. Scrambling off the bed, she picked the first door of three closed ones and got lucky.

The bathroom was as stunning as the other room. It was the size of her bedroom at home. Frosted windows covered one wall. The walk-in shower looked big enough to accommodate several people.

In the corner under the wall of windows sat a large whirlpool tub. Bottles of bath soaps and oils had been neatly arranged along the windowsill. She had other necessities to take care of first. Hurrying into the partitioned-off toilet area, she quickly took care of business. Once finished, she stepped up to the vanity and washed her hands.

As Ry slowly dried her hands, her robe gapped open, flashing a bit of color against her breast. Oh, shit. She'd forgotten the tattoo.

Ry yanked open her robe. Catching sight of herself in the mirror, she frowned. *Shit. Shit. Shit.* There was another wolf tattoo on her chest. This one covered her right breast and looked different from the first one. It was slightly larger, and his fur was a normal shade of brown. His eyes were brown too. Whereas the first had a playful look about him, this one was fierce. Instead of his tongue hanging out, his head was tilted and his lips drawn back to show his fangs. If he were real, he was in a perfect position to either bite her nipple or snap at anyone who tried to fondle her.

It was the middle brother, Colin. From her memories at the cave, she was certain the first tattoo represented Ian. She'd watched both of them shift from wolves into men. As she stared at the two tattoos, they both appeared to come to life. Their eyes blinked, their fangs flashed, a tongue stretched toward a nipple. Closing the robe as fast as possible, she sagged against the bathroom counter. *Oh shit, oh shit, oh shit, oh shit.*

That was her mantra as she slowly sank to the floor. Kneeling, she bent far enough down that her forehead rested on the cool tile. She rocked back and forth, one hand gripping and twisting her medallion. She hadn't been this helpless and confused in years. Her mother had told her once that she would rock like that as a little girl after they had adopted her. It was Ry's coping mechanism for when she was overwhelmed. Like now.

Except she wasn't that little girl anymore. *Suck it up.* She was an emergency room doctor. She'd worked hard to get where she was and she was not about to let a few crazy events siderail her. Pushing herself to her feet, she stared at the reflection in the mirror.

She needed someone to tell her what was so important about the little gold tree and why so many peculiar things were happening. Somehow, she knew the brothers were nearby. She'd get cleaned up, dressed, then leave the room to explore her surroundings. Maybe she could find a computer and with internet service to do her own search. Maybe someone had answers.

THIRTY MINUTES LATER, Ry stood in front of the bathroom mirror in a sundress and sandals. She'd lathered her freshly showered body with a flowery-scented lotion she discovered in the varied collection. Then she'd styled her hair and applied a bit of mascara, blush, and lip gloss. She rarely took the time to put on makeup and do more than pull her hair into a ponytail, but she was inspired today. Her normal jeans or slacks hadn't felt right. A cute dress, something a little sexy had appealed to her instead. Whatever was beyond that door, she would be ready to face it.

I've got this. Leaving the bathroom, Ry made her way to the wall of curtains. Pushing them aside, she found an entire wall of windows. She gazed out. This place was huge.

The view stretched for miles with grass, cacti, and mesquite scrub brush. Cattle moved in the distance while a herd of horses grazed near them. This had to be West Texas.

Near the house was an extensive garden filled with trees and flowers. Two small ponds and a swimming pool sat among the greenery. The epitome of peacefulness and quiet.

Stepping away from the windows, she did a quick inspection of the room. The furniture consisted of the bed, two nightstands, a loveseat, two large plush chairs, and a low coffee table with a tray of food. She snapped up the cup of sliced fruit. Devouring the strawberries, she continued her inspection.

There were three doors. She knew where two led. She'd discovered the huge walk-in closet when searching for clothes. All of her clothes from home were hanging on the racks, taking up less than half of the space. Her shoes stood in neatly arranged rows on several shelves. The rest of her clothes were folded in built-in drawers: bras, panties, socks, and everything else from her dresser back home. They had brought her entire bedroom. How long were they planning on making her stay?

Chapter 24

Ry made her way down the staircase unsure what or who she would encounter. She heard several voices before she saw who they belonged to. One was the distinct voice of War. Excitement raced through her. She would have her answers soon. Her uncle trusted War. She could trust him.

Turning a corner in the garden, she faced several men but her eyes narrowed on the only woman. As tall as the males, she had short-cropped black hair and eyes to match. An image flashed through Ry's mind, one of her pale naked body pressed against this woman's dark skin. Their mouths fused as their hands roamed over each other.

Ry blinked and yanked her gaze away. *Nope. Not going there.* She turned toward Ian and Colin, all thoughts of the woman disappearing. The two men stood across from her, staring at her, their gazes hungry and devouring. Her heart raced. Her mouth went dry. Her body ignited.

She'd taken a step toward them just before War said her name. Her step stuttered. Her brain did a somersault as she forced herself to stop moving toward her men.

My men. Where did that come from? A pleased sensation floated through her. She'd deal with that later.

Pivoting toward War's voice, Ry stared at a large, bald black man with tattoos covering his skull and neck. His arms were crossed over his chest, making his biceps bulge beneath his tight black t-shirt. The faded jeans did nothing to disguise his toned lower body.

Why am I looking at his body? Concentrate.

This man screamed *badass* in capital letters. If she hadn't heard story after story from Uncle Rick about him, she'd be cowering in her shoes. But she recognized that deep down this man was kind-hearted and a pushover. He might look like a terrifying biker dude but War was a pussycat.

She gasped as recognition slapped her in the face. She'd kissed this same man on the sidewalk when she was out jogging. *How many days ago had it been?* He'd deceived her by not announcing who he was or coming to her house. From the conversation she'd overheard upon walking in, these people were friends. They knew each other. War knew the three brothers but had not told her.

Anger bubbled through her. "War?"

A grin split his face. He spread his arms wide and gave a slight bow. "At your service."

"You're War?" She stepped toward him, stopping directly in front of him, her hands fisted at her sides. "Are you kidding me? I kissed you. You didn't tell me who you were."

War scowled but didn't respond, only ratcheting up Ry's anger further.

"You knew who I was on that street corner and you said nothing. And now I find you here, obviously friends with everyone. How long have you known Ian? Did you give him my address?" She waved her hands toward the small group gathered. "You're a liar. You've been playing me."

With a roar of frustration, she placed her hands on his chest and shoved him backwards. War went flying. He landed roughly fifteen feet away, on his back, sprawled out in a flowerbed.

Ry wasn't aware of the dead quiet until she heard a woman's voice.

"Damn, boss. She put you in your place."

War glared as he picked himself up, but he directed it at someone else. "Shut up, Emerson."

Out of the corner of her eye, Ry noticed another equally large man taking a step toward her. As she turned in his direction, a third man reached a hand out to halt him. Despite his powerful strength, the bigger man respectfully stepped back. The third man was old and frail. He would have been near six feet tall in his prime, but illness had clearly made him weak, thin, and a shell of his former self. Exhaustion creased the lines on his face.

"Ms. Hoffman, I'd like to introduce myself. I'm Robert Brinkman. I've been looking forward to meeting you." He held his hand out toward her. "Welcome. I hope you will consider my home yours and make yourself comfortable here."

The sincerity, warmth, and affection flowed from him despite his frailty. Her natural compassion took over as her irritation toward War and the other big man faded.

"Thank you, Robert. I love your home." Her right hand clasped his in a warm handshake. The second they touched an electric shock slammed through her.

She couldn't breathe. Her body felt as though it was surrounded by a pressure chamber. Then smack, it released her in an instant. Her hands were gripping his as she stared into his wide eyes.

Ry closed her eyes as the electrifying sensation surged

through her body, down her arms, and into Robert. A jolt of power zipped through her. Vaguely aware of his gasp, she heard voices filled with concern, a man's deep bass trying to get her attention, and Ian telling her to stay calm.

Then everything else vanished. She stood in a vacuum with Robert's hand in hers.

Nothing else existed.

She became aware of his body, his aches and pains. Mentally, she raced through his body; darting through his veins and arteries, major organs, blood, skin, and cells. Similar to watching a medical training video, only in real time.

She detected every bump, bruise, and ailment he had. She found a bruise on his shin, a cut on his palm, the hunger in his stomach, and his failing heart. Zoning in on his major organ, she reached out with her hand to cradle it, caress it, and analyze it.

Slow, weak beats accompanied the swishing of the blood through his arteries. In her mind's eye, she pictured the thinning walls of his heart and the partial blockage. Her fingers stroked the damaged organ, in imitation of the flow of life driving through it. With each caress, the blockage fragmented and disappeared. The walls of his heart thickened and strengthened. The blood pumping through his veins became faster. The beating of his heart grew strong.

Peace and satisfaction settled over her. As an afterthought, she slid a finger across the cut on his palm. It closed as her finger crossed it. A light brush on his bruised shin and it healed.

As abruptly as the experience had begun, it stopped. The cocoon she'd found herself in while mending his heart dropped away. She was back in the garden, holding Robert's hand in both of hers. They hadn't moved.

He looked stunned. Had he felt the healing energy too?

Ry yanked her hands away and stumbled backward.

She'd healed a man's heart without surgery or medicine or any modern technologies. She'd healed him with the power of her mind.

"OMG. Did you see that?" Tamping down her excitement, she forced herself to look at the small group of people surrounding her. They looked puzzled.

"See what?" Colin stepped closer to Ry with Ian moving to her other side.

Ry stood quietly for several minutes, forcing herself to take slow breaths. Her body was heavy and exhausted, though she'd woken barely an hour earlier. She wrapped her arms around her torso in an attempt to calm the excitement racing through her. She had healed a man and no one knew. This was different from healing Ian and Colin. There was no sexual energy. No overwhelming desire for sex.

This was pleasant and satisfying. The cocoon had sucked her in but she hadn't been afraid. She didn't know if she should shout with excitement, scream in horror or run away in confusion. If this was true, her life was changed. How many people could she heal? Her father would be the first. She had researched his cancer for months and now she would be able to give him back his life. She could heal everyone who came through the emergency room, anyone who showed up at her doorstep.

"You didn't see me do anything?" Her voice faltered. Her gaze darted from Ian to Colin. Ian opened his mouth to respond but War stepped forward, placing a hand on his shoulder to keep him quiet. Ian shrugged it off.

"You did nothing but stand still for several minutes with your eyes shut while holding Robert's hand." Ian hesitated before continuing. "What do you remember?"

Her mouth dry, Ry licked her lips. She shifted her gaze to Ian's chest, not wanting to look directly at anyone. They didn't understand what had happened. As far as they were concerned, she was losing her mind.

She steeled herself, attempting to remain calm, before looking up at the men standing before her. She had come downstairs to get answers but only found more questions. "War. If you really are my uncle's friend, I'd appreciate it if you explained what's going on. I've had enough of these games. It's not funny. Either explain or take me home."

Her voice cracked on the last word. She sucked in a breath. Her control began to unravel.

Ian frowned. His mouth opened slightly as though he was about to speak, but War placed a hand on his shoulder again.

"I could take you home, but the man who kidnapped you got away. We're afraid he'll try it again. Why don't we go inside and discuss this in private?" When she hesitated, he spoke again. "Colin and Ian can come too. They might have some answers."

Her initial excitement fading, Ry turned back toward the house but stumbled. Colin caught her, and swung her into his arms. He strode to the house with Ian, War, and Jamie following.

"I'm fine, Colin," Ry whispered against his neck, her arms wrapped around it.

"I'm sure you are, but I want an excuse to hold you." He pressed a kiss to her forehead and carried her inside and across the main foyer to the library.

Inside were comfortable looking chairs and sofas plus a large stone fireplace. Books lined the walls. Colin set her on one of the plush chairs facing the doorway. Ian knelt beside her while Colin stood behind her, his hand resting on the chair back. War and Jamie followed them into the room but halted several feet away. Ry sagged deeper into the chair. With each passing minute, she grew more exhausted.

"Tell us what you did to Robert," Jamie demanded.

"Back off, Jamie," Ian snarled. "You're not helping."

Ry lifted her head to look directly at Jamie. She spoke softly. "I healed his heart."

War frowned and stared at Ry in wonder.

Jamie blinked. Twice. "It's not possible."

"She healed her own broken hand, Jamie. She healed both Colin and my gunshot wounds."

Jamie turned and stormed out of the room.

War stepped closer to Ry. "Tell me what really happened to the statue, Ryder. We know Dunbar beat you for the information. Did it really disintegrate?"

RY RAISED HER GAZE, her eyes turning blue.

War had experienced this side of her twice. Once when she had lovingly kissed him, and then when she shoved him.

What mood will she be in now?

The woman in front of him spoke as if Ry was another person. "Ry didn't want to tell you."

War sucked in air. His world turned sideways. In the nearly three hundred years he'd lived, he'd never experienced an entity possessing someone. Was Ry still in her body somewhere? Details. He needed details. He needed to stay calm.

He swallowed. "Yes. I realize that. Tell me why."

The woman tilted her head while she studied him. "She didn't trust you. I've told her to trust her men, but she has a difficult time accepting her fate. Do you believe in fate, War?"

"Yes. What do you know about my fate?"

She smiled knowingly. "Enough. You'll be a large part of Ry's life. She'll need you for protection and guidance. Will you protect Ry with your life, War?"

War cleared his throat and swallowed heavily. Not much made him nervous but this conversation did. "Yes. I'll do what I can to keep her safe."

"Swear it. Swear it so she trusts you. She's listening. She's very determined and strong minded. She's learning how to push past my barriers."

He hesitated but knew he had no choice. With slow, precise movements, War went to his knees. In a semblance of an ancient tradition, he bowed his head for several seconds. Then he raised his gaze to Ry's face—or the face of whoever this was—staring at her blue eyes for a moment. He had no doubt that this woman would transform their world.

He spoke reverently. "I swear on the blood of my ancestors to protect Ryder Hoffman with my life for the rest of my time on this Earth and forever from the Afterlife."

The woman poised regally in front of him beamed in victory.

"A true ancient warrior's oath. I respect a man who knows the etiquette of allegiance."

She raised her hand to cover one of Colin's. Her other hand reached up to Ian's head, sliding her fingers through his hair. "I love these colors. The variations are unique."

She turned her face toward War. "Ry was telling the truth. The statue is a pile of dust at the motel. It disintegrated when she held it."

War frowned. "What does Dunbar want with it?"

"It's not the statue that is important. It's what was inside."

"I don't understand. What was inside it?"

She smiled wickedly. "I was."

Her face turned back to Ian, her hand stretching up to curl around the back of his neck and tug him close. Ian gave War a quick glance. "You should leave."

War watched as their lips met. Colin bent over her neck, his fangs extended. Uncomfortable with the turn of events, War hurried from the library. Jamie stood across the foyer with Markus and Emerson. They turned to watch him walk toward them.

He glanced around as he approached. "Where are Robert and the others?"

"Abby took Robert to her clinic. I told her what Ryder said about healing his heart. She's checking him out but she's insisting she needs to examine Ry."

War shook his head. "Not right now. You shouldn't go back in either."

Jamie glanced at the library door. "My brothers—"

"Are having the time of their lives. Trust me. Don't disturb them."

A woman's wail of pleasure emanated from the library across the foyer.

Emerson frowned. "We're back to that again? What's with this woman?"

War shifted uncomfortably. "We need to talk."

Chapter 25

Ian pulled her out of the chair and into his arms. Ry melted against him, his arms a comforting haven. She buried her face in his shirt and held onto him tightly, refusing to sob or tremble. Colin pressed himself against her back, adding his comforting presence.

Until now, she hadn't wanted to admit that there truly was another being inside her. The dreams made sense now —the ones of ancient men where she appeared to be someone else. The times she blacked out. The woman under the tree in her dream was the same woman controlling Ry's dreams and the encounters with Ian and Colin.

As she stood in the warm comfort of the two brothers' arms, the now-familiar tingling sensation started in her chest. It spread across her breasts, tightening her nipples, then spread down her belly, warming her insides, and traveling lower to fill her with a sizzling sexual heat. The speed at which she became aroused was astounding.

Ry closed her eyes and let her body relax against Colin. Her hands moved up to Ian's face and pulled him in for a kiss as Colin placed his hands on her hips and slowly moved her butt back and forth against his cock. She moaned against Ian's lips, deepening their kiss. Their tongues wound together, teasing each other.

Ian gripped the bottom of her dress. In one clean swoop, he pulled it up and over her head. Placing his hands on either side of her face, he continued to kiss her. Caught up in Ian's kisses, she scarcely noticed when Colin unhooked her bra, sliding it down her arms as far as possible. His hands cupped her breasts, testing their weight. His fingers teased her nipples.

She gasped; Colin's hands created incredible sensations.

Ian broke their kiss, his lips trailing across her cheek and down her neck. She tilted her head back, letting it rest on Colin's shoulder and allowing Ian access to her throat.

His lips continued down until he took one nipple in his mouth. With one brother holding her breasts and offering her up to the other brother, Ry's body tilted into overload. She cradled Colin's head with one hand while the other drove through Ian's hair and held him close. Her body writhed between the two men to the rhythm of their movements and Ian's sucking.

Ian switched to the other breast, pulling her nipple into his mouth. He tormented her with his mouth and teeth while Colin teased her other breast with his fingers. Her body exploded as she cried out and rocked against them.

"That's it, baby. Let go. We've got you," Colin whispered in her ear. They did. Between the two men, she wasn't going anywhere.

As she relaxed in their arms, Ian moved back a step and finished removing her bra. Her eyelids fluttered close when Colin's fingers pulled on her nipples again. A moan of pleasure sounded loud in the room.

"Easy, sweetheart. We both want you. It's my turn to be

first." Colin nuzzled her neck, nibbling on her. "What do you say to a little playtime?"

She remembered the ancient men in her dreams. The three men who looked like brothers had wanted to play games too. Was she doomed to repeat the past?

Colin's free hand slid down her side, along her ass, then eased a hand inside her panties. His fingers delved between her folds, teasing her sensitive nub and coaxing moans from deep within her chest. She dripped with excitement. He inched one finger inside her, circling it around, then sliding it in and out with slow, deliberate movements.

"Please." She begged for more than a single finger, surrendering to pleasure.

"Please what? Tell me, sweetheart. Tell me what you want." Colin slid two fingers inside her. Ian's hand joined his, rubbing her clit. Did these two brothers do everything together? *Wow.* The sensations rippled through her and sent her body into overdrive.

The brothers understood which way the other moved; what caress would elicit a response from her. They coordinated their efforts to guide her quickly to another climax.

She craved more.

Her hands wrapped around Colin's forearm, tensing. One breast received attention from Colin, the other from Ian. Both had a hand between her legs.

They released her and stepped back but kept their hands on her body so she didn't collapse. Ry swayed slightly until she steadied herself. She stood in the library stark naked while they remained clothed.

"You're not playing fair." She looked from one to the other with a smile. "You're both still dressed. I want to see bare skin."

In seconds, they were both gloriously naked. She

reached for them, then hesitated and stared at their elaborate tattoos. Although similar, Ian's covered his left breast with Colin's on the right. Identical in location to the tattoos she had of them.

Colin grinned. "You like what you see?"

She definitely liked. The tattoos gave them an air of mystery, seduction, and danger. They also drew her to them. She wanted more. She could only nod in response.

"Turn around and face Ian," Colin ordered.

Ian pulled over a chair and sat. As Ry turned toward him, he motioned her closer, then took her hands and placed them on the chair arms, causing her to bend forward. From behind her, Colin gripped her hips and tugged, pulling her legs backward and widening her stance.

Ian leaned forward to brush his lips against hers. "You like being kissed, don't you?"

"Yes," she whispered. Ian's kisses added to the pleasure rioting through her. She leaned more forward, bending over and exposing her butt to Colin. His hands caressed her ass, squeezing and cupping her. He slipped his fingers between her legs again.

She spread them apart farther, giving him greater access. She moaned into Ian's mouth as Colin explored her. With no warning, his fingers drew away and his cock pressed in. Ry pushed her hips back. Ian kept his hands over hers to keep her from drifting away.

Colin moved fast, plunging inside her repeatedly. There was no gentleness like with Ian. No slow and sweet. It was fast, deep, and raw. She loved it.

She pulled her lips away from Ian's, begging for more. A few days ago, she wouldn't have realized just how much she would enjoy a threesome. An orgasm ripped through her body, Colin's name a moan as she tumbled into ecstasy.

Ian recaptured her lips as she came down from her high. In a daze, she felt Colin slip out of her body when Ian picked her up by her waist. He sat her on the edge of the desk as he continued to kiss her.

Ry enjoyed the soft play of his lips on hers after the wild ride with Colin. Then Ian filled her, pressing her back onto the desk, releasing her lips. With her hips slightly off the edge, he eased himself into her body.

Little tendrils of pleasure shot through her as he stroked inside her. The complete opposite of Colin. Slow and torturous but deep and penetrating, Ry kept pace with Ian. Her cries of passion were no less heartfelt than they had been with Colin. Ian slowly built her up, then left her hanging for a moment before letting her explode again. Her back arched and this time she shouted Ian's name to the heavens. Then her world went dark.

She woke to discover herself in Ian's arms. With his shirt wrapped around her, he carried her up the stairway to her bedroom. Colin followed with their clothes bundled in his arms.

In her bedroom, Ian set her on her feet beside the bed. Her legs unsteady, she reached for the bedpost. Colin dropped the pile of clothes on the floor and kicked the door closed behind him. They stood in front of her. She grinned. Two naked, gorgeous, and hard men were at her disposal.

Without thinking of the consequences to her actions, she knelt in front of them, taking their cocks in her hands. She leaned over Ian's hard length and breathed lightly on him. Colin ran his fingers through her hair.

Above her, Colin said, "It's going to be a long day, baby. Pace yourself." She laughed along with them, excitement settling over her, then wrapped her mouth around Ian's shaft.

Chapter 26

Thursday

Ry woke to the late morning light. She lay in her bed alone, which suited her fine. The two men had worn her out and yet she was oddly energized. As Ry remembered what transpired during the night, she grew uneasy. Until now, she would never have had sex with two men at the same time. Her loss of inhibitions around the brothers astonished her.

She definitely enjoyed the sex but she worried it was addictive. Hugging her arms around herself, she remembered Colin and Ian coaxing orgasm after orgasm from her. They allowed her to sleep, but she couldn't for more than fifteen or twenty minutes before she woke craving more. They might have started what happened in the library, but she initiated it every single time in her bedroom.

They hadn't argued. Ry laughed to herself lightly. No, they definitely hadn't argued. They'd taken turns although they were complete opposites. The brothers obviously had shared women before.

Colin's lovemaking was fierce and wild. Ian remained slow and passionate. Colin enjoyed her on her knees while stroking her butt. Ian liked her riding him, making the pleasure all about her. Colin remained in control, dominating her. Ian let her set the pace, let her regulate what they did. The brothers behaved the same as in her dreams.

She liked these two men. They teased her, talked to her, cared for her. They laughed together. They held her while she slept, gently stroking her hair and back. They even ran a bath for her with scented bubbles. She'd luxuriated in the steaming water while Colin ran downstairs for food and Ian ran a loofah over her body. She could tell this was more than sex for them too, especially Ian. She wanted to turn to Ian with her problems and questions.

With a sigh, she rolled out of bed, ready for her body to protest. It didn't. There was no pain, no soreness, and no stiffness. Why did that not surprise her? Her body continued to heal itself no matter what happened, just as it had healed her eyesight initially and then again after Dunbar beat her. She needed to get to her father. Maybe if she spoke directly to Jamie, he would understand the urgent need.

Taking her time, she wandered into the bathroom. While the shower warmed up, she did a quick inspection of her body. Colin had bitten her several times, his fangs sliding into her flesh, but astonishingly no sign remained. The punishing pressure of his hands on her body had left no marks or bruises.

Finishing her shower, Ry dried off with a large towel and wrapped it around her body. Running another towel across her hair, she stepped into the bedroom only to pull up short when she discovered a tray of food sat on the coffee table, steam floating up from the mug. She dropped the towel and tugged on her bathroom before picking up the coffee and inhaling. Caramel latte. Her favorite. Someone has gone out of their way to learn her favorites. The coffee, the strawberries, the pancakes. She took another sip, closing her eyes as she savored the rush of caffeine and sugar. With a sigh, she opened her eyes and set the mug down.

A buzzing from beside the bed caught her attention. Her phone. Hurrying over, she grabbed it and answered. The voice on the other end was truly Lauren this time.

"Where are you? Are you safe?"

Warmth spread through Ry at hearing her best friend. "I'm good. I'm safe. I'm having breakfast of pancakes with strawberries and cream."

Lauren whispered, "Don't say anything weird. Don't do anything out of place. I think they're listening." She raised her voice slightly. "I thought I lost you."

Ry paused, taking in her friend's comments. Attempting to be casual, she continued the conversation. "I thought I lost you. What happened? How did those men kidnap you? Are you okay?"

"I was hit over the head by those goons when I left the hospital. War has a friend, Abby, who's a doctor. She made me stay here at my house. Another friend of War's, Zack, has been staying with me. I didn't know War had so many buddies."

It was a casual way of reminding her of the same questions she'd had the day before... before she'd healed a man and spend the night with two others. "I haven't met those two but I've met more of War's friends. I called him out on it but I don't think he cares."

Lauren huffed. "That's an understatement."

Ry murmured. "What's going on?"

In the same low tone, her friend replied. "I've been hearing things from Zack and the two other men at my place. They are all related or something. They talked about clans which is totally freakish."

Now that Ry knew the brothers were werewolves, she understood the term. What were the others? Maybe they were planning on turning her and Lauren into wolves or who knew what. Ry noted the concern in her friend's voice. She moved to the coffee table and sat beside it on the floor.

She picked up a strawberry but didn't eat it, staring at it and considered her options. She finally whispered, "I need answers. I'm in over my head and I don't know what to do. I tried to find out yesterday but things got ... sidetracked."

She confided, "I don't know how much of this you'll believe, but I can heal people. I fixed a man's failing heart yesterday." Her excitement growing, she continued. "I'll be able to heal my dad. Can you believe it?" Not waiting for an answer, she rushed on. "What I'm figuring out is that the statue had an entity inside it. A woman. When I held it in the motel room, it disintegrated on me. That woman now seems to be inside me."

Silence. She could almost hear crickets as she allowed Lauren to digest her words. She finally spoke. "I don't know what to believe right now. I've had some time to deal with it but it's all so confusing."

"Something like *Invasion of the Body Snatchers*?" Lauren was serious.

Ry sighed but smiled. "Yes, something similar to that. Only this invader craves sex."

"Are you saying that she's responsible for all the sex you've been having—your dreams included?"

"Yes, all of it. It freaked me out at first, but I'm not going to let this control me. The woman confirmed her presence with War yesterday. Ian and Colin were there. And this time, I heard her. I can't control the desire. Once it begins, I have to let it run its course."

"Wait. Two men? I mean, seriously, Ry, you're doing a one eighty as far as your sex life goes in a matter of days."

"I'm trying to explain it."

"This woman inside you is a nymphomaniac?" Lauren considered the situation. "Have you dreamed about any of the others? You originally said there were three brothers."

Ry blushed as she busied herself with her latte.

"Oh shit. You have."

"I've had dreams about Ian's oldest brother, Jamie."

"I haven't met him. What's he like?" Lauren asked.

Ry snickered. "You would call him Mr.-Stuffed-Shirt-Solid-As-a-Rock-I'm-Better-Than-the-Rest-of-You-and-Totally-in-Control dude. I doubt the man would loosen up enough to enjoy himself. He walks around here like he has a stick up his butt." Except Ry's dreams told a different story.

Lauren chuckled then abruptly grew serious. "That would mean you'd have three brothers in your bed. You'll have to tell me everything when that happens. Three men. Ryder Hoffman, I would never have believed you'd do something like this."

A frown crossed Ry's face. "I didn't ask for it and I have no idea how to make it go away." She slowly shook her head. "It all sounds far-fetched, but I can't deny it anymore. It's not a hallucinogenic. It's an ancient curse."

"Whatever happens to you, Ry, I'll be with you. You're not getting rid of me until this is settled and your life is back to normal."

Ry blinked back tears. "Thanks, Lauren."

"Finish eating then track down War or someone who can answer your questions. I'll work on Zack to get to you. Then we'll see about escaping this craziness. Whatever you do, stay safe."

Chapter 27

J amie stood in the library listening to Abby describe her father's incredible recovery. Robert had a healthy heart. She had no way of explaining it, but all the tests she ran proved it. Ryder had healed him.

The woman in question was upstairs having breakfast. It was time to discuss her fate.

When Abby finished, the others in the room waited for Jamie to speak. As the alpha of the pack most affected by the situation, Jamie ultimately had priority over the others in the decision. The statue had been in the possession of someone in his pack. Two members of his family were intimately involved with Ryder.

This woman was coming between them all. Even here in the library the factions were evident. Emerson stood next to the fireplace while War paced in front of it. Colin and Ian glared from where they stood together near the desk. Abby and Robert squeezed into a tight family circle across the room by the sofa. Markus was the only one who didn't appear to be threatened.

Markus spoke first. "We need to accept she's not human anymore and prepare accordingly."

Colin growled at him. "I realize this is difficult for you to understand but Ry has done nothing. She's a pawn."

"She might be a pawn but her strength is growing."

Colin and Ian snarled and stepped forward to protest. Jamie held up one hand, and they halted, scowling.

"All the men around her are in trouble. We need to take steps necessary to protect our packs," he warned.

Jamie turned to Robert. "Have you made any headway in locating someone who knows about the statue?"

"The historian from Spain is on an archaeological dig in Colombia. He's written a few articles about it, though. From what I can tell, his father knew everything about the statue. The father is dead now, but the son supposedly kept all his records. Markus has already sent men to Colombia. Once we talk to him, I'm sure we'll have a clearer picture of what's going on."

Jamie watched War pace. War had sworn to protect the girl, but he'd also promised Jamie he would kill her if she became a risk to their people. She was a risk. How many more men would she pull into her sexual web?

He'd watched his brothers panting over her yesterday. They'd been unable to resist her. It wasn't uncommon for the brothers to share women, but they had spent the rest of the afternoon and the entire night with her. He needed to decide Ryder's fate soon.

Jamie appreciated the fact that the logical thing for all the packs would be to kill Ry. Here on Robert's ranch would be the best place because they could dispose of the body easily. They'd take care of her friend too.

Robert stood and moved in front of Jamie. "This is your decision to make, but I'd like to point out a couple of things. Ryder healed me. I would have been dead within six months without her. Now I'm looking at an entirely new life. If she can do that, what can she do for our packs?"

Jamie crossed his arms over his chest. The potential usefulness of her new ability hadn't escaped his consideration but he wasn't convinced. "What else?"

"Dunbar wants the statue. Why? For a woman that will enthrall his men? I don't think so. There has to be another reason. I'm convinced the sex isn't her true purpose. It has to be her healing power. Or something more. This could just be the tip of the iceberg, so to speak."

Jamie placed a hand on Robert's shoulder. This man was his mentor. He'd been there for Jamie when his parents had died. He was willing to listen to his suggestions. "I'm pleased you're better, my friend. I don't want to lose you."

Robert chuckled. "It'll take more than a faulty artery to kill me."

"I'm glad to hear it," Jamie said. "You're right. As much as I'd like to finish this now, we need to wait for the historian before we decide. We'll keep an eye on everything she does. We also need to limit her access to people, except for Colin and Ian."

He turned to look at his brothers and quickly hardened his heart. He was sending them into battle, even though that battle would be in the bedroom. "You two will occupy her time any way possible to keep her away from the rest of us. Understood?"

His brothers nodded. Ian looked particularly eager to join Ryder.

Jamie turned back to Markus. "When will your men find the historian?"

"Probably later today. Tomorrow at the latest."

"Good. The rest of us will stay away from her until we understand the threat she poses."

A light tapping on the door caused all heads to turn.

RYDER WANTED everything out in the open. It was time to uncover what these people knew and what they were hiding. She walked into the library where she found the group of men and women who had swarmed into her life in a matter of days. They all looked guilty, including Ian and Colin.

Correction, Jamie scowled with annoyance. "What can we do for you, Ryder?"

"I want to go home. My life is in turmoil. I need to heal my father. But none of you seem to care. You all obviously know each other." She stared pointedly at War. "What's up with all the secrecy?"

"Now that we know what happened to the statue, we're locating someone who understands its history," War replied but ignored her question. "Once we realize the implications of the statue, everything will make sense."

She shook her head. "I'm tired of all this. Tell me everything you know now. All the details. Don't leave anything out."

She looked from face to face, waiting for someone to answer. When no one did, her anger flared as her hands clenched into fists. Gritting her teeth, she worked to control herself.

"Why can I heal people?"

When no one answered again, she continued, her voice growing louder and stronger as she ticked off items on her fingers. "I want to understand why I have tattoos, why I'm having sex with two brothers who don't seem to mind sharing while I'm lusting after the third brother, and why I continue to be kidnapped."

Ian reached for Ry in an attempt to soothe her. "We can discuss this, but you need to calm down."

She yanked her arm away. Before she realized what she was doing, her hand balled into a fist which she aimed at Ian. Someone grabbed her forearm, halting her movement. Stunned, Ry swiveled her head to glare, but felt nothing. All the emotion rushing through her vanished like a wisp of smoke smothered under a glass jar. Puzzled, she let her gaze travel up the length of her arm until she was looking directly into the man's face.

She recognized him from the day before, but she didn't know his name. He was as tall and broad-shouldered as War. He had a pleasant face with black hair buzzed at the sides of his head, in a modern version of a mohawk.

His voice was deep but cold and calm. "I don't want to hurt you, Ryder, but if you threaten the others, I will take measures to protect them."

"I wouldn't hurt anyone." She was surprised at how quiet her voice was when a minute ago she was screaming.

"You raised your fist in anger to Ian. The last time you were angry, you flung War across the garden. We don't need a repeat of that."

She nodded while gazing up at him. Deciding that having no emotions was a blessing, Ry stepped closer. "I wouldn't hurt Ian. Who are you?"

"Markus Armstrong. Security."

"Why do I feel nothing when you touch me?"

It was his turn to be surprised. "What do you mean ... nothing?"

Ian and Colin stepped around the others to stand in

front of Ry.

"What's wrong, Ry?" Colin asked.

She shrugged slightly. "One minute I'm furious and out of control. The next, he touches me and I sense absolutely nothing. It's like I'm in an emotional dead zone."

Markus hesitated, then withdrew his hand from Ry. The instant she lost contact with him, emotions slammed into her—anger, confusion, annoyance, animosity. Ry gasped and doubled over. She felt as though someone had punched her in the gut, something she remembered from her experience with Dunbar. Ian and Colin grabbed her.

Sucking in air, Ry slowly straightened. The unpleasant impact of her emotions returning dissipated. She brushed off the brothers to stand on her own. Looking up at Markus again, she took in a deep breath.

"I can't say I liked that much, but it stopped my anger. We'll have to remember that little trick next time."

"Hopefully there won't be a next time. You must learn to control your emotions and whatever seems to control you," Markus said sternly.

"It'd be nice if someone would tell me what you're doing to get this woman out of my head."

"How much do you remember of her?" War asked. "Is she always there?"

Ry shook her head. "She shows up in my dreams and talks to me. Sometimes it's as if I'm watching things happen through her eyes. Half the time, I don't realize it's happening until it's over." She shot a quick glance at Ian and Colin. She only remembered parts of their time together at the clearing.

"Your extreme emotions seem to come from her." Jamie frowned. "We've sent men to Colombia to locate the historian. He's supposed to know everything documented about the statue. Once we hear from him, we'll have a better grasp of what to do with you."

Ry turned her gaze to him, but found it difficult to look at him without experiencing the now-familiar lust creep along her skin. She reached for Markus's wrist. The lust disappeared.

With a sigh, she turned her head back to Jamie. Nothing. Absolutely nothing. She smiled up at Markus. "I think I'll keep you nearby."

He grunted but she noticed a slight lift at one corner of his lips.

Looking at the annoying brother, she asked, "What happens if this historian of yours has no answers?"

Jamie watched her for several seconds. In that moment, she realized whose hands held her fate, and the situation was precarious at best. She remembered his words *we'll have a better grasp of what to do with you*. He hadn't said, "What to do *for* you."

"Let's take it one step at a time," he said. "I think you need to get outside for a while. Why don't you go for a stroll? Get some fresh air and exercise. It'll do you good. I'm sure you'll feel better afterward."

Jaime wouldn't tell her anything else. It would be a waiting game until the historian arrived. At her agreement, he looked past her. "Ian. Colin. Take Ryder outside."

"SHE'S GETTING DANGEROUS." Markus rubbed his wrist. "She'll be as powerful as a shifter at this rate. Whatever this is, it's transforming her in more ways than we thought."

They had waited until the two men left the library with Ryder before starting a new conversation.

Markus continued. "I'm concerned about the identity of the second unknown factor from the farmhouse. I don't like the fact someone ripped the heads off experienced shifters and we have no idea who."

Robert sighed. "Hopefully that historian can provide some answers. In the meantime, we need to learn how to manage her before she gets out of control. If she can toss War fifteen feet now, think about what she'll be able to do if she gets stronger. I don't entirely mean physical strength either. She needs you, Jamie."

Jamie had been silent and distant, but at the sound of his name, he looked over at the others. "Me?" He shook his head. "No, I'm trying to avoid her. Do you see the looks she gives me? I'm her next snack."

"Exactly. Think about it, Jamie." Markus spoke this time. "She admits she's attracted to you. You're the alpha and elder of your pack. If you become her lover, which seems to be where this is going, you could gain her confidence and her trust. She'll have an older, more experienced man to look to and confide in."

Jamie laughed harshly. "Older man? Like a father figure? Give me a break, Markus. I don't plan on sacrificing myself for the greater good. She has a mind of her own. She doesn't need me to 'manage' her. That's my brothers' job. Besides, she'll do whatever she wants to, whenever she wants to."

He shook his head. "No. I'm more concerned about what will happen if we do become lovers. Her physical strength and healing ability have only grown *after* she's had sex with Ian and Colin. What will happen if I get introduced into the mix? I'm not ready to find out until we understand more."

Deciding he needed some air, Jamie left the group and headed outside, going the opposite direction his brothers had taken Ryder.

Chapter 28

Within fifteen minutes, Ry found herself sitting on top a beige colored horse. When Jamie had suggested getting some air, she thought he meant a nice pleasant walk. Except they headed straight to the stables. Ry was not a horse person.

Bubblegum appeared to be gentle and moved slow as they left the paddock area. Colin sat a horse next to her, talking to Ry, giving her instructions and encouragement. Ian sat on a horse on her other side, lending an extra hand to keep her in the saddle when needed. They rode away from the house out into the open pasture with the cattle and horses.

Riding for roughly an hour, they stopped at a small stream. Several trees had taken root near the water's edge and provided shade. Ian helped her dismount. He attempted to hold her close as her feet touched the ground but Ry didn't want contact with either brother. She moved away, pretending to talk and pet Bubblegum. He was trouble with his pirate look and multi-colored hair.

Colin stepped up to her while reaching for the bridle. "Let me water him. You can relax for a bit in the shade."

Unsure what to do as he led her horse away, Ry didn't hear Ian step up behind her.

"Come sit with me. We can put our feet in the water and cool off." Ian held his hand out, waiting for her to take it. Colin stood a few feet away, waiting for her to move.

Without taking his hand, Ry headed to the water's edge. She knew what happened when these two were around her. Hoping to avoid any sexual interaction, she pulled off her shoes and stepped into the cool water. She waded across the stream picking her way with care. She'd never been much of an outdoorsy type of person. Wading barefoot through a stream was a new experience.

The tension of the past several days faded away. Ry hadn't felt this carefree in years. On a whim, she turned toward Ian and Colin on the bank, bent down, and flung two handfuls of water at them.

The look of surprise on their faces made Ry burst into laughter.

"Oh no you don't." Ian hopped into the water and began splashing back. Colin stayed on shore, laughing until they start directly the water toward him. Within seconds, they were soaked but laughing hysterically. It was a free for all. Ry couldn't remember the last time she'd laughed so much or had such fun.

By the time they returned hours later, they were laughing and joking. Ryder was amazed yet encouraged that they had avoided fallen into a tangle of limbs. They'd been like normal people.

Exhilarated, Ry walked through the front door, the two men trailing behind. Jamie stepped out of the library, his arms crossed over his chest, a bored expression on his face.

"Dinner will be ready in an hour. We'll eat in the main dining room."

Surprised at his comment, Ry paused. She widened her eyes. "Oh goody. We get to eat at the grownup table tonight." She narrowed her eyes. "I'm getting a bit tired of eating in my room."

She pivoted on her heel and moved toward the giant curving stairway. She remembered her earlier comment to Lauren about a really big stick and slapped her hand over her mouth to keep the giggles inside. Halfway up, her laughter broke free and filled the air.

Outside her bedroom doorway, she paused with her hand on the doorknob. Ian and Colin stopped beside her, their expressions full of desire.

"You're not coming in here." She kept her hand on the doorknob but she wasn't opening it until they left.

"We could have some fun before dinner." Colin waggled his eyebrows and grinned.

Ry laughed. "No. I want a bath and you're not going to stop me. So go away. I'll see you in sixty minutes."

"Fifty-five now. Just enough time for a long bath." This came from Emerson as she marched down the hallway toward them. "Jamie sent me up to stand guard outside Ry's door and make sure you two go to your own rooms."

When no one moved, Emerson directed her glare at Ian. "You're wasting time."

Ian and Colin stalked off to their rooms, grumbling.

Smiling, Ry watched them walk away. Turning back, she became aware of Emerson standing near her.

Before she could say anything, Emerson spoke. "I'm to be your personal guard. I'll stay out here to give you some privacy. You've had little of it lately."

Ry gave a quick nod and hurried into her bedroom.

Leaning back against the closed door, she took a minute to collect herself. Ian and Colin had both mentioned how hard-ass Emerson could be but Ry didn't see it. Maybe it was a tool she used against the men in a male dominated profession. Emerson and Lauren seemed to be the only ones who understood her feelings and her lack of privacy.

Pushing away from the door, she made her way into the bathroom to shower off the horse smell before soaking in a hot bath.

Chapter 29

After a long, relaxing bath, Ry emerged from the bathroom wrapped in her bathrobe and towel-drying her hair. The horse ride had cleared her head and calmed her down. While in the tub, she'd decided she would speak to Colin and Ian about their alter egos—the wolves. They might think she was crazy, but she knew what she had seen. She took four steps into her bedroom before she noticed a man standing in the middle of the room.

He was tall like Markus and War but built more like the Stone brothers, only not so broad and with more of an athletic build. His brilliant red hair was pulled into a long braid that hung over his shoulder, stopping at his waist.

He stood, hands clasped behind him, legs slightly apart, looking like a soldier standing at ease. She got the impression he made nonthreatening his ideal look but she recognized a hardcore soldier underneath.

"Who are you? Where's Emerson?"

His gaze moved down her body to her bare feet, then back up to her eyes.

"You are a tiny thing, aren't you? Green eyes. I'd prefer blue, but it'll do." His voice was soft and had the same Scottish accent as the men in her dreams.

Blue? What the hell did it matter what color her eyes were? She blurted out the first thing that came to mind. "I don't know who the hell you are, but you shouldn't be here. Tell me who you are or get out."

He continued his calm study of her. "May I see your binding tattoos, Princess?"

Creepy did not begin to explain the sentiment flooding her system. *Binding tattoos?* Something told her that he meant the ones on her chest, and she was definitely not going to show him those. In addition, the "Princess" comment weirded her out.

"I don't think so. *Emerson!*"

The last word exploded in the loudest scream she could manage. If Emerson were outside the room, she'd be inside in a split second.

The door burst open. Emerson flew in with her gun drawn.

The man glanced up, looking over Ry's head. His lips twitched ever so slightly. Then he vanished— all before Emerson had taken two steps into the room.

Unbelievable.

Emerson slid to a halt, staring in amazement at Ry.

"Did you see him?" Ry yelled. "Did you? He was right there."

Emerson moved quickly to her side. She spoke as she surveyed the room. "Code Red. Code Red."

Footsteps pounded on the stairs and down the hallway.

Emerson grabbed her arm. "Are you okay? Did he hurt you?"

Ry shook her head forcefully. "No. Did you see him? Please tell me you saw him vanish."

Emerson scowled. "Yes. Calm down. I saw him."

Ry flung herself at Emerson, grateful she wasn't hallucinating or dreaming.

Several people stormed into the room, pulling up short as they saw Ry clinging to Emerson. She released her grip on the woman and ran to Ian, quickly stepping into his open arms. He embraced her, only to pull back and look down at her.

"Are you all right? What happened?"

She nodded numbly, confused at the situation. How could someone disappear like that?

War turned on Emerson. "What the hell happened? You were supposed to be guarding her."

"War. Stop." Ry placed her hand on his arm and tried to swing him toward her, but he didn't back down from Emerson.

"She's mine to discipline as I see fit. You stay out of this, *Ms. Hoffman*." He stressed her name as if doing so would put her in her place.

Ry stepped up to him, put her hands on his chest, and shoved herself between Emerson and War.

"I don't care. You have no right to shout at her. She was in here before I finished screaming her name, so *back off*."

War glared at her, then with a slight growl, he stepped back.

Then the realization of a stranger in her room and then vanishing hit her, making her shake. She wrapped her arms around herself and turned back to Colin and Ian, who steadied her. Leading her to a chair, they sat her down and knelt in front of her.

"Tell me what happened, sweetheart. What do you

remember?" Colin coaxed. He held her hands in his. Ian's hands rested lightly on her ankle, gently rubbing.

Gazing into Colin's face, she explained, "He was waiting for me when I got out of the shower. When I screamed for Emerson, he vanished."

"He who?"

"Some man with an accent and a long red braid."

From across the room, War cursed. Colin and Ian frowned.

Jamie spoke from behind his brothers. "Tell us everything that happened."

She gave them all the details she remembered, including what the man looked like, what he wore, and what his accent sounded like.

"When he asked to see my tattoos, I decided enough was enough. That's when I screamed for Emerson."

She looked up at Emerson. "You saw him. You said you saw him."

"I saw him, but only from the back. I saw no weapons and he vanished in an instant," Emerson confirmed.

"I need to see this," Markus announced, then turned and left the room. A moment later, Robert, Jamie, and War followed.

Ian spoke. "We'll figure out who he is. Give Markus a few minutes."

Ry looked at the two men kneeling in front of her, their faces suspiciously expressionless. She had a nagging misgiving that something was happening downstairs. She stood, only to have Colin and Ian gently push her back down.

"Sit and relax. You're frightened. Just calm down," Colin said.

She frowned at him. "Don't tell me to calm down. What

are you hiding? I can tell something's going on downstairs you don't want me to know."

She looked over at Emerson. "Where did they go?"

Emerson scowled as she glanced away. Clearly, Ry would have to find out on her own.

Again, she moved to stand, only to have the two brothers stop her by pressing her back into the chair. She was not about to huddle there like a frightened child and wait for them to trickle information to her only when they deemed it necessary.

"Let. Go."

The two men looked startled at her tone, but stood and stepped away. Ry was surprised they responded to her order. She'd remember that little trick for later.

She hurried to her closet and dressed. When she left her bedroom, the others followed.

RY FOUND the library door closed, with the sound of a muffled conversation coming from inside. There was no doubt in her mind that the other men were in the library. *What a surprise.* They seemed to live there from what she'd noticed.

She stormed inside without knocking. Markus grunted his annoyance. War cursed. Jamie slipped to the far side of the room, glaring.

"You shouldn't be here." War stepped toward her, trying to block her view.

"You're not being secretive, you know, barreling down the stairs and ending up here. What are you hiding?" Then she noticed what was on the big-screen TV over the fire-place. It was her bedroom, with the intruder moving around the room, inspecting her things. Lauren had been partially right; they were doing more than just listening.

She forced her way around War to stand closer to the fireplace, looking up at the screen. "Is that now or earlier?"

"Earlier, while you were in the bathroom," Markus replied in a no-nonsense tone.

She whirled on him. "You monitor my bedroom?"

No one answered. They didn't need to. Huffing, she turned back to the TV. The intruder was now bending over her bed, lowering his face to the bedding.

"He's smelling my bed?" Confused and disgusted, she turned to War, the closest one to her. "Is he smelling my bed?" Her voice rose.

War kept his eyes on the video, but nodded. Ry shuddered. *Ewww.* She turned back to the TV screen to see what else the red-haired man had done.

He continued to cruise around her room, then paused at the bathroom door, staring at it. Ry hugged herself tightly, realizing how close the intruder had been to entering her bathroom while she relaxed in the tub. Ian was immediately at her side, wrapping an arm around her and drawing her close. She rested her head against him, needing his reassurance.

The intruder stood near the bathroom door for several moments, not doing a thing. He finally moved on, continuing his exploration of her room. He entered the closet without hesitation.

Markus pressed a button on the remote he was holding, and the video switched to one showing her closet. Ry stiffened. What else were they monitoring that she had no clue about?

The intruder ambled around the huge walk-in closet, stopping in front of the built-in drawers, opening first one then another. He pulled out her underclothes one at a time. He held a pair of pink lace panties to his face. Ry struggled with being creeped out and furious. She was a lot of both.

He looked at several other pieces of clothing. He held some to his face, then put everything back as neatly as he had found it.

He glanced toward the door, then for no apparent reason he left the closet. Markus clicked the remote again, and the screen switched to the video from her bedroom, all in sync with the man's movements as they watched the intruder step out of the closet, closing the door quietly and making his way to the spot where she'd found him.

He took up his stance there, hands behind his back, waiting. A moment later, she stepped out of the bathroom, towel-drying her hair.

They watched the brief conversation, with Markus only stopping the video after the intruder vanished when Emerson burst into the room. He quickly rewound and paused it just before he vanished. The intruder was looking directly at the camera and smiling.

"How did he know about the security cameras? I didn't even realize they were there," Ry said.

War turned to Markus. "We need to double the guards. I want someone to review the tapes of all the rooms. I need to know if he's been visiting the entire *house* without us knowing."

Emerson added her suggestions on how many guards they should use, who they should be, where they should be placed, and who should review the tapes. Ry's anger grew rapidly at being left out. She would show them. She didn't need them. She'd go home and her uncle would protect her. At least he wouldn't be videotaping her bedroom.

Pulling away from Ian, she headed toward the door. She

was within three feet of slipping out before Emerson stepped in front of them, blocking their escape.

"Move out of my way, Emerson. I'm going home."

As soon as the words were out of her mouth, the entire room went silent.

Emerson scowled. "You won't be safe at home. Dunbar *will* find you."

"I'll go to my uncle. He can protect me. I don't need you anymore. We'll get our things and leave as soon as possible."

Robert hurried to her side. "You can't leave. Your uncle can't protect you."

Ry turned on him, rage flaring. "Really, Robert? Is that what you think? Because at this moment, you can't protect me. That man was in my bedroom. He *smelled* my things. My bed. My underwear. I'm not sure Rick could do any worse."

She turned to War, the one man here who had promised to protect her. "Normal people can't appear and disappear. *How are you going to protect me from that?*" She wasn't sure if she meant it as a statement or a question. Either way, the entire situation frightened her.

She would not get hysterical. She remembered what happened when she became upset. However, they had a madman popping in and out of her bedroom and nobody had any idea how he'd done it. The panic escalated the more she thought about it.

She turned away from all of them, trying to slide past Emerson at the door. Ry refused to look at anyone. She didn't want to discuss this. She wanted to get away.

Markus moved toward her, smoothly and quietly. In one swift movement, he was on one knee in front of her with his head bowed. Similar to War, he was schooled in old-world manners. His behavior surprised her. He was the last one she would have expected this from.

"I swear on the blood of my ancestors to protect you, Ryder Hoffman, with my life for the rest of my time on this Earth and forever from the Afterlife."

As Ry looked down in surprise at Markus, War addressed her.

"Ry, you do understand that your uncle can't protect you, don't you? You'll put him and your parents in danger by going home. Dunbar will find you and take you back within twenty-four hours. This new guy would waltz into your house and take you in seconds. He didn't this time because there are a lot of us and we videotape everything. We can protect you 24/7 with guards constantly watching you."

She spoke quietly, with determination. "Has anyone been watching the videos of me in my bedroom?"

"You're overreacting. We have to protect you. This," he gestured back to the TV with the intruder's face still plastered on it, "is the best way to protect you."

He hadn't answered her question.

Ryder tilted her head, waiting for an answer.

"Answer her truthfully, War." Markus, still on his knee in front of her, frowned at him.

"No. No one has been viewing any of the videos except of the grounds and main rooms within the house." He watched relief spread across her features. "We didn't think it was necessary ... until now."

Chapter 30

Ry made her way to the garden for some much-needed fresh air. Halfway down the path, she halted and stood quietly, then closed her eyes and took several deep breaths. The wind brushed lightly through the branches. The birds chirped in the trees. Bees buzzed around the flowers. Water gently bubbled nearby. Far away, several voices were talking and shouting.

Ry concentrated on the sound of the water as she tried to calm down. She lost track of time. She could have been there anywhere from ten to twenty minutes, but she eventually relaxed enough to breathe evenly. The tension eased out of her body.

When she opened her eyes and could look at Ian and Colin without anger, she knew she had accomplished her goal. She smiled at them, then turned back toward the house.

She wanted to go inside and discuss the surveillance of her bedroom with Markus and War. Instead, she noticed the additional guards. Every several hundred feet stood a man with a weapon. They had moved in quickly and quietly while she had been meditating, her eyes closed.

"That happened fast," she murmured.

Ian shrugged casually. "The guards? When War and Markus speak, people jump to attention."

Colin stepped close to her. "It's only a temporary measure. War and Jamie want to move us to a different location, hoping to throw these guys off."

She glanced at Colin. "Where will we go?"

Ian answered as he stepped closer, his body brushing against hers. "They won't tell us until we're on the jet and in the air. Markus and War will contact several locations to make arrangements, but none of them will know which one we'll go to until we're there."

She laid her head on his shoulder, her every movement with the men natural. "What about all the men here? Will they come with us?"

"Some. The ones who work for us will follow. War will bring most of his men. Many of these men work for Robert. I'm sure he'll send several."

Ian took her hand, raising it to his lips. "Be prepared for more guards. You can't change War or Markus on that account."

She sighed and straightened. "Keep them out of my bedroom."

She looked toward the house again, this time noticing Jamie standing on an upper balcony, watching her intently. Before she commented to his brothers, the red-haired intruder materialized directly behind Jamie.

Several things happened within seconds. She yelled and pointed at the two men on the balcony. Ian, Colin, and all the guards looked to where she indicated.

Jamie swiveled around to defend himself.

The intruder reached for Jamie, who collapsed unconscious, the madman catching him. Both men disappeared, with Jamie sagging in the intruder's arms.

It was over before her scream faded.

Two of the guards nearest the house exploded in a flurry of shredded clothes. Almost instantaneously, two large black leopards emerged from the shredded cloth and raced up a tree next to the house. They scrambled across the large branches nearest to the balcony and leaped onto it.

Ry exhaled. "Oh, wow." Her heart raced. The overwhelming terror she'd experienced at seeing Jamie vanish warred with her astonishment and fascination at seeing two men transform in seconds into large predatory cats.

She gripped both Ian and Colin's arms as she watched the two cats prowl the balcony, sniffing the area. The balcony doors opened and War stepped out. Spotting her in the gardens below, he spoke sharply to the two cats, then turned back toward the doorway, a scowl plastered across his face. With the cats preceding him, he rushed back inside, slamming the balcony doors closed.

Leopards and wolves. Her heart thudded but her mind embraced the concept. She'd accepted that the brothers were shifters. Why not the others?

"Ry." Ian's voice interrupted her musing.

She frowned, then murmured. "What did you say?"

"I was trying to get your attention."

"Sorry." She glanced from Colin to Ian. "Jamie. We have to save him."

Everything they had been talking about became inconsequential. They had to help him. She understood without a doubt that she needed him. "He had a needle or something.

He had to have. Jamie collapsed too fast for it to have been anything else."

Colin looked at Ian with a questioning glance. "It's possible. It all happened fast. She was at a different angle than we were."

Ian nodded his agreement.

"We need to watch the videos." Colin placed his hand at the small of her back. "Why don't we go inside and see if War knows what's happening?" It took little encouragement on his part to get her moving.

Ry tried to shove aside thoughts of what types of beasts these men could shift into. Jamie was in the hands of a madman and needed rescuing. She needed to stay strong and calm for him.

Ry took stock of everything in a few seconds. Jamie had rescued her from Dunbar. Regardless of this new revelation that he was a shape-shifter, Jamie had been there for her. Despite all his doubts about her, he had protected her. She could do no less.

Walking into the house, she slowed, her step stuttering. Not until they reached the main foyer did she come to a complete halt. She had witnessed two men shifting into large wild cats, not werewolves. Those cats had blown her theory all to hell. Who were these people?

From everything she'd studied in medical school, morphing from one species into another defied all logic. Not to mention being physically impossible for a creature on two legs to morph into one on four legs.

Except she had seen several men shift with her own two eyes.

Did they call it shifting? Or morphing? Or changing? Were they animals living as men, or was it the other way around? Were there women too? Was War one of them?

Could everyone at the ranch shift? What about kids? She hadn't seen any children on the ranch, but maybe they had a special shifting school for kids.

Dear Lord, *crazy* did not describe the thoughts scurrying through her head.

Chapter 31

War had already cued the video from the balcony when Ry stepped into the library. She decided he must have a fetish for watching security camera footage.

She kept a small distance between her and the others, except for Markus. If she freaked out, he was prepared to touch her and send her into the zone. Personally, Ry was not keen on any more freaking out. She'd done enough recently.

A few minutes into the video, Markus quickly zoomed in on Jamie's neck. Yes, Red had used a needle—clearly, he had come prepared. Whatever had been in it was fast-acting. With any luck, it wasn't deadly.

After ten minutes of dissecting the footage, Markus shut the video off and turned to War.

"We continue with our plans. Jamie knows we'll be leaving tonight. If he gets away...." Markus scowled. "*When* he gets away, he'll know where to look."

War nodded. "Agreed. Get the men prepared for moving. Colin and Ian," he turned toward them, "you're still in charge of Ry. Keep her busy. Get her packed. Have her ready to move at dusk. Understood?"

They nodded. There was no questioning the two men now in charge. She realized they were planning on leaving Jamie behind.

"No." Ry caught everyone's attention. "No. You can't leave him." She looked around at the group standing there. She knew she sounded desperate, but she couldn't help it. Ry took a slow, deep breath. "He rescued me. You can't leave him to his fate with this Red guy."

Colin spoke. "Ry, we understand your concern. It's not an easy decision. Jamie and all of us have faced life or death situations before because of who we are. He knows the plan. He would be the first one to tell us to leave. He would not want to risk your safety."

"You don't understand. I need him. I've had dreams about him. Him, Colin, and Ian. All three. Without him, it doesn't work."

"What doesn't work?" Ian placed a hand on Ry's shoulder.

"I don't know. All of it is important. Three brothers. Three wolves. They have to be important if I've been dreaming about the three of them before I knew Colin and Jamie existed. I need Jamie to complete whatever the dreams have been telling me."

She watched as they considered her comment. They were hesitating. She could see it.

Markus decided for them. "We get prepared to go, but we wait. At the first sign of trouble," he pointed at Ian and Colin, "you get her ass out of here. You understand?"

They nodded.

Markus looked at Ry. "You won't give them any trouble, will you?"

She shook her head. If she didn't agree, they would haul her off to who knew where without a second thought. They would leave Jamie behind.

"Good," Markus continued. "Jamie will beat the crap out of me, but we'll do what we can to find him, or hope Red brings him back. If she's dreaming about him, he must be vital to this entire situation." He turned toward her. "Are you good? Do you need help calming down?"

She shook her head. "Where's Lauren? I need to know she's being protected."

"At her home. Zach is guarding her."

Good. The less Lauren knew of this discussion, the better.

Deciding to be blunt, she turned her gaze toward the brothers. "Are you two werewolves?"

They shuffled their feet. Ian ducked his head.

Markus responded instead. "It's about time you asked questions. No, they are not werewolves."

She swiveled her head to look up at him, blinked, then relaxed and smiled. Of course not. Men couldn't shift into animal forms.

"Not in the traditional sense, at least," Markus continued. "Colin, Ian, and Jamie are wolves. I'm a bear. Those two men, the black leopards you saw, are part of War's pack."

The image of Ian shifting from a wolf into a man flashed through Ry's mind. She remembered the intense and immediate visceral reaction she had while watching him and Colin shift or bite her.

Ry's legs wobbled, but she stood her ground while Markus continued to reveal more. "We're called weres or werekind or shifters, depending on who you ask. We prefer shifters. We're born this way. It's not something you can get by being bitten on a full moon, so don't worry about shifting into a wolf or anything." Markus grinned.

"Geez, Markus," Ian hissed.

"Nothing like holding back," Colin growled.

"Someone has to tell her. You two aren't," Markus snapped. At least he'd been honest with her.

"Shifters? I've heard of them in stories and fables. Are you like those?"

He shook his head. "It depends on the story, but probably not. We keep to ourselves and stay quiet. There are so few of us left anymore, a couple thousand worldwide. We don't let humans know we exist."

"Red and Dunbar. What are they in all of this? Are they...?"

"Shifters? We haven't determined what Red is yet. We usually can smell other shifters, but he seems to be able to mask his scent. In addition, we don't pop in and out of rooms like magic. According to Devon, Dunbar isn't a shifter. He's human."

"Red could have hurt me, but he didn't. Why not?" Ry asked, confused.

"*Yet.* Red hasn't hurt you *yet*. We don't understand his motives or where he stands in all of this or what he wants with Jamie. We suspect he's working for Dunbar but until we understand his motivation, we can't give you a proper explanation."

Her thoughts in turmoil, Ry clamped her mouth shut. They couldn't explain anything. They couldn't get her to her father. They couldn't let her leave. What in hell could they do for her?

Chapter 32

Jamie woke. Thirsty, he licked his lips for moisture with little success. His tongue felt thick. Drugs. He vaguely remembered a slight sting in his neck before he passed out. As he gradually came back to full consciousness, he could feel the strain of pressure on his arms and shoulders.

Looking up, he found he was hanging from the ceiling. He wore handcuffs, with a chain draped between them that led back up to the ceiling to a hook. Chains bolted to the floor wrapped around his ankles securing his legs. Suspended, his feet weren't touching the floor, forcing his arms to take his full weight.

In his shifter form, he could change into the smaller human form and slip his way out of most situations. The restraints would slip off. But this was different. In his human form, he couldn't shift into his larger wolf form with something restraining him—like handcuffs and chains. It would constrict and tighten as his body grew.

Someone understood what they were doing. He was in deep shit.

Struggling, he put his feet under him and stood, relieving the strain.

He was naked. Great. Things couldn't get any better. He tugged and shook the chains, testing their strength. They were solid.

Jamie took in his surroundings. The sterile, stark-white room was made of concrete. There were no windows. There was one door, directly in front of him, made of steel, and a drain in the middle of the floor. The only piece of furniture was a stainless-steel cart, similar to one that might be used in a hospital, the whips, chains, daggers, and knives on it weren't hospital equipment.

Similar implements of torture covered an entire wall. There were two other locations in the room with chains hanging from hooks in the ceiling. Another wall also had expanded assortment of chains, handcuffs, and hooks.

Awesome. A frigging torture room.

Yep, things couldn't get any better.

As if on cue, Red stepped through the door. Barefoot, he wore only a pair of faded black jeans. A mapping of scars crisscrossed his bare chest, back, and shoulders. Thick, uneven ones standing out. Thin, smooth ones barely there. All showed a lifetime of abuse. He didn't look at Jamie as he headed to the table with its load of instruments.

This man had appeared out of thin air at least twice at Robert's house. Probably more times they didn't even realize. Jamie had tons of questions, starting with how Red did the nifty little disappearing trick—and what he wanted with Ry. What was the connection between the two?

"I wouldn't mind knowing how you do that vanishing act of yours," Jamie probed.

Red studied the torture instruments on the table,

finally picking up a cat-o'-nine-tails. As he turned toward Jamie, he ran the leather through his hands, gently caressing it.

Jamie tried again. "I enjoy a bit of bondage like a lot of us shifters do, but you're not my type. Sorry, but I have to refuse."

Red stared at him with a blank expression. He needed a different approach. Ryder was the key.

"Maybe you can teach Ry your disappearing act."

Red's expression never wavered. "In due time, the Princess will learn to control her power."

That definitely got Jamie's attention. "Tell me about her power."

Red blinked at him before a slight smile crossed his lips. "You'll learn in time."

He turned away.

"Did Dunbar order you to torture me? What does he want with Ry?"

"Dunbar knows nothing. This is entirely my undertaking."

Jamie tipped his head to the right, puzzled. Although Red was now answering questions, getting information out of him was like prying a can open with his teeth.

"Was kidnapping Ry your own undertaking too?"

Red's face blazed with rage. His entire body stiffened. He gripped the whip, causing his knuckles to turn white.

"No. That was his idea. I had nothing to do with it. If I had, I would have taken her myself and put an end to the debacle."

"And ripping the heads of those shifters? Your idea? Or the gunman who shot my brother?"

"The demons have their own agenda. I shot your brother."

Anger rippled through him. And what was this about demons? Interesting. Jamie knew nothing about their kind.

"You work for Dunbar." He made it a statement.

"I owe Dunbar my life. He is my master," Red admitted.

Amazed, Jamie asked, "You're his slave?"

Red hesitated, looking uncertain. "He is my master but I have my own life. I do what I want."

"So, this is what you want. To hurt me."

Red shook his head slowly. "I don't want to hurt you, but it's necessary. You're an obstacle in my path. I must remove the obstacle."

"And killing me will get you closer to Ry."

Red frowned. Jamie could tell no one challenged him often, at least not verbally. Red thought for a moment, then shrugged. "I can see why you are an alpha and an elder. If I let you continue to talk, you'll soon know all my secrets."

Jamie straightened the best he could. He would not let Red's acknowledgement of his titles slide without using it to his advantage. The man had done his research.

"Let me go and help us against Dunbar. I'll bring you into my pack, no questions asked."

Red moved around behind him. Jamie's muscles tightened in anticipation of a lashing from the whip. He was no stranger to it, but he didn't wish for it.

In addition, the fact he was naked wasn't helping matters any. The big man behind him with a whip handle was disconcerting.

Red stepped close to Jamie. He didn't touch him, but he was close enough that Jamie had no problem hearing him whisper, "I plan on beating and cutting you. I'll make you bleed until you are close to death. But you won't die. The Princess needs you. She must heal you and take you as her Guardian. You will provide the Princess with a stronger force and more power. She needs her Guardians for protection. Having them will bring me one step closer to my goal.

"What I do benefits the world. I can't let you continue to avoid the inevitable. I've seen you keep your distance as her power pulls you to her. You are the current bottleneck and I plan to remove it. I am the last Guardian and I won't wait forever for you to make up your mind."

Red stepped back and began a steady rhythm of strokes on Jamie's back. No spot went unscathed. He occasionally stopped the whipping to select a knife, which he then plunged into Jamie repeatedly in places designed to cause more bloodletting and more damage.

Within an hour, Jamie sagged in his restraints, half-conscious and barely alive.

Chapter 33

Ian and Colin kept Ry busy. After preparing a small bag of clothes and essentials for each of them, they headed to the rec room and played pool, then foosball. Occasionally Markus or War would enter and talk briefly with the men, then leave. When she wasn't occupied, she paced the floors. If she thought she was going crazy earlier, this was worse.

Four long agonizing hours after Jamie's disappearance, she was unable to concentrate on what they were doing. Ian and Colin led her up to her room. She realized the two brothers had bed-related activities on their minds, but she persuaded them to play cards instead. Although she gave in and agreed to strip poker.

Despite their off-color comments and them losing on purpose, she knew they were on edge. At first, she thought the men were callous and uncaring about their brother's situation. Then she looked closer. They exchanged concerned glances between each other. Occasionally one or the other would stand and gaze out the wall of windows. They were constantly checking their phones. When a text did come through, they both jumped and rushed to read it. A steady underlying current of nervous energy ran through them.

Both men were down to their jeans. She was certain they were both going commando, which meant the next one to lose would be naked. She didn't think she could concentrate after that.

Ry still had her shirt, bra, and panties. She was positive they let her win occasionally.

She wasn't sure what alerted her to the intruder's presence. Red's arrival was similar to a sudden drop in the temperature. One second, they were alone. The next, Red stood across the room near the bed. He held one arm around an unconscious and very naked Jamie, barely keeping him upright. His other hand held a wicked-looking knife to Jamie's chest, near his heart.

Ian and Colin sensed them an instant after she did, which surprised her. Red halted their approach with a movement of the knife. They didn't like being powerless, but for Jamie's sake, they didn't move. A low growl emanated from both men.

Ry slowly stood. She was not about to upset Red and have him stab Jamie. Red looked directly at her, ignoring the two brothers. Holding his gaze, she took a step toward him, then another. She advanced five steps before he ordered her to stop.

She immediately halted, not letting her gaze waver from his face. Then he did something she hadn't expected. For the first time since they'd met, Red showed emotion. His gaze cruised down her body, then back up, his expression full of lust, desire, and longing. Her t-shirt barely went to the tops of her thighs, exposing her white panties when she moved a certain way. He didn't speak until he finally let his eyes rest on her face.

"Eventually, Princess, it will be me you take to your bed."

Everything happened in seconds.

He shoved the knife into Jamie's chest and vanished.

Jamie fell to the floor with a heavy thud.

Ry screamed in agony and raced to him. She became aware of Colin and Ian reaching him at the same time she did. Colin cradled his brother in his arms while Ian gripped Jamie's shoulders.

Ry dropped to her knees next to Jamie and pressed her hands to his chest. His heart wasn't beating. Calm settled over her.

"Pull out the knife, Ian." She could do this. She had to do this.

Ian didn't question or hesitate.

As the blade slid from Jamie's chest, she concentrated on his wounds, focused on picturing his wounded heart, just as she'd done when she'd healed Robert. She could "see" where the knife had nicked it. The blood seeped from the tiny incision. She mentally reached her hand out to touch it and gently traced the small cut, sealing it.

She tapped his heart lightly and watched in amazement as it began to beat. Then she continued probing his body for the rest of his wounds. Only then did she realize the extent of the damage.

Red had beaten Jamie and stabbed him repeatedly, seemingly more to weaken him with blood loss than to kill him outright by hitting a major artery.

Ry healed wound after wound. Her hands and arms turned red from his blood. She smeared it on her shirt and her face as she wiped away the sweat. Finally, she finished healing the last wound. She opened her eyes and found Jamie's calm brown eyes watching her.

In a split second, he had her on her back, his bloody, naked body pressed between her legs. Her body throbbed, knowing what was coming. She remembered the encounters with Ian and Colin. The brothers had been injured the first time they had made love to her.

Jamie rose to his knees, running his gaze over her. He reached for the bottom of her t-shirt and ripped. Seconds later, with a quick flick of his fingers, he shredded her bra down the middle. Then, with two quick movements, he shredded her panties.

He pulled her to her feet, stripping off the remnants of her clothing. With no regard of who else was in the room watching, he turned her around and placed her hands on the footboard of the bed. Taking hold of her hips, he roughly tugged her backward until she bent over.

Jamie laid himself carefully over her back. His weight pressed on her. He placed his head near her ear. His lips brushed over it, against her neck. His fangs scraped her skin.

"Tell me what you want. Beg me for it." His voice was guttural as though he was talking through a growl.

Ry quivered with anticipation. Somewhere deep inside, she had known this moment would come. He had been the more aggressive lover than his brothers, more demanding, in her dreams. Reality was imitating those visions.

Her mouth went dry. Ry swallowed hard and licked her lips. She answered in a hoarse whisper. "I want you. I want you inside me, Jamie. Bind me to you. Please."

He brushed her hair away from her neck, baring the back and side. With a smooth but powerful move, he pressed his cock into her wet entrance in a long, slow slide. Ry felt every inch of him. Once he settled inside her body, he paused and let her adjust to his size. Her pussy pulsed around him.

His mouth moved sensually against her neck, his fangs lightly dragging against her skin. She tried anticipating his movements.

"I hate you for doing this to me." Then he sank his canines into her neck.

Ry exploded in an orgasm as his fangs entered her flesh. He hadn't even moved inside her.

JAMIE WATCHED the tattoo bloom on her neck under his mouth. He felt an answering tingling sensation on the back of his. Satisfaction flowed through him from knowing they were marked. Red had been right. He had been avoiding this. Now it was done. The immense pleasure was unlike any he'd ever experienced—both sexual and emotional. Sensations he hated admitting, even to himself.

Releasing her neck, he retracted his fangs, trailed his tongue across the wounds, and began sliding in and out of her at a smooth, steady pace. He wanted to prove he was not either of his brothers, in or out of bed.

His movements were deep and steady as he gripped her hips. Ry moved with him but let him set the pace. He sensed her orgasms before they rippled through her. One would barely cease before another began. He paused, allowing her to clench tightly around him. As soon as she relaxed from the climax, he began moving again.

HER ORGASMS RAN TOGETHER. Ry cried out his name more times than she could remember. As her world turned to black and faded away, his grip on her tightened and he came deep inside her.

When she felt his release, her body erupted into a billion particles of energy. It was so much more than a normal orgasm. Every fiber, every cell in her body felt like it exploded. As she shattered, her power expanded. It swept through her cells. Stars burst behind her eyes. The world tilted on its side. Her knowledge of reality became inconsequential.

Ry opened her eyes to discover Jamie squatting several feet away studying her, breathing heavily. Colin and Ian were beside her. They brushed her hair away from her face and gently stroked her body. She smiled at their concern.

Looking relieved, Ian gathered her up and carried her to the bathroom. Once there, they discovered the shower was large enough for all four of them. After they cleaned the blood off, they used the rest of the night to explore her newly expanded energy and power.

Chapter 34

Friday
 Jamie stood in the library in front of the big-screen TV, gazing at the image of Ry's bedroom in real-time. She snuggled against his brothers in the king-size bed. They were all naked, various body parts tangled up with each other and the sheets as they slept. He could see one breast with a tattoo, bare legs, and part of her hip.

He'd woken thirty minutes earlier and needed to get out of the room. He'd ended up here. Although he'd attempted to stay away, Jamie now couldn't quit watching her. He felt what Ian and Colin had described to him, an overwhelming necessity to protect her.

He heard War and Markus whispering in the hallway. Normally, he wouldn't have been able to eavesdrop from that distance but he was amazed at how heightened his senses were now. Had this happened to his brothers after they received their tattoos and joined with Ry? Or had this only happened to them now, after he completed the group of four?

All three brothers had sensed the power and magic

expand within her when he and Ry had bonded. How long before they would see more examples of her newly acquired strength and skills?

He massaged the back of his neck. The tattoo tingled, like a spider crawling on his skin. It was larger than the ones his brothers sported. He also sensed her in his head, how content and happy she was at this moment. The same sensation Ian and Colin previously mentioned. They could sense where she was and what her mood was.

He stayed watching the monitor as War and Markus came into the room, only turning around when War spoke.

"Nice tattoo."

Jamie couldn't stop the smile tugging his lips. He'd known these men for years before he came into his role as the elder of his pack, more years than he wanted to remember. They'd fought battles together, gotten drunk together, screwed women together, almost died together.

He reached a hand back to rub the tattoo of the tree. It spread out across the back of his neck and shoulders, as if it draped over him. It was in the same spot as the wolf now imprinted on Ryder's neck and shoulders.

"When is the historian arriving?" Jamie asked. Although he already knew the answer from Markus and War's conversation in the hallway, he wanted the subject changed.

"The jet landed and Robert drove out to collect him, so he'll be here shortly." Markus stepped forward as he spoke, watching the TV monitor. Jamie turned toward the screen too. She had moved slightly, curling up against Ian.

Ian pulled her into his arms and cuddled her close. Colin spooned up behind her, reaching his hand below the sheets, between her legs. In seconds, her expression transformed from sleepy to aroused.

Jamie clicked off the screen and turned back to the other two men.

"I haven't had a chance to talk to you two about my encounter with Red. He had some interesting things to say."

The two men gave him their full attention.

"He mentioned Dunbar. It wasn't clear if Red is his slave but he was annoyed that Dunbar had kidnapped Ry. Both of those men seem to have their own agenda. Red's is to be Ry's lover."

"Then why doesn't he just snatch her? He's had plenty of opportunities," Markus asked.

"Because he seems to think there's a pattern. He claims he's the last. He shot Colin to get the ball rolling. He hurt me because I wouldn't willingly crawl into her bed."

"Interesting," War said. "So, he's bidding his time and throwing men into her path."

"One other thing. He mentioned demons at the farmhouse."

Both men frowned but Markus responded first. "Demons? What the hell do we know about demons?"

"I've never heard that demons were real. You'd think we would know, don't you?"

"The sulfur we smelled. They're the ones who ripped the heads off. Who else could it have been?"

Jamie heard cars approaching the house. The three men tabled their discussion until later. They remained still while voices grew louder in the foyer.

Moments later, the library door opened. The man who followed Abby into the library was six feet tall, his face handsomely chiseled, ash blond hair, eyes a light brown, almost gold. A tiger.

Robert followed him inside. Before he closed the door, Jamie saw four of Markus's toughest men in the hallway, dirty and tired, but all business after hauling their prey home.

The newcomer looked around the room, glaring at everyone, taking in who was there. "Who wants to explain why someone yanked me from my bed and hauled me here?"

He was furious, but kept his anger under control. Control was something shifters learned at an early age.

Robert broke the silence. "Christian Dupree, these men have questions for you. This is Waru Swift, Markus Armstrong, and Jamie Stone." Robert motioned to each man as he introduced him. No one moved to shake hands. Formality was no longer required or appreciated.

CHRISTIAN LOOKED at each man as Robert introduced him. He openly stared at the tattoo reaching around the sides of the Jamie neck. Although tattoos weren't unusual—hell, the big, bald man had several on his head and neck—this man's tattoo was the most unique he had ever seen.

A shiver of anticipation flickered in his gut. It couldn't be. It was impossible. His father died waiting for the day this type of tattoo would appear, and he had always hoped Christian would see the day this happened. He continued to stare at Jamie, waiting for him to speak.

Jamie didn't disappoint.

"Tell us about this statue." He took a photo off the nearby desk and handed it to Christian.

Christian took the paper and scrutinized the picture. Although he was dancing on the inside, he let a sneer cross his lips. He wasn't about to tell them anything without knowing more about what had happened. His family had kept the secrets of the statue for generations for a reason. The power it contained was not to be taken lightly or put in the wrong hands.

"Seriously? You brought me here because of a statue?" He waved the paper in the air. "Do you realize how many people ask me silly questions about this statue every year?"

Jamie's expression turned curious. "No. How many?"

Christian smiled wickedly. "None. Until a week ago. You, three other shifters, and one human."

"Dunbar, I presume."

Christian dipped his head. "You would presume correctly."

"What did he ask? What did you tell him?" Jamie demanded.

Christian hesitated, watching Jamie. "Why should I tell you?"

Jamie scowled before he pulled his t-shirt over his head and turned his back to the others. This gave them a clear view of his tattoo. It ran from his hairline down his neck and upper back and spread across his shoulders.

Christian whistled. "Holy fuck."

Jamie turned around, pulling his shirt back over his head.

"Do you have any idea what that tattoo means?" Leaning forward, Christian spoke softly, barely containing his excitement.

"No, which is why we *yanked* your ass out of bed and hauled you here."

Christian licked his lips. His mouth had gone dry. The tattoo was real, which could only mean one thing.

"Dunbar wanted to determine if the legends were true. I couldn't confirm or deny anything. They've always been legends. He asked me to tell him the stories. I referred him to a book I wrote several years ago. It has the basic legends and some general stories about the statue but none that would explain the tattoos. Those stories I kept to myself."

He motioned toward Jamie. "That's a binding tattoo. No one has seen them in over two thousand years. Probably closer to three. It was a ritual initiated by a queen to bind couples together. It meant they were true mates and no one could tear them apart. No one else would interest them. If one mate died, the other would follow shortly from despair. They were bound together, body and soul."

"One man and one woman?" War interjected.

Christian nodded. "Yes. At least that was the basic concept. The only exception was the queen herself. She had several guards she took as lovers. She bound them all to her."

He looked from War to Jamie and his face lit up with excitement. "It's unlocked, isn't it? The statue. Someone's awakened the magic. The three other shifters who asked about the statue mentioned they had sensed a surge of magical power. It selected a host. She bound you to her, didn't she?"

He watched Jamie intently. He knew he was right, but he needed the verbal confirmation. Jamie idly watched him back. The man was stone-cold.

"Okay. What do you want from me? My sworn silence? A blood oath? My firstborn?"

When no one answered, Christian sat on the sofa, perched on the edge, gripping his hands together. Slowly releasing his breath, he raised his head to look at Jamie again.

"What if I told you something no one knows?" He didn't wait for a response. "The magic from the statue is now in the new host. I'm assuming it's a woman. Over time, the power *will* grow with each lover she takes. That's the secret to the magic. She'll become extremely powerful. How this plays out will depend on what type of person she is and whom she chooses as Guardians. The original queen ruled her kingdom for hundreds of years. Imagine what this woman could do with the right men supporting her."

War spoke up. "We've heard the stories, the rumors, of the Tree of Life. Of a human destroying our ancestors and enslaving them. Is this the same tree? Should we expect the same outcome?"

Christian pursed his lips together and looked between the men standing in front of him. He stood. "Yes and no. I will do *anything* to be a part of this. You name it, I'll do it. But I won't tell you everything until I meet her."

Chapter 35

A rock dropped and settled in the pit of Jamie's stomach. If Ry's possession continued to follow the history of this queen, more men would share her bed. More men to insinuate suggestions in her ear. More men to sway her decisions and have her second-guessing herself. With his brothers, he would always have the final word. He'd always be right. Now he wasn't so sure.

"Robert, would you mind seeing to our guest, please? I believe he's hungry." At Robert's nod, Jamie turned to War and Markus. "Do whatever you have to, to secure him. He's coming with us."

Jamie moved to the door, stopping with his hand on the handle.

"We leave in two hours."

As he left, carrying the remote with him, he had no worries. Everyone would be prepared to go when the time came to leave. In the meantime, he had something to take care of. A way to ensure his word would be final with Ry.

Once upstairs, he slipped into the bedroom and found

his two brothers still lying in bed, dozing with Ry. He stood next to the bed, watching her for several minutes.

After the conversation with Christian, he understood what he had to do. There would be more men in her life. He suspected War. Red seemed confident he would be the last. Who the others in the middle would be, no one knew. Regardless, he realized with the power she wielded already someone would need to manage her. Markus had been right.

There was one way he could gain control, though—if it worked. Their society had a pecking order. If she tied herself to someone more powerful than Jamie, he would have no control.

He tapped each brother on the shoulder to wake them. At his nod, they slid out of bed and tugged on their jeans. The three men stepped into the hallway.

Jamie brought them up-to-date. "The historian is here. We'll be leaving in two hours. I want you both to work with Markus and make sure everything is ready to go."

"What are you going to do?" Ian asked.

"I need to spend some time with Ry. If we have to split up, I want her to go with you two." Jamie hoped it was a reasonable request. If they didn't leave the bedroom willingly, he would have to order them. If he ordered them, they would be suspicious. They'd figure out soon enough what he was planning and they would not be thrilled.

Colin nodded agreeably, but Ian hesitated. Jamie realized in that instant that Ian felt more than an obligation to Ry. The young pup was in love. Jamie controlled his expression. Under normal circumstances, he'd be smacking his brother upside the head. Shifters never fell in love with humans. Too many bad things happened with those relationships, namely that the human eventually died.

"She'll be fine, Ian. I promise." Jamie wouldn't hurt her. She was too valuable to the clans.

With a frown, Ian followed Colin. Jamie watched them leave before he returned to the bedroom. Setting the remote on the nightstand, he undressed and climbed into bed. Then he set about waking her and making her his mate and alpha female.

R Y WOKE to hands gently stroking her body. Opening her eyes, she saw Jamie gazing at her. He was alive and all in one piece. He lay beside her smoothing his hand over her hip and side with light strokes. She smiled, raising her hand to his face.

He gently kissed her palm. "Do you trust me? My brothers and me. Do you trust the three of us?"

She had never given her trust freely. Her mom said it came from when she had been a child and abandoned by her birth mother. But she trusted these men. They had rescued her and protected her.

He hesitated while she caressed the side of his face and thought about her answer. Ry turned her gaze to the rest of the room. "I trust all three of you, but where are Ian and Colin?"

He rested his hand on her hip. "They went downstairs. I've been talking to the historian who knows about the statue. He told me some things you need to understand. Like the tattoos; they are called binding tattoos."

Ry shivered. "That's what Red called them. He said he wanted to see my binding tattoos."

He nodded. "It's a way to bind us to you."

She frowned. "I don't understand."

Jamie hesitated, seeking the right words. "The tattoos

serve two purposes. First, to bind us to you, which means we will protect you with our lives."

"Protect me? From what?"

He smiled. "Anything. Anyone."

He slid his hand up to her left breast and traced Ian's tattoo with his fingertips.

"The second purpose gives us an indicator of where you are and how you're doing. We'll sense if you're upset or angry or in what general direction you are. I hope we can strengthen that power over time so we can locate you easier if needed."

"I can sense you, too, but it's been hazy. Since you and I...." A blush crept along her cheeks. "It's more sensitive. I can feel your emotions."

He pinched and held her nipple between his fingers. Exquisite pain throbbed through her breast. Ry sucked in her breath, arched her back, closed her eyes, moaning. He released the pressure and allowed her to ease back into the bedding. It took several seconds before she opened her eyes to discover him smirking. With a quick dip of his head, he sucked her nipple into his mouth. His suckling brought her close to the edge of climax before he pulled away, denying her a release.

He kept his face close so when she opened her eyes, he was right there.

"I hate you," she whispered with a smile.

Jamie chuckled. "I know you do. Trust me. It'll be worth it in a few minutes."

Curiosity filled her as she wondered what he had in mind. He pressed her down into the mattress and held himself over her.

"You are so beautiful." Jamie followed the compliment with a growl from deep in his chest. He nuzzled her neck, his lips making their way to her ear. She didn't know what was more exhilarating, his growl, his aggressiveness, or his hard cock lying against her thigh.

"Don't freak out. Touch my shoulders and upper back. I want to get you accustomed to the different ways we can shift. Just know, I'll never fully shift when we are having sex."

Hesitantly, she ran her hands over his back, alarmed to touch a light covering of fur. She froze, unsure of what was happening.

Jamie tried to reassure her. "It's only a partial shift, just my upper torso. Feel it. I can control how much I change and what I change."

Stroking his shoulders, she realized the luxurious wolf pelt replaced his human skin only in the section he'd described.

"Oh wow. It's so soft."

"We start shifting when we hit puberty. I've had many years to perfect the little changes." He demonstrated by shifting his face ever so slightly—his eyes, his nose, his ears, his fangs.

Ry gasped but didn't pull away. Ready to experience whatever she could about these men, she relaxed under his ministrations.

ENCOURAGED at the bright interest shining in her eyes, Jamie lowered his head to trail his tongue down her breasts to lick one nipple, then the other. He dragged a fang against one than the other, hearing her hiss. Her excitement ratcheted up with each nuzzle and caress.

"Bite me. Hard. Please."

"Not yet, sweet. Not yet." He pulled back, turned her

over, then positioned her on her hands and knees, her legs spread wide. "That's a pretty sight. You're wet." He dragged a finger through her folds. Ry whimpered and pressed back into his hand.

"Easy, sweet, in due time. First, you need to know what I plan on doing." His finger slipped inside, causing her to moan low in her throat. He spoke as he stroked her in slow, precise movements. "There's a way I can fuck you that you will never forget. I'll be human but my cock will swell, giving you more pleasure than you've ever experienced."

He pushed his finger deeper, hooking it to press on her g-spot, stroking it every so lightly. He leaned his body over hers, whispering in her ear while she began to tremble. "You want more, don't you?"

She moaned. "Yes."

"You can't get enough, can you?"

A whimper was her only reply before her body convulsed into another orgasm, her pussy clinging to the single digit inside her.

Jamie removed his finger, running his hands over her tight ass. He had to admit that if he was going to be hitched by an unknown source to a human, she was what he would have wanted. She was beautiful and had a sexy body. He would definitely enjoy fucking her and claiming her as his alpha mate.

He hesitated a moment before placing his mouth over one tempting butt cheek. His fangs elongated, then ever so gently he punctured her skin and slid them into her flesh. Her body stiffened, her muscles rippling with the power while her pussy tightened on nothing. She arched back into him, whimpering at the emptiness inside her. Jamie disengaged his canines and pulled back.

"Are you ready for my cock?"

Her moan confirmed her need.

Jamie positioned himself at her entrance and pressed his cock inside. He paused, letting her get accustomed to his size. Little by little, he used his shifting capabilities and began to enlarge his cock. Ry trembled with anticipation; it was already a tight fit. As his size increased, he moved. He pulled out a few inches, then pressed back in.

He knew the moment it was too much for her. Her body tensed. Her moan was not a pleasurable one. Jamie stopped increasing his size, held still, and rested a hand on her lower back.

"It's okay. Just breathe. You've got this."

Ry shook her head. "It's too much."

He had to distract her. Thinking quick, he landed three quick swats to her right ass cheek. His instinct was correct. She pressed back into his hand, her moan sliding into a groan of pleasure.

"That's it. You like a bit of spanking, don't you?"

Her positive reply was barely more than a moan.

He smacked her other ass cheek. Her pussy tightened on his cock.

"There you go. Once we get to our new location, I'll show you all about bondage."

She shifted her hips, attempting to force him to move. He chuckled and pulled his cock out ever so slightly.

He leaned over her back, his voice low and seductive. "I'll decorate your nipples with jeweled clamps. One on your clit. I'll have you walk naked through our home. Ready for my brothers and I to take whenever we want."

Jamie chuckled, realizing that she was getting excited by his talk. He continued making suggestive comments, keeping the one-sided conversation going while he started his initial intent again—making her his alpha bride in an ancient ritual.

Before she could hesitate again, he moved fast and deep, fucking her with an increased intensity. Even with his larger than normal size, she took him, letting him slide in, begging for more.

He growled low in her ear. "Mine. My mate. My alpha. My other half. I claim you."

A burst of power pounded through him as he sunk his fangs into her shoulder. He held her down and thrust repeatedly into her, demanding she accept him and his wolf. The mating ritual between two shifters could last for days as they shifted between human and animal forms. The man and woman would make love in both forms, but their animal form made the deepest connection between the two.

The first time the mated couple had sex, they typically did so while shifted, and it lasted anywhere from a few moments to hours depending on the circumstances. He didn't have days or hours. This had to work. He couldn't remember if any shifter had ever tried the mating ritual with a human. If it didn't work, he'd be one of several men in her harem. An unknown. One of the pack.

He'd growled the ancient mating oath to her. He could only hope she didn't need to say anything to make the ritual work.

"Jamie," she cried out as his teeth sank deeper into her shoulder and triggered another climax. When he released his seed inside her, he felt powerful. He was in control.

Her screams of pleasure filled the air. Releasing his fangs, he threw his head back, his howl carrying through the room. Ry collapsed onto the bed with Jamie buried deep inside her. His weight pressed her into the mattress, but she was beyond caring. She'd passed out.

He tried lifting himself off her, but he couldn't. Jamie frowned. The swelling of his cock prevented him from slipping out. This never happened unless both mates were in their animal form. It was a way to assist conception. It shouldn't be possible since Ry couldn't shift. Yet, here he lay, unable to pull out.

"What the fuck did you do?" Jamie looked up in surprise at the sound of Ian's voice. His two brothers stood near the bed watching him in amazement. Colin leaned closer to get a better look.

Jamie growled, slapping at his brother's shoulder to shove him out of the way. He wrapped his arms around Ry and moved them both so they were lying on their sides. If she woke and saw his cock was so swollen he couldn't remove it, she'd panic.

Colin was the calm one. "Relax, Jamie. It'll go away in a minute."

"This isn't supposed to happen." Jamie hissed between his teeth. It was painful. He tried shifting to release the pressure. The pressure became worse. He froze.

"I think you got what you wanted, though. Look at her shoulder." Colin nodded toward Ry.

Jamie nudged aside her hair so they could see. Bite marks were imprinted into her flesh. As they watched, the fresh wounds healed into scars. The power flowing through her seemed to have accepted him and his claim. When she had healed herself previously, all evidence of her wounds had vanished. This time, the bite mark remained; a permanent scar.

Several minutes later, his cock softened and he slipped out of her body. Ryder moaned at the loss, opening her eyes.

Chapter 36

Something had changed between them when Ry and Jamie convulsed in a climax. She instinctively knew her life could never be the same.

For a while, she had hoped they would catch Dunbar and she would go back to her previous life and her work at the hospital. Then she'd had hopes of healing her father. In that moment with Jamie though, she understood she would never be able to go back. These three men had claimed her body, her life, her soul, and, oddly enough, her heart. She could never walk away from them.

Jamie lay beside her, spooning. He was back to his normal, human self. She hadn't split in two. The other two brothers stood beside the bed. Colin looked grim. Ian looked furious. She wondered why. She hadn't expected them to be jealous of each other, not after the previous night.

As she reached a hand out to Ian, he pivoted and stormed out of the room. Ry felt his absence to her core. A stab of pain twisted in her chest. She pulled away from Jamie, curling into a ball.

. . .

JAMIE SMILED. She was bound to him beyond the tattoos and the power she wielded. Although she could never shift forms, she was one of them now, a member of his pack, his mate. He was the alpha male and she was his alpha female. Any shifter would recognize her status from her scent. The scars on her shoulder were additional, undeniable proof.

He held off until she fell asleep before dressing and leaving the bedroom. Colin followed. As he stepped out of the room, he found Ian pacing at the other end of the hall. Ian turned toward them, beyond agitated.

He barely contained his fury. "I don't fucking believe you. How could you do that?" He planted himself in the middle of the hallway, his fists clenched at his sides, his eyes blazed with anger.

"Ian. Let me explain." Jamie spread his hands out in a peaceful gesture. He sauntered toward his youngest brother to soothe him. When Jamie halted, Ian took him by surprise and punched him. One quick fist to the jaw. Jamie stumbled backward two steps before he caught himself. He stared at Ian in surprise. Sure, the brothers fought and argued from time to time. This was different. Jamie suspected his little brother had sincere feelings for Ryder.

Ian continued his outburst, trying to keep his voice down. "You knew what she means to me. *You knew.* Yet you did it anyway."

Colin stepped between them. "I'm sure Jamie has his reasons, Ian. He wouldn't do something so asinine without a good explanation. Would you, Jamie?"

The glare Colin shot Jamie made him wonder if Colin believed his own words. Ian snorted in disgust and continued to glare at his oldest brother.

Jamie sighed. He looked from one to the other before settling his gaze on Ian. "You know nothing with her is genuine. Half the time, it's not even Ryder you're screwing."

Ian took a menacing step toward Jamie but halted when Jamie held out his hands. "Listen. I talked to the historian. If she continues following the path of that woman inside her, she will accumulate more men as Guardians. That's what we are—Guardians."

The blood drained from Ian's face.

"I suspect Waru will be one. I've noticed how he watches her. In addition, that Red guy claims he will be her last Guardian. I'm not sure if there's any significance in being the final one, but I wanted to stake a claim. *We* needed to stake a claim. Through me, we will protect her."

Ian growled at Jamie and flashed his canines. "Damn you. You could have asked first. Did you give her a choice?"

Colin frowned at his older brother. "I agree. We should have discussed it."

"I could have, but it would have wasted time. I knew what your reaction would have been. If I had discussed it with her, she would have balked. We're leaving soon and I needed to complete the mating ritual. In less than a week, she's taken the three of us as Guardians. How fast do you think the others will happen?"

Jamie looked from one brother to the other. Hell, he was alpha. They were supposed to heed what he said, not question him. This was as much for their protection as it was for hers. One day they would realize it. Until then, his word was law.

"Ry is my mate, and I will protect her. Think about that when she attracts more men as Guardians. Fuck you both." He snarled and stabbed a finger at Ian. "You can be the one she loves." He turned to Colin. "You can be her best friend. I'll be her alpha. We'll see who protects her best."

He brushed past them to the top of the stairs and looked back at them. "Just to be clear. Because of the healing she's done, if she gets pregnant, I *will* claim the child as mine."

Chapter 37

"What a fucking bastard." Ian glared after Jamie, thunderstruck by his brother's actions. Colin moved to walk past Ian, but instead halted beside him.

"You know he means well." Colin always played the mediator between the brothers.

Ian snarled. "No, I don't. He's only looking after himself. He wants to stay in control." He would not willingly accept this new turn of events. She was *his*.

Colin sighed. "Do you remember the stories about the two brothers back in the eighteen hundreds? The ones who went to war, but neither wanted to leave the same woman behind?"

Puzzled, Ian glanced at him. "You're talking about how they both mated with her. If one died, the other would still have a link to her."

Colin smiled in the direction Jamie had disappeared. "Exactly." He slapped a hand on Ian's shoulder. "Try completing the ritual without her passing out." He marched away, clearly knowing that his brother would be busy for a while.

Ian slipped into the room and found Ry tugging on her robe.

"Where do you think you're going?" His voice seemed loud in the stillness. Ry's head shot up. A weak smile crossed her lips.

"You're angry. Why?" Frowning, she held the two edges of her robe together, not bothering with the tie.

"It's nothing. Brother stuff."

Releasing her robe, Ry walked toward him. Her hands rested on the sides of his face as she looked intently into his eyes, watching him for several moments.

Ry's touch soothed him. "It's more than that. You were livid. I can see how angry you still are. I can sense it. You and Jamie both. Tell me what happened."

He couldn't tell her that his brother had taken her as his alpha bride without her permission. Ian hoped that Ryder would have protested and refused. He raised his hands to her waist, sliding his palms under her robe and against her soft skin.

Rising up on her toes, she cruised her lips along his jawline. He dipped his head to capture her lips with his.

"Hmm," Ry moaned into his mouth. Ian deepened the kiss as he slipped the robe off her and wrapped his arms around her naked body. Hers glided around his neck. He marveled at how perfectly they fit together.

When they broke the kiss, Ian buried his face in her hair, breathing in her scent.

"I need you to make love to me, Ian."

Pulling back, he gazed down at her. The smile she gave him lit up his soul.

"I want you to love me slow and easy. Take your time. I

need to know how much you want me." Her voice was soft and sexy. She tilted her head to the side. "Can you do the same thing as Jamie? With the fur and size and all? It was ... intense."

Stunned by the look of trust shining in her eyes, he hesitated. Could she be feeling the emotion—love—that he was?

"I can."

"Then do it with me. It was exciting with Jamie, but I want the same thing with you. I want to see you, the real you."

He squeezed his eyes closed tight. She trusted him. She wanted him. She accepted his other half. How much of this was Ryder and how much was the entity? He didn't want to know.

Opening his eyes, he gazed at the beautiful woman before him. Her green eyes encouraged him. "I don't want to frighten you. Seeing one of us shift partially can be shocking."

"I saw Jamie. I wasn't frightened," Ry insisted. Her voice dropped lower. "I want to see you, Ian. All of you."

He pressed his lips to her forehead. If he did this, Jamie would be pissed. To hell with his brother. This was his woman. He wanted to prove that to her.

"I love you," he whispered.

Ry blinked at him, then a bright smile spread across her face. She opened her mouth to reply, but he quickly pressed his lips to hers. Ry sighed and kissed him back. A moment later, he released her, then scooped her up into his arms. She giggled when he gently tossed her onto the bed. He yanked his clothes off and with a grin, followed her down, covering her nakedness.

"I had to stop you from repeating the words. Not yet. I

want to prove to you first how much I love you. Do you understand? No pressure."

Ry nodded. She spread her legs, letting Ian settle between her thighs. He showered her with tender kisses. Her head tilted back as a soft moan escaped her lips.

Ian slowed his movements. He wished he had all the time in the world to show her how much she meant to him. His kisses roamed over her tattooed breasts. He still marveled at how close the images resembled him and his brother. Sucking in one nipple, he gently manipulated it with his lips and teeth. Moving to her other breast, he licked it, swirling his tongue around before nipping the tender bud.

Ry's moans became whimpers and pleas for more. When she tried to reach for him, he pressed her back, capturing her wayward hands.

"I'm in control. Lie back and relax." He chuckled at her pout, but Ry complied. This was not their typical encounter, their love making was usually fast and furious. The men's goal had always been to get Ry to climax as fast as possible and as many times as possible. Now he took his time. He planned to show her the extent of his love and desire.

Ry's breathing steadily grew labored while her body trembled. Ian was in tune with her and sensed her orgasm before she did. Her body arched up, a whimper on her lips, her fingers dug into the sheets, and her legs opened wider.

Ian scooted down and nestled between her thighs. He skated his fingers lightly against her skin; drifting along her hip, across her belly, tracing along the crease between her legs, dipping into the slickness. She trembled with every touch; her hips surged up for more contact. With a delicate touch, he spread her folds, then blew gently.

Ry shivered and groaned, begging for more. "Lick me. Taste me. Please."

Chuckling, he lowered his head and pressed his lips in a gentle kiss on her clit. She jerked. Another light kiss then a lick. This time she held still, whimpering and pleading for more. Licking again, he tasted her unique flavor. Working with slow movements, he savored her with licks and tiny nibbles. She quivered, her hands furrowing into his hair; digging in and holding tight. His name falling from her lips again and again. Until he pressed a finger inside her core. Then she screamed, her hips bucking against him.

"Shhh. Relax. Let it flow over you."

With his murmurs, she settled and met his strokes with an eagerness he treasured. His single finger became two. Then three. Their movements synced, his tongue teasing, her hands encouraging. Then her body stiffened and arched. Her pussy clamped down on his digits and squeezed with her orgasm.

He halted his movements, except for his tongue which continued to lightly stroke causing her body to quiver ever so slightly. He relished her taste, her wetness dripping from his fingers.

Her fingers tugged on his hair, urging him. Releasing her, he crawled on hands and knees up her body. Hovering over her, he dropped a kiss to her lips. Her eyes fluttered open. "Ian."

Grabbing one of her ankles, he pulled it around his waist. She copied the movement with her other leg, wrapping him up tight against her. His cock nudged her entrance, then slipped inside when he pressed forward. He moved once, then twice before settling deep in her.

Ian began a partial shift. A luxurious wolf pelt sprouted

over his back. His cock increased in size. He felt Ry's body shift to accommodate him. The feat amazed him.

"Bite me. Please. I need it," Ry begged, sounding like an addict who needed her next fix.

He positioned his head near her shoulder, next to the spot where Jamie had marked her. Slowly, he sank his canines into her. The sharp fangs punctured her delicate skin and slid through her flesh. It was instantaneous. Ry's body shook with her climax.

Ian groaned. He couldn't last much longer. He tried thinking of algebra. A topic that usually worked, but failed him this time. Within seconds, he came. Ry's heels dug into his backside. Her legs tightened around him. He collapsed into her warm embrace.

After several minutes, he moved to roll his weight off her, but froze. He was stuck, the same as Jamie had been. Astonished, he looked down between them as he shifted back to his normal size and shape. It didn't help.

He looked up at Ry. She broke into a fit of giggles.

"I'm sorry. I can't help it. It's so ... unexpected." She laughed.

Ian chuckled. "If you don't mind, I don't. It'll correct itself shortly. Once we both relax."

He gazed into her eyes and brushed a wisp of hair from her face.

Ry went silent. Her hands ran over his back as she watched him intently. In a soft voice, she spoke. "Ian. Is it crazy that I think I love you?"

Ian froze. *The L word.* Did she mean it?

A smile crossed her face as she watched his reaction. Leaning close, she placed her nose against his. A smile twitched his lips. He gently pressed a kiss to her lips.

"I love that you love me," Ian murmured.

Ry's eyes closed as she sighed. When she reopened them, he saw the happiness shining there. His heart was ready to burst. He'd never been so content. With a tranquil sigh, they relaxed, eventually sliding apart and falling asleep in each other's arms.

Chapter 38

Colin roused her with light kisses. Opening her eyes, Ry smiled and wrapped her arms around his neck. She pulled him close, deepening the kiss.

Pulling back, she whispered, "I like the way you wake me. Can you do that shifting trick for me? The one Ian and Jamie did."

Surprised, Colin realized she didn't understand what it meant. Jamie or Ian would have to explain it to her. "Sorry, another time. But right now, I need to get you on the jet. You have fifteen minutes to get dressed and be downstairs."

She looked surprised as she yawned. "Fifteen minutes? Are you serious? I want to sleep some more."

Colin grinned and slid off the bed.

"Orders are orders." He swatted her butt to get her moving. "Don't go back to sleep."

"I won't."

He stood for a moment watching her, hands on his hips. Reluctantly she sat up and moved to the edge of the bed, her legs hanging over. Waving Colin away, she waited until he left, then lay back down and curled up with a pillow. She was not ready to get up yet. Five more minutes, that's all she needed. A little more sleep and a quiet dream or two. She needed to talk to Ian too. She needed to understand why the brothers had argued. She didn't want to come between them.

Dreams rushed in as sleep overtook her.

PANIC WRAPPED *a crushing hold around her heart. She struggled to breathe as she sat on throne, slumped over, incapable of moving. A tea cup lay on the floor, the liquid forming a puddle. She couldn't lift a finger to stop whatever was coming. The silence is deafening and terrifying. Overwhelming grief buried her under its weight. Deep down, she realized this was another dream through the other woman's eyes but the emotions were strong and all too real.*

A man headed down the long hall toward her. He's tall, broad-shouldered, handsome, confident—too confident. He smiles in triumph. He's won.

Until a child's small hands pressed a cold, solid object into her palms. A tiny voice whispers, "Your statue, my Queen. Camden told me to deliver it only to you."

Instinctively, she knew she held the gold statue, the place she would store the queen's power for protection until summoned. The boy would stash it and keep it safe. If the man rapidly approaching got his hands on the statue and power, he would use evil to destroy the kingdom and then the world.

The power is unimaginable, growing in strength for years. She feels the boy's soft lips on her cheek and hears him whisper "I will love you forever, my Queen" and then he's gone—taking the gold statue.

Weak, empty, and cold, her body refuses to respond. Tears flow down her cheeks from the utter desolation.

Shouts can be heard in the distance. The guards and warriors are coming to her rescue but it is too late. He is directly in front of her, demanding someone catch the boy. She sends a quick prayer toward the heavens that the child escapes and the guards and warriors will save her.

He turns with an evil smile and plunges a knife into her heart. As it sinks into her body, her last thought is of the men she loves... her Guardians.

R Y BOLTED UPRIGHT, gasping for air, crying terrified sobs. She'd felt the knife thrust into her chest. She rubbed her hands over her heart. No, it hadn't been her chest, but she'd felt it. She continued to sense the blade slicing into her flesh.

She squeezed her eyes shut. She'd felt it all—the despair of knowing the fate of her Guardians, the overwhelming sadness at realizing they were dead, the relief in knowing the young boy aided her, and the denial that someone she recognized had plunged a knife into her heart.

"Ry? What's wrong?" Colin stood over her.

She'd missed the fifteen-minute warning Colin had given her earlier. Instead of being ready to roll, she sat in bed struggling to breathe.

He sat beside her on the bed. "Calm down. Relax. Take slow, deep breaths."

As he tried soothing her, he reached for the phone next to the bed. He kept it on speakerphone and dialed. A voice she didn't recognize answered.

"I need Abby in Ry's room *now*. She's having a panic attack." Not bothering to wait for an answer, he hung up and turned back to the bed.

He slid his hands up and down her arms while

murmuring calming words. She continued to gasp for air. Her heart rate sped up with each breath. Tears streamed down her face. Terror that she would die, too, flooded her.

Seconds later, the door was flung open. Jamie raced in with Ian on his heels.

"What happened? I sent Abby a text message to get here now." Jamie's demanding voice bombarded her already sensitive senses.

"I don't know. I came in and found her like this. She won't calm down. She keeps rubbing her chest and gasping for air," Colin answered.

Ian turned and ran out the open door. Ry could hear him bellowing for Markus and Abby.

She closed her eyes. Why did her chest ache? It'd been a dream. A replay of the stabbing continued to cycle through her mind. She groaned in pain, doubling over as she felt the knife sink in again. Ry tried to scream in agony, but she had no breath. Seeing Ian standing next to Colin on the opposite side of the bed, she reached for him. She clung to his hand while Ian slipped onto the bed.

"Keep your eyes open, baby. Look at me. Markus and Abby will be here in a second. Here. Squeeze my hand if you understand me."

She squeezed as tight as possible.

Ian smiled. "That's it, baby. Hang on."

He cocked his head as though hearing something she didn't, then turned back to her. "Help's here."

Ry couldn't see who it was with the three men crowded around the bed. Ian wrapped his free arm around her and tugged her body close to steady her trembling. She felt a small hand rest on her shoulder, then a needle pinch. It took seconds for Abby's choice of drugs to work. Ry gasped once, twice, then a third time as she slowed her breathing. The fourth breath was a deep inhale. Listening to Ian's voice, she slowly exhaled.

"That's it, baby. Nice and slow. You've got it."

He brushed away her tears. She leaned forward, resting her head on his shoulder. He wrapped both arms around her trembling body. Colin's hands caressed her back and arms.

"What did you give her? Can she travel?" Jamie's voice rumbled through the room. "I was hoping Markus would be here to calm her."

Abby spoke. "Markus is at the jet. It's a mild sedative to relax her, and yes, she'll be able to travel. What happened? Does anyone know?"

Colin stood from the edge of the bed. "I walked in and found her sleeping, but before I could step over here, she sat up gasping for air and crying. I could tell she was panicking, but I have no idea why."

"Ian and I felt her pain and raced up here, but Colin had already called you," Jamie replied.

Abby brushed Ry's hair away from her face as she sat on the edge of the bed. She smiled as Ry turned her gaze to meet the doctor's.

"Can you talk yet? Your breathing is back to normal."

Ry didn't want to think about her dream. She was comfortable in Ian's arms. She relaxed and did her best to stop imagining the knife plunging into her chest. Curling up closer to Ian, she tucked herself into a ball. Someone pulled the sheets up around her, slipping them around her nakedness.

"I was dreaming." She closed her eyes, remembering the throne room. She remained in Ian's arms, not wanting to leave the perceived safety of them.

Abby continued to be gentle. "Can you tell me about it?"

Ry wasn't sure if she could tell her the details or not. When she spoke, it was in a soft, trembling voice. "He stabbed her. I felt the knife sliding into my chest. It was as if it was happening to me."

"Who was stabbed?" Abby encouraged.

"The woman from my dreams. They killed her guards."

She drew back to look up at Ian.

"She's the one who put the power and energy into the statue. They wanted her magic. This boy took the statue and hid it so they couldn't find it. They killed her anyway."

Her tears ran unchecked as she remembered the woman's warranted fear.

"He stabbed her in the chest with a knife. I could feel it. I could feel all of it." She shuddered and rubbed a hand over her chest.

Ian gave her a reassuring hug. "Shhh. It's okay now. We're here. It was a dream."

He rocked her, murmuring as Ry slowly calmed. When the crying stopped, she snuggled in his arms, safe and warm. The drugs had kicked in.

Jamie addressed the others. "Colin, make sure everyone's ready to leave. We need to get out of here on time. I'll heat up the shower."

Ry raised her head, pushing away from Ian.

"I'm fine. You want to leave tonight. I can get dressed."

"I know you're fine, but we have time," Jamie said. "Ian will take a shower with you so you're not alone." He gently brushed the back of his knuckles against her cheek.

She closed her eyes as Ian continued to cradle her and press his lips to her forehead. She couldn't get the fear she had experienced out of her head. Tears gathered at the corners of her eyes, unable to bear the thought of all those men dying. The utter desolation of the woman in her dream had been heartbreaking.

What if her men died? *Yes, they are mine.* Ian, Colin, and Jamie.

Ian carried her into the bathroom. He handed her to Jamie, who held her while Ian stripped. Once naked, Ian took her back into his arms and stepped into the shower. The water falling on her was soothing and warm.

A moment later, Jamie stepped in too. She looked up at him in surprise.

"You didn't think I'd let Ian have all the fun, did you?"

She managed a smile.

They held her, lathered her, and cleaned her. Their ministrations made her feel treasured. After the shower, they dried her off and wiggled her into the clothes Abby had laid out. Sweatpants and a t-shirt would be comfortable for the journey. They skipped her underclothes but pulled socks on her feet.

Jamie carried her downstairs with Ian following. Abby and Colin stood in the foyer with Robert and a man she didn't recognize, but something about him caught her attention. She turned her head to stare as Jamie headed to the front door.

Her voice a whisper, she tried getting Jamie's attention. When he didn't slow down, she wiggled, trying to get down. "Jamie. Stop."

He halted to keep her from slipping out of his arms. He muttered curses under his breath, but she had already turned to face the unknown man.

He had to be the historian.

Ry addressed him, "It's you. You know what's going on, don't you?"

His eyes widened and he glanced at the others nervously.

"Ry," Jamie growled, "we'll talk to Christian once we reach our destination."

Christian. That was his name.

"Who was the woman? The woman with the statue."

He licked his lips. Did she make him nervous? She tried to look friendly by smiling, but she was too drugged to be sure if she was smiling or scowling.

Exasperated, Abby chided Jamie, "Tell her. It might settle her down. You have to tell her sometime."

Jamie scowled, but he nodded to Christian. "Go ahead."

Christian cleared his throat. He appeared more frightened of Jamie than of her.

"The statue belonged to a queen who ruled roughly three thousand years ago."

"What was her name?" Ry asked.

"Mara. Queen Mara."

"How did she die?"

"Stories report she was stabbed in the heart by a neighboring rival."

Chapter 39

I t was true. She rested her head against Jamie's neck, hiding her face as she clung to him. He began walking again. This time, Ry let him. She had dreamed the Queen's death. She was the woman through whose eyes Ry had experienced her dreams. She was the woman under the tree who told her to trust her Guardians.

The Queen's Guardians had died trying to protect her.

"It seems the tattoos serve two purposes, from what he told me. The first purpose is that binding us to you means we will protect you with our lives."

She remembered Jamie's words from earlier. He hadn't called himself and his brothers Guardians, but she knew. They were her Guardians. The Queen had many more Guardians depicted on the tapestry in Ry's dreams. Would history repeat itself again?

She lifted her head to look at Jamie. They approached a car with Colin and Ian walking beside them.

"You knew, didn't you?" she asked Jamie softly. "You knew there will be more men. More Guardians."

His gaze darted to her, then focused straight ahead.

Stopping beside the car, he waited for Colin to open the back door. When he did, Jamie bent down and slid her onto the seat while Ian climbed in on the other side. Instead of pulling away, Jamie hesitated.

His face was near hers. She could see the turmoil in his eyes. It was the only sign that he had mixed feelings about telling her the truth. He watched her for several seconds before speaking.

"Yes. I planned on telling you once we reached our new destination."

Ry smiled to herself. He was protecting her already. She didn't mind. Maybe it was the drugs, but she understood his motives.

She wrapped her hand around his head and pulled him close. Just before her lips met his, she whispered, "Thank you for being my Guardian."

She saw a quick flash of surprise in his eyes before she kissed him tenderly. Jamie's response was equally gentle. When he pulled away, his gaze searched her eyes for a moment. Then with a slight jerk of his head, he stepped back and closed the door.

Ian pulled her onto his lap while Colin slid into the front passenger seat and Jamie into the driver's seat.

The drive was short, five minutes max, to Robert's private airstrip. Two jets sat on the tarmac.

Markus and War moved around the jets in the dark, making last-minute inspections. Jamie parked the car a short distance away while Ian gathered her in his arms.

As soon as they left the car, Markus turned toward them. Ian carried Ry as the three brothers headed to one jet, meeting Markus near the stairs.

Markus brushed her hair away from her face. He looked up at Jamie.

"She looks drugged. What happened?"

"Nightmares. I'll tell you about it when we get in the air."

Markus nodded.

War emerged from the dark. Ry turned her head to greet him, but held her tongue when he glared at Jamie.

"I can't believe you. Did you seriously think no one would figure out what you did?" His voice was rough and gravelly.

"Back off, War." Markus turned and planted himself between War and Ry.

War growled, flashing his fangs. "You have no right, Markus. This is between Jamie and me. I'm responsible for her. She's my friend's niece. I should take her with me and see how you like it."

Jamie's response was swift and decisive. "Touch her and die." Ry gasped with surprise.

War reached for her. Jamie shoved him away. Before she realized what was happening, there was a flash of fangs and fur as Jamie and War shifted into their animal forms and threw themselves at each other, their shredded clothing flying. Right before her eyes, a huge wolf and an enormous black leopard were at each other's throats. They rose on their hind legs, scrambling to get a solid grip on the other. The growls and snarls were deafening.

Ian hurried up the stairs into the jet with her in his arms. She struggled to slip free, but there was no stopping him. Colin closed ranks behind them to make sure no one followed. Markus took up a defensive stance at the bottom of the stairs. No one would get inside the jet without his permission.

Ry heard the battle outside as Ian set her down in a luxurious seat. Scooting over to the window, she watched the two animals charge and slash at each other. Breaking apart, they circled. They bared their teeth, hissing, growling, and snarling.

She rose onto her knees, her palms pressed against the window. Pain slashed her to the core. They were quarreling over her. These two friends were ripping, biting, and clawing each other. She turned her head to look at Ian, who stood in the aisle, bent over, watching the action.

"Why are they doing this? Please, Ian, make them stop."

"Don't worry. Markus will put a stop to it. They need to get out some aggression first."

No. It was unacceptable. Ry realized that she'd been drifting along over the past few days, not taking a stand, not making her opinion known. She had enough. She refused to be passive and let this entity take over her body and soul. And right now, that started with standing up to these men and controlling the situation.

Ignoring the protests from Ian and Colin, she walked toward the back of the plane to the exit. Her chilly look had them both clamping their mouths shut before following her outside and down the stairs. The wolf and leopard stood on the tarmac, sides heaving, glaring at each other. Nearby, sitting on his haunches, was a grizzly. A massive animal who could only be one person—Markus.

Putting on her best and most courageous doctor persona, she stepped off the stairs.

"Enough!" The single word cracked through the air, capturing the attention of man and beast alike. All eyes turned toward her.

Her gaze traveled from one animal to the next, pausing enough to show her annoyance and disappointment.

"Shift back to your human forms. I want to talk."

Jamie was first, followed by Markus. War snarled, flashing his fangs before he cooperated. The second they were in their human form, Ry realized her mistake. Three magnificently naked men stood before her in all their glory. As her gaze drifted to each one, their cocks went to half-mast.

If she had thought the Stone brothers were well equipped, she had a lot to learn. The length and girth of the other two men's cocks caused her core to tighten and her heart to stutter. They couldn't be normal. Dragging her eyes away from the distractions, she focused on War's forehead. He had started it.

"Do you want to tell me what made you so upset?"

War, obviously realizing how he affected her, strutted forward still scowling. They were all comfortable with their nakedness, something she'd noticed with the brothers as well.

"You should ask Jamie that question. He knows exactly what he did."

Lowering her focus to his eyes, she laid down the law. "I don't have time or the patience for these childish antics. I asked you. Answer me."

He blinked, obviously not expecting her to stand up to him. "Jamie performed a mating ritual with you. I'm assuming you were aware that you are now his mate."

What? That had to be what happened the last time she was alone with him. Was it the same with Ian? Could she have multiple mates? She had multiple Guardians.

She crossed her arms over her chest. War was no longer just her uncle's friend. He was now a potential Guardian. She'd felt the tug of attraction when she was near him. But she wouldn't accept him controlling her any more than she would accept the woman in her dreams taking over her life. Or the three Stone brothers.

"And what would you say if I told you that Ian did the

same ritual? And once we're in a safe location, I plan on repeating it with Colin."

War narrowed his eyes but didn't respond.

"I'm not a complete fool but I do have a lot to learn." She directed her gaze at Jamie. "I'm not going to take any more of this lying down. Pun intended. I plan to fight back. If I can't control what's happening to me, I will at least direct its process and direction."

Dropping her arms, she turned and faced Ian and Colin. "I can't change what's happened but I want to know every-thing. All the details. All the gory, nasty bits and pieces."

Turning again, she gazed at Markus. God, he needed to put on some clothes soon. Her nipples tightened even though she kept her eyes focused on his face. "I expect you all to work with me, not control me or the situation."

Full circle, she turned again to face War. "If you don't have any other complaints, I think it's time we left before Red shows up."

A satisfied smile on his lips, he bowed and straightened before answering. "No more questions or complaints. You can count on me."

He pivoted and hurried across the tarmac to the other waiting jet, his tight ass flashing her until he disappeared into the darkness.

Not willing to watch the other two naked men, she walked past Ian and Colin back into the jet and found the seat she'd vacated. Hands trembling, she gripped the armrests so no one could see.

Ian took the seat across the aisle from her while Colin sunk into the seat in front of her. He swiveled toward her, his gaze direct and unwavering.

"If you were serious about the mating ritual with me, I would be honored."

Her eyes widened. She had been right. "Yes. Of course. What's one more husband?"

When Colin and Ian broke out in amusement, she relaxed and giggled.

Markus, now fully dressed, paused beside her. "Nicely done, Princess. You handled that well."

She shuddered. "Please do not call me that. It's what Red called me. It's creepy."

He settled a large hand on her shoulder and gently squeezed. "I'm sorry. That was thoughtless of me. But you did handle it very well. I'm proud of you."

Ry gazed up. Although he was touching her, the dead zone wasn't completely surrounding her. Maybe it was because his grip was through her clothes. Regardless, the earlier desire intensified. An answering look of desire filled his eyes. He stepped back, dropping his hand and putting space between them.

Ian interjected, "Did you mean the part about having a lot to learn?"

She paused, trying to remember what she'd said. "Yes. I want to learn about you as shifters. I know nothing and I need to rectify that situation."

He glanced down the aisle behind her. When she twisted in her seat she found Jamie, fully dressed, standing there.

"You better tell her."

She looked back at Ian, who had a secretive smile on his face, darting a glance between Markus and Colin. "What am I missing?"

Ian leaned forward, his arms folded on the armrest. "Shifters have heightened senses—taste, eyesight, hearing." He paused. "And smell."

She frowned, wondering if it was true about animals smelling fear.

Markus answered with a suggestive grin. "What he means is that we can smell your arousal."

Ryder blinked. *Oh fuck.* "So outside...." She held up a hand, stopping four masculine voices from replying. "Don't."

Her mouth went dry thinking about the past several days. "I'm just going to let that sit for a bit. We don't need to discuss that further."

"It does put men and women on an even playing field. With humans, you know when a man is aroused. It's obvious."

"Yeah, some more than others." She slapped a hand over her mouth then snickered. Markus threw back his head and barked out a laugh. The other men chuckled. She enjoyed their teasing banter.

"Maybe we should get this jet in the air. We are in a hurry, aren't we?"

Markus headed toward the cockpit, making her wonder if he was the pilot. She hadn't seen anyone else on the jet.

Jamie came into view and squatted down so he was eye level with her. "I need to explain my actions. I was only protecting you, Ryder. If it's true about more Guardians, you will need someone who will keep your wellbeing in mind."

She stared into his calm eyes. Nothing fazed him. "Which is why I'm glad Ian did the same ritual and why Colin will complete it also." Annoyed with Jamie, she changed the subject, "Where are we going?"

"Alaska. We have a place there. Lauren and Zach will arrive before us. Abby and Christian will arrive later tonight. War and Emerson will arrive tomorrow."

"You have it all planned."

"Not me. Markus."

"I'd like to talk to my parents. They'll be worried."

Ian replied, "You already emailed them. Explained about a fantastic chance you have to spend several weeks in Scotland at a castle. You'll be learning from a world-renowned doctor, and getting first-hand experience."

She craned her head around Jamie to look at Ian. "I did not."

"No, but I did. From your email account. Your parents called earlier, before we left. Lauren answered. She told them you were in the shower. She chatted with them about the castle. What a fabulous opportunity it is for you. She talked about how she was going to take off from work for two weeks and visit you. Very convincing."

"I don't believe you."

"Listen to me, Ryder. You are not safe. Lauren is not safe. None of us are. We have to cover our tracks, put Dunbar off our scent, and protect you. Did I tell you that Red works for Dunbar?"

Horror slammed into her. She shook her head.

"He mentioned it when he tortured me. Except he's going rogue. He seems to have his own agenda, and if he can pop in and out of rooms, he's our greatest threat."

Ian knelt beside Jamie. "I won't let him hurt you, Ry. I swear. But you have to trust us. Trust Lauren. She's trying to protect you. If your parents know where you are, they could be injured or even killed."

"My uncle. If you told him...."

"War doesn't want him involved. They'll play poker tonight. It's Friday. War wants to learn what your uncle knows. Then he'll meet us."

"I need to heal my dad. I can do that now. Just take me to him long enough for me to heal him."

Jamie answered. "We can't. Not yet. Once we get settled, we'll make plans to either bring him to you or both of you to another location. We can't risk it yet."

She sat stunned, unable to move. They had made plans without telling her what was happening or where they were going. All she knew for sure was that she loved Ian and trusted him. Her life would never be the same again. But did she want it to be?

Through a twist of fate, she'd found excitement and a completely new world of people. The medical insights alone would be phenomenal. What she could do to heal people had extreme potential.

She had the soul of an ancient queen inside her, dragging her into the unknown. There would be no turning back. She hoped she wouldn't make the same mistakes—like trusting someone who wants to take a knife to her heart.

Three men. It was laughable. She'd avoided men all her adult life so she could concentrate on her work and career. Now, her work and career were on hold while three men promised to protect her and cherish her.

EPILOGUE

The three men cautiously moved into the room. Dunbar stood, hands behind his back, waiting for them to line up in front of him. They had failed him and they understood the consequences. Sweat dotted their foreheads and upper lips. One in particular. The human.

Dunbar's gaze swept the three men, then fixated on the one who had fucked up the most. The man had panicked when things got tough. Typical human. Dunbar couldn't accept failure.

With no remorse or hesitation, he swung a handgun to his front, aimed, and shot the human between the eyes. Neither of the other men moved. Not even a flinch. They were their own breed of monster—shifters.

Dunbar had no love for the beasts, but he used them mercilessly. Like humans, shifters could be bought. You just had to understand their price.

"The only reason you two are still alive is because you tried. He didn't. He pissed himself when the wolf charged the windshield."

One snickered, but at Dunbar's glare, he quieted and shuffled his feet.

"No more humans. Now that we know she has shifters with her, we can't afford any more mistakes. Get out of my sight. Be prepared to roll on my command when she's spotted. They will move her."

Both men turned. "Take that piece of shit with you and get rid of it." They grabbed the body by the feet and lugged it out.

Dunbar sank into a chair. He was probably overreacting, but it was time to call in his specialist. Time to fight fire with fire. He snickered. His beast would burn the woman's new shifter playmates to a crisp.

At ease and comfortable, he crossed his legs, lightly tapping one foot in the air. He looked up when another man came into the room, halted several feet away, then knelt. As he bowed to Dunbar, his long red braid swept over his shoulder and reached the floor.

"Master, how may I serve you?" His voice was soft and low with a slight Scottish accent. Even after all the centuries as a Dunbar family slave, the man had never lost that bit of his identity. Everything else, including his name had eroded away years ago. The man was at his disposal. This slave would locate the bitch or Dunbar would kill him. Dunbar had a responsibility to his slaves to keep them in line and discipline them.

"You're late. What delayed you?"

Never raising his head, the red-haired man remained calm and collected as he answered. "My apologies, Master. There were delays with the flight due to weather. It was out of my control."

"You understand she escaped me? I had her in my possession. She wouldn't have gotten away if you had been there." Dunbar slapped his palm on his thigh, his anger getting the better of him.

He'd had to leave the woman behind as the shifters swarmed the dilapidated ranch buildings and rescued her. What he didn't understand was how they had found her. Had someone betrayed him?

"I arrived as soon as possible, my lord. I am here. I will do my duty."

Dunbar tapped his fingers on his leg. Standing, he strolled to the side of the kneeling man. In a swift, snakelike movement, Dunbar clutched the man's braid and yanked his head back. The redhead did not call out in pain. His green eyes stared straight ahead, devoid of any emotion.

Dunbar leaned closer. "Do not fail me or I will lock you back in your cell for another thousand years. Do I make myself clear?"

"Yes, Master. Perfectly clear."

The emotionless eyes unnerved Dunbar. He had been around this man, this creature, his entire life. The man had served Dunbar and his family without question but only because he had been enslaved. Dunbar had never been comfortable around the shifter, but he was the master and he would make sure this animal knew it.

"Good." Dunbar released him with a shove and stepped away. "Now find me that bitch."

The End

GET A FREE NOVELLA FROM SHARLA WYLDE

Building a relationship with my readers is one of the best things about writing. I occasionally send out newsletters with details on new releases, special offers, and other bits of news. If you sign up for my newsletter, you will get a free novella – *Dragon Wings*.
This is the prequel to *Awakened* which introduces you to one of the shifter clans.

You can get the free novella, for free, by signing up at this link:
Dragon Wings - https://dl.bookfunnel.com/lqob1p7yea

DID YOU ENJOY THIS BOOK?

You can make a big difference

Reviews are the most powerful tool when it comes to getting a reader's attention. Much as I'd like to, I don't have the power of a New York publisher. I can't take out full-page ads or billboards. (Not yet, anyway.)

But I do have something more powerful and effective then that – a committed and loyal bunch of readers.

Honest reviews of my books help bring them to the attention of other readers.

If you've enjoyed this book, I would be grateful if you could spend a few brief minutes leaving a review (it can be as short as you like) on the book's page where you purchased it.

Thank you very much!

A NOTE FROM SHARLA

Thank you for reading *Awakened*. I **loved** writing this story. It was so much fun. I'm plotting out the next book in the series which will bring in more shifters and guardians for Ryder to accept and the Stone brothers to acknowledge. I can't wait to write it.

I hope you enjoyed *Awakened*! Stay in touch and get updates by visiting my website: https://www.sharlawylde.com/

I'd love to hear from you. You can find me here:

Email: Sharla@SharlaWylde.com
    Web Page: https://www.sharlawylde.com/
    Facebook: https://www.facebook.com/WyldeSharla
    Twitter: https://twitter.com/SharlaWylde
    Pinterest: https://www.pinterest.com/SharlaWylde
    BookBub: https://www.bookbub.com/profile/sharla-wylde
    Instagram: https://www.instagram.com/sharlawylde
    Amazon: amazon.com/author/sharlawylde